"Are you flirting?"

Though Piper colored, she d[...]
Maybe not. I'm trying to find [...]
with each other. I also notice[...]
question."

Cord laughed; he couldn't help it. "I'd have to be dead not to find you attractive," he told her. "But don't worry, I won't let it get in the way of the job I have to do. Or finding Renee. Both are too important to me."

Color still high, she finally smiled back. "Fair enough. Now how about we call it a night and regroup in the morning?"

Though it was still early, he nodded. "Okay. Good night."

She sighed. "I'm probably going to regret this, but..."

Before he could ask what she meant, she crossed the space between them, grabbed him and pulled him down for a kiss. Her mouth moved across his, nothing tentative about it. A wave of lust swamped him. Damn if it wasn't the most erotic kiss he'd ever shared.

Standing stock-still, he let her nibble and explore, until he couldn't take it any longer.

**We hope you enjoy this dramatic miniseries—
The Coltons of Texas: Finding love and buried
family secrets in th[...]**

**If you're on Twi[...]
think of Harlequi[...]
#harlequi[...]**

Dear Reader,

Living in Texas, I truly enjoyed writing a story set in my adoptive state. And every time Harlequin asks me to write a Colton story, it's like getting the best present ever! I love the Coltons.

When Piper Colton is framed for the murder of her adoptive father, she runs. Everything seems stacked against her but she's determined to find out the truth. And when she meets Cord Maxwell, the handsome bounty hunter tracking her, sparks fly.

Cord is a true Texan. Rough around the edges, brash and sexy as sin. He also is a man of honor and high principles. Watching him try to hold fast to those values while attempting to assist Piper, all the while battling an intense attraction, was fun. The story unfolded like a movie and kept me on my toes.

Piper Colton is a free spirit. Adopted by the Colton family at a young age, she has goals and plans. Getting arrested for murdering the man who was the only father she's ever known and having some of her family actually believe her to be capable of such a heinous act is like being punched in the gut. But she's strong and brave and true. She's a worthy heroine for a man like Cord Maxwell.

I hope you enjoy their story!

Karen Whiddon

RUNAWAY COLTON

—

Karen Whiddon

H HARLEQUIN® ROMANTIC SUSPENSE

Special thanks and acknowledgment are given to Karen Whiddon for her contribution to The Coltons of Texas miniseries.

ISBN-13: 978-0-373-28201-2

Runaway Colton

Copyright © 2016 by Harlequin Books S.A.

Recycling programs
for this product may
not exist in your area.

Printed in U.S.A.

HARLEQUIN®
www.Harlequin.com

Karen Whiddon started weaving fanciful tales for her younger brothers at the age of eleven. Amid the gorgeous Catskill Mountains, then the majestic Rocky Mountains, she fueled her imagination with the natural beauty surrounding her. Karen now lives in north Texas, writes full-time and volunteers for a boxer dog rescue. She shares her life with her hero of a husband and four to five dogs, depending on if she is fostering. You can email Karen at KWhiddon1@aol.com. Fans can also check out her website, karenwhiddon.com.

Harlequin Romantic Suspense

The Coltons of Texas

Runaway Colton

The Coltons of Oklahoma

The Temptation of Dr. Colton

The Coltons: Return to Wyoming

A Secret Colton Baby
The CEO's Secret Baby
The Cop's Missing Child
The Millionaire Cowboy's Secret
Texas Secrets, Lovers' Lies
The Rancher's Return

Silhouette Romantic Suspense

The Princess's Secret Scandal
Bulletproof Marriage

The Cordiasic Legacy

Black Sheep P.I.
The Perfect Soldier
Profile for Seduction

Visit the Author Profile page at Harlequin.com for more titles.

As always, to my beloved husband, Lonnie.
You are the inspiration for every love story I write.

Chapter 1

"I was framed." Back ramrod straight, clenching her hands into fists so her adoptive brother and sister wouldn't see how badly they shook, Piper Colton kept her voice perfectly level. "You have to realize that."

"Framed." Marceline Colton snorted, making her elegant, gem-encrusted earrings swing. "Right. Piper, you were arrested. The police wouldn't have arrested you unless they had sufficient evidence. I think finding Eldridge's bloody shirt in your closet might have been the final clue."

"I saved up to buy that shirt for him one Christmas when I was sixteen. You know that."

"Now it's evidence," Marceline continued, her voice as icy as her pale blue, flawlessly made-up eyes. "Apparently enough evidence for them." She sneered, her bright red lipstick a bright slash of color in her alabaster face. "Where's your trademark optimism now?"

"It's all circumstantial. They don't even have a body." Piper spoke with confidence, despite the fact that her own family's suspicion hurt her heart.

"I'm sure it's just a matter of time before they find the

body," Marceline declared. Even at home, every strand of her golden-blond hair appeared perfect. When Piper had been younger, she'd been envious of Marceline's movie star appearance. Now, understanding the amount of work that went into maintaining that look, it only made Piper feel tired. Plus, Marceline might be gorgeous on the outside, but her inner self was an entirely different matter.

"That's true," Fowler Colton agreed, his cold blue eyes intense. As usual, he wore one of his custom suits and perfectly pressed black Stetsons. "Come on, Piper. You can tell us. Did you kill Eldridge?"

Though Piper wanted to double over at the amount of pain his question caused, by sheer strength of will she managed to remain expressionless. Her natural optimism hadn't fled—it had just gone into temporary hiding. "How can you ask me such a thing? Why on earth would I murder my own father?"

"Adoptive father," Marceline reminded her. "You're not a real Colton, after all."

As if she could forget. Not possible, with Marceline finding a way to remind her of that fact at least once a day. Piper figured this was Marceline's way of dealing with her own insecurity, since Marceline hadn't been born a Colton, either. However, since her mother, Whitney, was actually married to Eldridge Colton, Marceline clearly figured that put her one step above Piper, who'd been orphaned when Whitney and Eldridge adopted her.

"Think of what you're doing to poor Whitney," Fowler said, the disapproval in his voice matching the disgusted expression on his face. "She took you in, adopted you, cared for you, and you repay her by killing her husband. You ought to be ashamed of yourself, Piper."

Piper opened her mouth and then closed it. She had the strangest urge to laugh, but reined it in lest they label her insane, as well. "You know me, Fowler. How could you think I'd kill anyone, let alone Eldridge? I won't even squash a spider."

Marceline snorted. "Well, obviously this time you must have figured you had more to gain."

Looking from one to the other, Piper shook her head. "No matter how many times I tell you I didn't do it, you'll never believe my innocence, will you?"

"Nope," Marceline responded promptly. She and Fowler exchanged identical smug smiles, making Piper wonder if they'd high-five each other next. She'd long ago given up on trying to figure out why the two of them disliked her so much. At least she still had T.C., Reid and Alanna, her other siblings. She'd bet they'd believe her.

"You know I've been mourning Eldridge," Piper began, hoping to try again. "I love—loved—him. Why would anyone believe I'd harm him?"

"Maybe you know something we don't." Marceline smirked. "You've been spending a lot of time with him. Did you convince him to change his will and leave you a lot of money?"

The idea was so ludicrous Piper gasped. "Are you kidding me?"

"Not hardly." Marceline watched her like a hawk watching a mouse. "You've always envied those of us who are better off than you."

"I give up." Piper threw up her hands. "Clearly, there's nothing I can say that will make you believe I'm not a killer."

"Convince us," Fowler said. "Give us the reason that shirt was in your closet."

That was easy. "It was planted."

"By whom?"

"I don't know," Piper cried. "I need your help to find out who would do such a thing and why."

"I don't believe you." Marceline curled her brightly painted lips in disgust.

"Neither do I." Fowler and Marceline exchanged knowing glances before he turned back to Piper. "And if your own family thinks you're guilty," Fowler continued, "how are you ever going to convince a jury that you're not?"

Piper stared, praying her eyes didn't reveal the hurt. She felt as though she'd been punched in the stomach. Leave it to Fowler. Nothing like going for the gusto. Except as he usually managed to do, Fowler had hit upon the crux of the problem.

Because he was right. If she didn't take matters into her own hands, she'd be going to jail for a crime she hadn't committed. It would be up to her to find the real killer and quickly, before her hearing.

"Cat got your tongue?" The vitriol in Marceline's voice made Piper wonder for the hundredth time what she'd ever done to make her older adoptive sister despise her.

Like Marceline, Fowler waited, his gaze hooded and secretive. As long as she'd known him, the eldest Colton had constantly worked every angle, pulling invisible strings behind the scenes to help him obtain his goal, whatever that might be.

Still, they were family and their accusations felt like a knife straight through her heart.

Looking at the two people who should have been on her side, even if blood didn't form any ties, Piper finally understood she was wasting her time. She could explain and rationalize until she turned blue, but Marceline and Fowler had already made up their minds. They believed her arrest had been warranted. They actually thought her capable of murder—not just murder—but the slaying of someone she loved.

This knowledge hurt more than she would have believed possible. While Marceline had never been kind to her, to consider her a murderess?

In that instant, Piper realized what she would have to do. For a person who always, without exception, did the right thing, running would be a bitter pill to swallow. But better than going to prison for a crime she hadn't committed.

Even worse, she hadn't gotten a chance to fully mourn Eldridge yet. Of course, until she actually saw his body, she refused to believe he was dead.

Too bad the police didn't think the same way.

Pushing away the sheer terror turning her blood to ice, she managed to incline her head, hopefully gracefully, as she moved toward the stairs. "I'll be in my room if anyone needs me."

Though both siblings continued to glare at her, neither responded. She didn't dare breathe until she'd gotten out of their sight.

All her life she'd known if she wanted to get something done, she'd have to do it herself. This temporary snag would be no exception. Since no one else seemed inclined to locate the real killer, she'd simply have to do it herself. Even if she had to break the law to find the truth.

Once she reached her room, she hurried inside and locked the door. Then, she dug her old backpack from her closet and began to fill it with her clothes. She took three pairs of jeans, five long-sleeved shirts and two short-sleeved, underwear, bras and socks. She'd recently purchased a new pair of sneakers and hadn't worn them yet, so they went on top, along with black flip-flops.

Removing her slip-on flats, she put on socks and her favorite pair of boots. Texas weather this time of year could be mercurial. Heat waves and cold snaps made it difficult to predict what she'd need, so she took a little of everything.

Tying a lightweight jacket around her waist, she gathered up her favorite cosmetics and dropped that bag into her oversize purse.

Now, she'd need to slip out of the house and get to the bank. Though she hated to empty her savings account, especially since she'd gotten so close to having enough to open her own business, she didn't see that she had a choice.

Not if she wanted to stay free long enough to find out who really had kidnapped or killed Eldridge Colton.

If the day got any worse, Cord Maxwell figured he'd have to close up the office and go home. Not only had he failed to turn up a single lead on his missing niece, Renee, but after he paid the electric bill, he wouldn't have too much leftover for food.

"Maybe you'll have to start sharing your dog food with me," he told Truman, the mangy mutt he'd rescued from the Kaufman County shelter a year ago. In pure Truman form, the skinny dog didn't even bother to open his eyes.

Earlier today, when Cord had taken Truman for his midmorning walk, some snooty woman in designer clothes had sniffed and called Truman ugly. It had taken every bit of restraint Cord possessed not to tell her off. Instead, he'd managed a mild "Beauty's in the eye of the beholder, now isn't it?" Then, unable to resist a scornful sweeping glance that hopefully told her he found her lacking, he led Truman away. Cord couldn't understand how anyone couldn't see the beauty in Truman's caramel-colored eyes and jaunty plumed tail.

At least he had a forty-pound bag of Truman's favorite lamb-and-rice dog food. Cord would go hungry if he had to, but his dog would always be fed.

Money again. Everything circled back around to that. He'd been in tight spots before and made it through by using credit cards to fill in the gaps. If he had to, he'd do that again.

Except for the one debt that required cash. Today he had to go visit Lorraine Berens, the once-wealthy widow his father had scammed out of money. He'd gone to her upon learning what his father had done and sworn to make it right. But this time, instead of making his usual payment of restitution, he'd have to explain his sad financial situation and promise to make it up to her as soon as he could.

Without any real work looming on the horizon, he wasn't actually sure when that would be. He'd been so consumed with his search for Renee that he'd turned down too many jobs without thinking of the consequences.

Sinking down into his worn leather desk chair, he stared at the too-silent phone and willed it to ring. If only Renee would call and let him know she was all right. At least maybe then he could stop his gut from constantly churning.

Renee had been a surly sixteen-year-old when she'd come to live with him after the death of both her parents in a drunk driving accident. Her mother, Denice, had always been a hard partier, which had gotten worse when she'd married Joshua Barnes, who played bass guitar in a band. She'd quit when she'd gotten pregnant, but by the time Renee turned two, Denice had gone right back to her old ways. Cord rarely heard from her. She'd been driving drunk when she'd caused the accident that had killed her and Joshua and left a rebellious teenager an orphan.

Cord had tried—he really had—but he'd had no idea how to be a father to a sixteen-year-old who thought she was too cool for him and his life in a boring small town. His attempts at setting boundaries and rules had come too little too late and were laughed at and scorned.

For two years, every time they'd argued, Renee had told him she couldn't wait until she turned eighteen. She'd given him plenty of warning, he'd give her that. But still, he'd been surprised as hell when he'd come home from work to find her meager belongings had vanished, along with her.

In that instant, he'd seen her future. He'd tried to help his older sister, but failed. He couldn't let her daughter down. He had to find Renee and save her from herself.

Looking around the small, wood-paneled office from where he operated his business, he knew he'd risk everything he had to accomplish that.

He could almost see Sam shaking his head. Sam Ater had started S.A. Enterprises, Private Investigation and Fugitive Recovery. Years ago, when Cord had been assigned to him on a high school internship, Sam had taught the teenager everything there was to know. Cord would forever be grateful for Sam, who'd seen something in an insecure, poor teenager back in the day. Sam had taken Cord in and taught him the business. Unlike many of his classmates, Cord hadn't the funds or the desire to go to college. The military held no appeal, either, but thanks to Sam, none of that mattered. Once Cord graduated, Sam had offered him a job.

Cord had a place to go after high school. Sam had not only given him a job, but a lifelong career.

Cord had gotten licensed and found his true vocation. He'd enjoyed going to work every single day. The business Sam had built, a respected fugitive recovery agency as well as private investigation firm, was an operation that not only operated within the law, but had an 89 percent success rate, something that placed them in the top tier of their industry.

The two men had formed a team. Cord had considered Sam a friend as well as his boss.

Sam had passed away a couple years ago from lung cancer, shortly before Renee had arrived. It had been a quick death, two weeks after he'd been diagnosed.

Somehow Cord kept the business running and had been there, helping his friend as much as he was able. The day Sam died, Cord had closed S.A. Enterprises and gone fishing, since he'd promised Sam he would. Well, more beer drinking than fishing, though he'd kept a pole in the water. He'd mourned Sam out at the lake, saluted him and the moon with a beer can, and returned to work the next day sober, sad and hungover.

Sam left everything to Cord. Cord had been honored, realizing he'd had mighty big boots to fill.

Thinking of his old friend brought back the sense of loss. He had to wonder, what would Sam think if he could see him now?

While Sam would never have suspected Cord would let the finances get this bad, Cord knew the old man would have understood Cord's need to find the runaway teen. Both men knew firsthand the kind of evil that walked in the world.

Still, if he didn't want to lose the business Sam had spent years building, Cord needed to figure out a way to keep it running while he searched for his niece.

Sighing, he leafed through his notebook and reviewed

all the places Renee wasn't. He always kept meticulous notes.

The names and phone numbers of the jobs he'd turned away were in a manila folder on the corner of his desk. He couldn't say how many times he'd eyed the damn thing and thought about opening it. Maybe one or two of them might still need his services. Though he'd bet they'd all hired somebody else. The problem was, he needed a fairly quick and simple job that wouldn't interfere with his search for Renee.

He grabbed a can of diet cola from the mini-fridge and popped the top. Taking a long swig, he knew he'd better get out of the office and take another shot at locating Renee. He'd broaden his horizons this time. Since he'd already checked all over town, he'd head toward Dallas. Since Dallas was a big city, the sheer size and number of suburbs would complicate things. He figured he'd search suburb by suburb first, hoping Renee had found a waitressing job in one of the smaller communities.

The front door opened, hinges squeaking. Though Sam had always kept them oiled with WD-40, Cord had stopped after Sam died. He actually liked the sound. He figured it let him know when someone entered or left the office.

A well-dressed man stepped inside. His business suit looked custom-made and expensive, just like the ostrich skin cowboy boots he wore on his feet.

"Cord Maxwell?" the man asked, glancing around the sparsely furnished room. "I'm—"

"I know who you are." Cord got to his feet, taking one more swing of his Coke before placing it on his desk. "Fowler Colton, CEO of Colton Incorporated and Eldridge Colton's oldest son."

Fowler nodded, no doubt accustomed to being recognized. He took another step closer, his carefully blank expression revealing both nothing and too much. "I'd like to hire your services."

Surprised, especially since someone with Fowler's money could hire a top-notch firm from a bigger city like Dallas or Fort Worth, Cord waited to hear the rest. It'd probably be the kind of job no one else would want to do.

Fowler cleared his throat. "Before I tell you what—who—I need you to find, I'll require your promise to keep this confidential."

"That goes without saying." Crossing his arms, Cord realized the other man didn't remember him at all, despite the years he spent on the ranch when his father had been a ranch hand. Of course not, since even when he'd been younger, Fowler had always given the impression that he paid no attention to those he considered beneath him. And poor children of ranch hands, such as Cord, definitely fell into that category.

"I need you to find Piper." For the first time since he'd shown up, raw emotion flashed across Fowler's aristocratic features. Guilt, Cord realized, as his gut twisted. What the hell did Fowler have to feel guilty about?

And then Fowler's words hit him. *Find* Piper?

"I heard she was arrested in connection with Eldridge's murder." Cord kept his tone casual, even though the instant he'd heard the news he'd known something was horribly wrong. The Piper he'd known as a kid wouldn't even hurt a fly. No way he believed she could have actually killed another human being, especially not her adoptive father. He couldn't think she would have changed so drastically, even though it had been years since he'd seen her.

"Yes. She had to spend the night in the county jail.

Some of our siblings got together and posted bail and brought her home."

So far so good. Even though he'd said "some of our siblings," which meant Fowler himself hadn't been involved. Though he wondered why, Cord couldn't really say he was surprised. Fowler had never been big on family loyalty. Hell, as far as Cord could tell, the other man didn't have a single loyal bone in his body.

"Marceline and I were pretty rough on her," Fowler continued, his thin lips twisting. "We sort of barraged her."

"About what?"

Now Fowler wouldn't meet Cord's gaze. "We told her we were convinced she's guilty."

Now *this* was getting interesting. "Are you?"

"Convinced she's guilty?" Fowler lifted one shoulder in an elegant shrug. "I don't know. I mean, she could be. But then again, Eldridge didn't have a lot of friends."

Like father, like son.

"I feel horrible," Fowler continued, though the lack of inflection in his tone made Cord question whether he meant it. "Marceline can be brutal when she fixates on something. She showed no mercy. Piper appeared pretty upset. She usually looks on the bright side of everything, but not this time. I think we're the reason she ran."

Ran? "What?" Cord couldn't contain his shock. "Are you telling me Piper jumped bail?" *Which meant her siblings would be out serious money if she didn't show up in court.*

Fowler nodded, grimacing. "Yes. No one's seen hide nor hair of her since she got home from jail."

"Since she got out of jail." While Cord hated parroting back what the other man said, he simply could not take all this in. He never would have believed Piper Colton, rich, all-American girl next door, would in a million years do something like this.

Except she had. At least, according to Fowler.

"Okay." Wary now, Cord dragged his hand through his hair. "Why are you here, Fowler? If you're asking me to find Piper—"

"I am. You are a fugitive recovery agent, aren't you? I've done my research. Not only are you highly respected in the criminal court community, but your success rate is 89 percent. And I'm willing to pay well."

Of course he was. Since it just so happened that Cord really needed the money. "Our standard fees are—"

Again Fowler cut him off. "That doesn't matter. I'm willing to give you double what you usually charge."

"How much was her bail?"

Fowler recoiled, peering at Cord down the length of his impressive nose. "I fail to see how that concerns you."

"Seriously?" Somehow, Cord kept from snorting. "If you did your research as you claim, you'd know my fee is 10 percent of the bail."

"Her bail was set at fifty thousand."

"Which means you'll pay me five thousand. Up front."

"No." Fowler shook his head. "Like I said, I'm willing to double that."

Though Cord knew he should keep his mouth shut, he didn't. Fowler wasn't the type to throw away money. "Why?"

"This is a delicate matter. Piper may be a fugitive and I don't really know if she's guilty or innocent, but she's a Colton. No matter what. This matter must be kept quiet." Fowler cleared his throat and lifted his chin.

Suddenly, even though he had past-due bills to pay, Cord didn't want to get involved. When he'd been a kid on the ranch, Piper had always been kind to him, even though he'd grown up shabby. "Look," he told the other man. "My niece is missing. She ran away a few weeks ago, right after she turned eighteen. I'm sorry, but my first priority is finding her. I don't have time to hunt down Piper."

"I'll offer you triple."

Fifteen thousand dollars. Nothing to sneeze at, but since most of the fugitives Cord searched for had bails set at one hundred thousand, he regularly made ten grand a case. This still wasn't enough to divert Cord's attention from locating Renee. He wasn't sure any amount would be enough.

After all, it was his fault she'd taken off. He'd done a piss-poor job of looking after her when she'd come to live with him. "I'm sorry, but I can't," Cord began.

"Fine." The snap in Fowler's cultured voice warred with the grudging respect in his eyes. "You drive a hard bargain. Thirty thousand dollars. Cash. Up front."

Damn. No one paid up front. Usually, the fee was paid only once the fugitive had been apprehended.

Though Cord wasn't sure if Fowler was playing games, he knew he had no choice. Plus, while he was searching for Piper, he could continue the hunt to find his niece, which had turned out to be more difficult than he'd anticipated. Renee had no money and nowhere to go, yet he couldn't seem to locate even a hint of her whereabouts. "I accept," he said, before the other man could change his mind. "I'll locate Piper. What do you want me to do with her once I find her?"

"Bring her home immediately, of course. Everyone is really worried about her. We're all willing to help in whatever way we can. Let her know I'm willing to pay all her legal fees."

While Fowler's tone sounded earnest, something just felt off.

None of his business. "I don't want the entire amount before I do anything. You can pay 10 percent up front," Cord said.

Though Fowler's derisive expression said he thought Cord was an idiot, he nodded. "Agreed."

After the two men shook hands, Fowler pulled a thick wad of money out of his suit pocket. While Cord was processing this, Fowler peeled off thirty one-hundred dollar bills and handed them over.

Though he knew to do so would be goading the other man, Cord couldn't help himself. Slowly, methodically, he began counting the bills out loud. "And three thousand," he finished, pinning Fowler with his gaze. "The balance is payable immediately once I locate her."

"How long will this take?" Fowler didn't bother to keep the impatience out of his voice. "Thanksgiving is in a couple of weeks. I'd like to have the entire family at the table."

"When's the court date?" Cord countered. "She'll be back well in advance of when she's supposed to appear in court."

At the question, the uptight businessman actually appeared uncomfortable, shifting his weight from one foot to the other and tugging at the collar of his starched white shirt. "I don't know," he finally admitted. "But I will find out and get back to you."

"Sounds good." Ready for Fowler to leave, Cord headed for the door. He turned the knob and pulled it open. "Thanks for coming. Once you get me that court date, I'll give you weekly updates on the search."

Fowler frowned. He didn't move. "Weekly? I'd prefer daily."

"Not possible. I can't spare that kind of time. It would take away from the actual searching. I'll call you once a week, more if I have news."

"Fine." Fowler stalked to the door. "And remember, keep this quiet. No one needs to know about this, no one but the two of us."

Chapter 2

It took a lot of effort—head up, shoulders back, carefree smile—but Piper Colton figured she looked pretty damn confident, the way a Colton should. Not at all like she felt inside, all shaky and nervous, her heart pounding as loud as a runaway colt's hooves. Usually, she'd learned if she pretended self-assurance, she felt that way, too. What had once been a coping mechanism had become a way of life.

So what if she was often accused of wearing rose-colored glasses? She figured seeing the good in the world was much better than constantly looking for gloom and doom.

Except now. Getting arrested—finding out when they placed the handcuffs on her wrists that this wasn't some kind of prank her brother T.C. had cooked up for her—had given her resilience a severe beating. So much so that she scarcely recognized herself. And now she found herself back to pretending to be the person she'd believed she'd become.

And soon she'd be a criminal for real. Ack. If she had a choice, she'd rather be doing almost anything than this—emptying her savings account so she could stay untraceable while on the run. On the lam. Usually, a turn of phrase could make her chuckle. Not today.

Approaching the bank counter, she summed up a smile for Colin Jameson, who'd recently graduated from high school and landed a job as a teller. He blushed when she smiled at him, but handled the transaction without a lot of questions, which was exactly what she wanted. If she'd gotten Mrs. Bell, the older teller would have peppered Piper with questions.

Accepting the white envelope containing her hard earned cash, Piper tucked it in her purse and turned to go.

To her relief and surprise she made it to her car without anyone stopping her. Once inside, she locked the door and took deep breaths, trying to stop shaking. She didn't know why she felt so guilty. It wasn't like she was robbing the bank or something.

Starting the car, she carefully backed out of the parking space, waving at Mr. Gumpert as if she hadn't a care in the world. Carefully keeping to the speed limit, she drove toward Dallas, even though she had no intention of staying there. At least not yet.

Only once she left the town limits behind did her heart rate slow. Though she knew she needed to make a strategy, truthfully she hadn't thought much beyond getting every penny of her cash. Now with that accomplished, she needed to deal with making some sort of practical plan. Starting with where to go.

Hiding in plain sight would be great, but not so much in a smallish town where her entire family was well-known. Since she wanted to try and find out who'd really killed Eldridge, she had to stay close. Not Dallas, since the hustle and bustle and huge size of the place made her nervous—once a country girl, always a country girl—but maybe one of the closer suburbs, near enough that running into the city wouldn't be a big deal, but far enough that she could go unnoticed.

Since Eldridge had operated mostly from downtown Dallas, she knew she'd have to start her investigation there.

Especially since the sheriff's office hadn't done much of a job investigating. Once they'd made up their minds Piper was the killer, they'd stopped looking for anyone else.

She still couldn't figure out what she'd done that had made her a suspect. In fact, when the two deputies had shown up to arrest her, at first she'd believed someone was playing a joke on her. The cold bite of the steel handcuffs had made her realize otherwise.

Still, trying to wrap her mind around her circumstances made her feel ill. Someone, somewhere, truly believed her capable of murdering the only man who'd been a father to her.

As far as she knew, her court date hadn't been set yet. She had until then to come up with the real killer or she'd need to have a better alibi than the truth if she wanted to stay out of prison for a crime she hadn't committed. Though truthfully, the idea of fleeing to Mexico was tempting, there was no way she was leaving T.C., Reid and Alanna on the hook for the $50,000 bail they'd posted for her. They'd lose all of that if she didn't show up in court. No matter what, she knew she couldn't do that to them. They'd believed in her and helped her when she needed it the most. She'd never forget that. Somehow, someday, she'd pay them back.

Pulling into a fast-food restaurant on the outskirts of town, she parked. Before she did anything else, she needed to have time to gather her thoughts. Though she'd been saving for close to a year to start her own business, she hated to blow through her savings if she didn't have to. She refused to let go of the hope she might still open her Piper's Funky Furniture store one day. Her hobby of fixing up and painting old junked-out furniture bright colors had taken off. Friends, and then friends of those friends, had purchased pieces from her online store. Enough of them to make her realize she needed to have a brick-and-mortar shop of her own. She'd actually saved enough to get started and had begun making plans to find a spot to rent after the holidays. She'd even accumulated some inventory—a couple of chests of drawers and a lovely china cabinet that she'd painted turquoise.

Now all of that would be put on hold. Hopefully, not permanently.

First things first. As a member of the Colton family, she was often recognized. She'd need a disguise, like a new haircut and color, maybe a pair of oversize eyeglasses.

And then she'd need a place to stay. Her best bet would be to find a cabin for rent, one of those summer places where prices would be slashed since it was off-season. She thought she'd head toward Lake Whitney, after checking on her phone and learning of just such a place.

Item number one. Alter her appearance. And no going about it halfway. She'd seen a trendy little salon outside of Terrell. Fingering her long, silky locks, she grinned. She'd always wondered what it would be like to have super short hair. Looked like she was about to find out.

Once she'd been seated in the stylist's chair, Piper gave the young woman instructions to give her an edgy cut that would be easy to maintain. She also requested hot-pink tips, though she asked to keep her pale blond hair color.

An hour later, staring at herself in the salon mirror,

Piper laughed out loud. She could barely recognize herself. "I should have done this years ago," she remarked.

"I agree." The quiet stylist brought a mirror around to show Piper the back. "The cut brings out your cheekbones and makes your eyes appear huge!"

"And I love the pink tips." Odd how such a simple thing as a haircut could make Piper feel like herself again. She paid in cash, tipping exactly 20 percent, though she wished she could give more. For now, she had to be frugal with her money. This was all she had until she found out the truth about what had happened to Eldridge and exonerated herself.

All she had to do was find the true murderer. Since she had few illusions that finding Eldridge's real killer would be easy, maybe she should hire a private investigator. Could she afford that? Or could she afford not to?

She thought back to a guy she'd once known. Cord Maxwell. He'd lived on the ranch as a kid since his father had been a ranch hand. Though she'd lost track of him over the years, she'd heard he'd gone to work with Sam Ater as a PI.

Walking out of the salon a good seven inches of hair lighter, she shook her head, loving the way air felt on her naked neck. She'd never worn her hair this short, nor had layers. She had to say, the tousled look and different colors made her feel like a totally different person. Since that's exactly how she needed to look, she considered it money well spent. All she needed now was a pair of oversize eyeglasses and hopefully no one would look twice. She drove to Walmart, walked inside and purchased a pair of frames with clear, nonprescription lenses. Slipping them on, she caught sight of herself in her car window and grinned. Perfect.

Now she'd taken care of a disguise, which hopefully

would buy her time to search for information about where Eldridge had been and who he'd seen the day he'd supposedly been killed. The one thing she didn't understand was how the police could assume he'd been murdered when they didn't even have a body. Since they couldn't seem to find one, she believed quite strongly that Eldridge wasn't dead.

The bloody shirt needed explaining. Who hated her enough to try and frame her for murder?

Rubbing her hands together, trademark optimism back in place, she needed to decide what to do next.

She had a small problem. Okay, maybe a big one. Despite watching lots of detective and true crime shows on TV, she actually had no idea how to start searching for Eldridge. If the police couldn't find him, how could she?

Of course, she didn't think the sheriff and his deputies had searched much once they'd decided to arrest her.

Her brief consideration of hiring Cord Maxwell came back around. Maybe it wasn't a bad idea. She needed a professional. Someone who did this sort of thing all the time. Someone with contacts, who could be discreet, and would accept a payment in cash.

She thought he might be just that person. The only problem—his office was on Third Street, back in town.

Glancing at her watch, she knew she had enough time to drive back toward town and stop at his office. But then she reconsidered. Not only did she run the risk of being recognized, even with her disguise, but what if Cord had heard she'd left town? This could be misconstrued as skipping out on her bail. He was a bounty hunter, after all.

Instead, she decided to call him. Once he'd verbally accepted her offer to work for her, he couldn't bring her in, could he? She thought it would be a conflict of interest. Or something.

Using her phone, she did a quick internet search for S.A. Enterprises and located their web page. Once she had the phone number, she put it in her phone. Her finger hovered above the green phone icon. Was she sure she wanted to do this?

Though a trickle of fear clogged her throat, she knew she had to make the call. Truth be told, she had nothing to lose and everything to gain.

When his office phone rang, Cord almost didn't answer it. He'd spent the last hour mapping out a search area. Since Piper Colton wasn't used to being on the lam, he figured she'd be easy to find. Of course, he'd believed the same thing about Renee.

Something, call it instinct or maybe just desperation, had him reaching for the phone. After he answered and heard the husky feminine voice on the line, he could hardly believe he could be this lucky.

Piper Colton. And she wanted to hire him.

"Wait, slow down," he said, barely able to make sense out of the torrent of words. "Maybe you should come in so we can talk."

She went silent then. For a few seconds at least, long enough for him to worry he might have blown it. "Or we can meet somewhere," he added, aware she might not feel comfortable venturing back into town.

"There's a flea market tomorrow in Terrell," she finally said, sounding remarkably upbeat considering her situation. "Meet me in front of the entrance at nine. It's usually pretty crowded, so I'll wear a yellow T-shirt."

Quickly, he agreed. Evidently, Piper Colton still liked to hunt down junked out furniture and make it pretty. He'd actually planned to begin searching at the Terrell Trade Days.

She ended the call before he could question her further. No matter. He could hardly believe this case would be so easy. Not even two days had passed since Fowler had hired him.

Grinning, he wished Sam were still here to high-five. Well-paying, quick and easy cases happened very seldom.

The next morning, Cord donned his usual jeans, work boots and T-shirt. Though he wore his pistol in the concealed holster, he knew he most likely wouldn't have to use it. One thing he'd learned over the years was that bringing in a fugitive was nothing like what was portrayed in movies and books. Nine times out of ten, the best way to apprehend someone was to talk to them. Explain the cost of their actions. And to listen when they attempted to justify what they'd done.

By the time he and Piper finished shooting the breeze, he anticipated she'd be eager to return home to face the music.

Years had passed since he'd seen Piper, and he remembered her as a skinny waif of a kid, all legs and elbows, with her long blond hair worn in twin braids. Oddly enough, in all this time he hadn't run into her in town. He supposed he might have seen her from a distance, but couldn't say for certain. He'd never been one to pay that much attention to the Colton family's coming and goings. Those folks operated on a different plane than the rest of town.

Despite the overcast morning, the unseasonably warm temperature enabled him not only to go without a jacket, but to wear short sleeves. Texas weather, always unpredictable. Eighty degrees one day, a hard freeze the next. As far as Cord was concerned, he preferred heat over cold.

Driving out to the flea market, he realized Piper hadn't been exaggerating when she talked of the crowds. A mile from the flea market and he sat in a traffic jam that rivaled Dallas's early morning rush hour.

Finally, he spotted a parking lot with openings. Handing over his ten dollar fee, he parked his truck. Now to find Piper Colton and talk her into returning home.

Long lines formed at the entrance. Realizing people were waiting to purchase tickets to get in, he muttered a curse. Whoever heard of paying admission to an oversize garage sale, which was all a flea market was as far as he was concerned.

Bypassing the lines earned him several frowns and glares. He ignored this, scanning the crowd for a woman in a yellow shirt.

Of course, there were several. The first, he discounted immediately as she had to be at least eighty. The next could be the right age, but she had three kids in tow.

And then he saw her. Piper Colton. Slender and beautiful and much sexier than he'd expected. She stood tall and confident, occasionally glancing up from her phone before returning her attention back to it. Though still athletic, she had curves in all the right places. She'd cut her blond hair short and tipped the spiky ends with hot pink, giving her an edgy look that he found erotic as hell. The stylish cut went well with her heart-shaped face, showing off her high cheekbones and making her green eyes appear huge, despite the large black eyeglasses she wore.

The pale yellow of her T-shirt made him smile. He'd pictured lemon yellow, not this watered down version that suited her coloring so well.

Striding toward her, he kept that smile on his face. She looked up, met his gaze, and he felt his entire world shift on its axis.

What the hell? Pushing away the momentary sense of disorientation, he held out his hand. "Cord Maxwell," he said quietly.

"Pleased to meet you." Though she slid her fingers into his and shook his hand, he noticed she didn't offer her name. The fleeting firmness of her cool grip on his fingers pleased him. There was nothing tentative in this woman, which was good. She'd need all of her strength to face the days ahead.

"I need your assistance," she began. "As I'm sure you've probably heard, my adoptive father has disappeared. Since you're a private investigator, I want to hire you to help me find out who kidnapped him and where he is."

Though he tried, he couldn't quite contain his shock.

"What'd you think I wanted?" she asked, her dry tone warring with her serious expression.

He gave her the truth. "I thought you might ask me to help you find information to beat the murder charge."

A subtle flash in her eyes before she looked down. Anger? Resignation? Maybe both. "You know about that."

"Yes." Debating if now would be the right time, he exhaled and went with it. "Your brother Fowler paid me a visit."

A combination of distaste and pain reflexed back at him in her expressive eyes. "What did Fowler want?"

"He hired me to find you."

She froze. "Do you think you might have mentioned that when I first contacted you?"

"I thought maybe we could talk first."

Barely had he gotten the words out when she spun to take off. He grabbed her arm. "Wait…"

"Let me go or I'll scream." She spoke through clenched teeth.

"Please. Hear me out."

"Release. My. Arm." She spat. "You're hurting me."

That last did it. Even though he doubted his tight grip was painful, he let her go.

Of course she took off. A fast walk, then a jog. He hurried along right behind her. No one in the crowd waiting in line to enter the flea market paid them any attention—if they did, Cord figured they'd assume a lovers' spat.

Piper's jog became an all-out sprint. As he did the same, he couldn't help but feel proud of her. She had no way to know he ran every morning. Or that he'd completed many marathons, too many to count.

Instead of catching her, he kept pace with her, keeping a few feet away. When she reached a white BMW, evidently her vehicle, she stopped and fumbled in her small shoulder bag for a key.

He made his move, stepping between her and the driver's side door. "Ten minutes," he said. "Just give me ten minutes of your time. I just want to talk."

Gaze raking over him, she shoved her glasses back up on her nose and considered. "I don't see what good that will do. If you're working for Fowler, you can't help me. Conflict of interest and all that."

"Maybe I can do both," he said. This got her attention.

"Fine. Ten minutes." Unlocking her car, she gestured at him to get in. "Start talking."

As he folded himself into the passenger seat, he realized she smelled like peaches. Which made him think of summer, his favorite time of the year. Biting into a plump, ripe peach with the juice running down his chin. And she, completely unaware of her appeal, eyed him with skepticism plain in every tense line of her body.

"I believe you," he told her. "I remember when we were kids on the ranch. You wouldn't even kill a bug."

She nodded, but didn't speak.

Neither did he. He could wait her out. Sam had drilled into him how patience solved more cases than anything else.

"But?" she finally prompted.

He hid his rueful smile. "When's your court date?"

"I have no idea. My sister said she was told I'd get notice in the mail. She is going to hire an attorney to represent me."

"Fowler said to tell you he'll pay all your legal fees." Might as well put that out there.

Her lovely eyes narrowed. "Why would he want to do that? He and Marceline made it clear they think I'm guilty."

"I think Fowler feels bad. He paid me a lot of money to find you and bring you back home."

Her pointed look told him what she thought about that. "And that's your cue to get out of my car."

"My ten minutes aren't up yet," he protested, keeping his tone light. "How about this. I'll work with you to find out what really happened to Eldridge if you agree to go back with me before your hearing."

"You want to make a deal?" The suspicion dripping from her voice made him smile.

"Yes."

"How do you know you can trust me?"

"I knew you way back when," he reminded her, even as he tried to reconcile the tomboy she'd once been with the confident and sexy woman sitting next to him. "I figure you couldn't have changed too much."

Head tilted, she considered him. "You know, despite

your kind memories of me, I'm not at all like you apparently think I am. I'm not a saint."

Her words brought a rush of selfish gladness, which he wisely kept to himself. It would be a sin to be a saint with a body like hers. "I never said you were."

"Despite that, to be honest I wasn't planning on skipping out on court. I wouldn't do that to T.C., Reid and Alanna."

"That's what I thought." He considered her right back, suppressing the tingle of desire he felt. "My suggestion is a win for both of us. I'll help you investigate what really happened to Eldridge, and you can help me—" He stopped, unable to believe how close he'd come to telling her about Renee.

Of course she picked up on that. "Help you what?"

Should he? Why not. Like her, he had nothing to lose by telling her. "Since my sister died two years ago, I've been trying to raise my niece, Renee," he said, keeping all emotion out of his voice. "She ran away a few weeks ago. I've been looking for her ever since."

Piper swallowed. One corner of her sensual mouth quirked in the beginnings of a smile. "Without success?"

"Exactly."

He could see her thoughts written plainly on her face. "I normally have a very high success rate. But just because I'm licensed as a private investigator and fugitive recovery specialist doesn't mean I never run into trouble."

"Good to know." The ghost of a smile vanished before it ever actually came into being. He found himself wishing he could have seen it.

"Why not?" she finally said, apparently coming to a quick decision. Her lack of prevaricating was another trait he admired. "Sure, I'm in. I'll help you find your niece and you help me learn the truth about what happened to Eldridge."

He noticed again she didn't say murder, which made him realize she truly didn't believe her adoptive father was dead. The flicker of interest he had at the thought was the first he'd experienced in any case since Renee had disappeared. Worry and guilt had basically consumed him, blotting out the potential for anything else.

"Sounds good," he managed, realizing he'd gone a bit too long lost in his thoughts. He held out his hand. "Partners?"

Without hesitation she shook. Once again, he felt that sizzle along his nerve endings and the touch of her fingers in his. Weird. But he could deal with it.

"Where are you staying?" he asked, now that they'd sealed the bargain.

"The Budget Inn off I-20."

"Let's go gather your stuff. You're staying with me from now on."

Arms crossed, she shook her head. "If you think that authoritative command is going to make me fall right in line with your plans, you're dead wrong," she drawled. "In fact, whenever someone tries to order me around, I want to do the exact opposite."

A laugh escaped him; he couldn't help it. "I like you," he said, surprised.

"I'm reserving judgment until I know you better." There it was again, the smile sneaking onto a corner of her mouth.

He found himself holding his breath waiting for it. When she looked down instead, he pushed away his disappointment. "Fair enough," he said. "We're a lot alike. I think we'll get along just fine."

"Maybe." She didn't sound too concerned. "Now I'm

going to go back to the flea market and check it out. After that, I'll think about considering your kind offer of shelter."

Chapter 3

As she browsed the flea market, pretending an extreme interest in just about every booth, from homemade baked goods to used tires, Piper ignored her keen awareness of the large man silently shadowing her. Due to his size and the masculinity he radiated, he drew a lot of stares from other women.

Though she couldn't blame them, she wasn't sure what to think of Cord Maxwell. As he'd pointed out, they'd known each other as children, but she also knew a lot could happen to a person in the years between childhood and adulthood.

Despite that, she'd kept distant track of him, the way most everyone did in a small town. She knew he'd inherited Sam Ater's business when Sam died and had heard Cord had a good reputation as a steady, honest man. She'd planned to hire him, after all. Until she'd realized he not only knew she'd been arrested for murder, but that Fowler had beat her to him.

Did that mean she could trust him? As she examined a beautiful, amber-colored jar of local honey, she considered. Cord had told her the truth up front—that he was working for Fowler—despite the possibility that doing so might make her run. That had to count for something, right?

She'd always been a big believer in trusting her instincts. And her gut feeling told her she could trust him.

Decision made, she turned to tell him, only to catch him regarding her with such intensity that his eyes had darkened. Unbidden, she felt an answering shiver of awareness before squashing it right back into nothing.

"We have a deal," she told him, about to offer him a handshake but thinking better of it at the last moment.

"I'm not nuts about staying in the same place as you," she admitted, swallowing hard as she brazened it out. "It's too intimate."

He stared at her for a second before a slow grin spread across his rugged face. "Intimate? Only if you make it so. You'll have your own room and bathroom. The only common areas will be the kitchen and living room. More like a roommate scenario. There's nothing remotely intimate about that."

His expression and voice said one thing, but the heat in his eyes said another. Her face warmed and she knew her skin had turned the color of a ripe tomato. She considered herself a strong, self-sufficient woman. Surely she could resist this tug of sexual attraction she felt whenever she so much as looked at him.

"You're probably right." Squaring her shoulders, she didn't let a single trace of regret sound in her voice. "All right. Let me pick up my gear and I'll follow you there in my car."

Though he nodded, he stared at her like he thought if he granted her access to her vehicle, she'd jump in and speed away. Irritated, she glared back at him. "My word's as good as yours, you know."

"That obvious, huh?"

"Yes. I guess you might have to deal with a lot of low-lifes in your profession, but I'm not one of them."

This clearly surprised him. One brow raised, he studied her. "I wasn't thinking you were a lowlife. I can see you're not. But you are a survivor. And I can tell you'll do whatever you have to in order to continue to survive."

Surprised and secretly pleased, she nodded. "Good read. We truly are two of a kind, because I can tell you're the same way. And from what little you've told me, I think your niece is a survivor, as well. I'm sure we'll find her soon."

The mention of his niece caused his expression to darken. "Maybe what I need is a feminine perspective. Once we get to my place, I'll tell you everything about her. Then maybe you'll have some thoughts about where she might have gone."

Though she doubted he was aware of it, he sounded so lost, so worried, that her heart went out to him. She truly hoped she actually could help him bring his niece home.

She drove back to her motel with him right behind her. For the first time since she'd left the ranch, she didn't stress so much over the possibility of anyone following her. At least now that she'd teamed up with Cord, she'd have one other person on her side. Sometimes that alone could make a huge difference.

He waited in his truck while she went into her room and gathered up her meager belongings. She checked out, paying cash, and strode back outside. Once in her car, she gestured to Cord to lead the way, and off they went. At least he didn't live in town proper or anywhere near the Colton Valley Ranch. Though he didn't have a place on the outside of town like her family, his home on the southern fringes near the county line ensured she wouldn't run into any of the Coltons or their friends.

As they turned into a long, winding drive, the sight of his house sitting beneath tall trees caused something to shift inside her. "Perfect," she exclaimed out loud, even though no one could hear her. His home on the outside, all perfectly fit logs hewn from rugged timber, suited him perfectly. If the situation had been different—no, she wouldn't let herself go there.

She'd keep things friendly, but professional. After all, this was a business partnership, sort of.

"What are you going to tell Fowler?" she asked the instant she got out of the car.

To give him credit, he simply shrugged. "Nothing, yet. I'm not going to lie, but he doesn't need to know I've found you until closer to the court date. Since notice will be mailed to your home, we're either going to have to rely on Fowler to tell me, or you'll need to contact one of your siblings. Is that all right with you?"

Once again she appreciated his honesty. "Sounds good." Keeping her tone light, she followed him into his house.

Inside, she stopped and stared. The same log walls, with matching polished pine floors, gave the interior a rustic, welcoming feel. His oversize leather furniture, along with the still life painting of wildlife, gave the room a masculine feel. The only thing lacking was a woman's touch.

He laughed, making her realize she'd spoken out loud. "I'm sorry," she said. "Sometimes my thoughts travel from my mind to my mouth before I can think."

"It's okay." At least he continued to smile, so she knew she hadn't offended him. "I actually remember that about you."

"Seriously?" She frowned, trying to decide if her bad habit had been around even in childhood. Guessing it probably had, she let it go.

"Yep." He squeezed her shoulder, his expression friendly. "It's one of the things I always liked about you. No subterfuge."

Apparently he remembered more about her than she did him. Mostly she remembered feeling sorry for him, a young kid like her, left so often to his own devices by a father who stayed drunk more than sober.

"Thanks." Taking one more look around, she eyed him. "Where am I staying?"

"This way." A short, L-shaped hallway branched out from the living room. They passed one doorway, which at a quick glance appeared to be an office-combination-workout room, and stopped at the second. "My guest bedroom, now yours. Feel free to add any womanly touches you feel it needs for as long as you're here."

Gazing up at his smiling face, something shifted inside her. "I will," she said, her tone brisk. "I'm going to unpack first. I don't like things wrinkled."

"Of course. When you're done, meet me in the kitchen. We have a lot to discuss, not just about Renee, but about Eldridge, too."

She nodded, heart still up in her throat, and quietly closed the door. Then stood there like a fool and listened to the sound of his footsteps as he went down the hall.

Sighing, she went over to her backpack, unzipped it and emptied it onto the bed. Hanging up her meager collection of clothes—kudos to Cord for providing hangers in the closet—she checked out the hall bathroom before heading out to the kitchen. It would do. It all would do for the short time she intended to stay here.

Cord stood as she approached, drawing her gaze to

his broad shoulders, muscular chest and arms. With his shaggy head of dark hair, he looked primitive and dangerous and, if she was honest, sexy as hell.

It dawned on her that maybe she'd made a mistake agreeing to stay with him. Then, as he met her gaze and flashed that half smile, she took a deep breath and told herself to quit being an idiot.

"Would you like something to drink?" he asked. "I have coffee, tea, bottled water and Coke."

"Water, please." Taking a seat, she gazed up at him, refusing to be overwhelmed by his blatant sex appeal.

Handing her bottled water, he straddled the chair across from her. "Let's start at the beginning. What evidence do the police have on you that made them arrest you?"

"A bloodstained shirt was found in my closet."

"Eldridge's?"

She nodded. "I gave him that shirt for Christmas several years ago. He rarely wore it."

"What else?" Watching her closely, he took a long drink of his water. She almost lost her train of thought, watching the movement of his throat as he swallowed.

"That's it, as far as I know."

"A shirt alone isn't enough. Do they have some sort of confession?"

A humorless laugh escaped her. "No. But not for lack of trying. Two officers badgered me for hours. At one point I considered agreeing to what they wanted me to say, just to get them to stop. But I knew that's what they wanted. And, since I didn't kill Eldridge, there was no way I was about to claim I did. They need to get off their lazy rear ends and find the real killer."

His grin floored her, making her chest ache. She couldn't figure out how this man could distract her so easily, at a time when distraction was the last thing she needed.

"I agree." He sounded almost cheerful. "And there has to be more, or the DA won't let them charge you. I've got a friend who works in the sheriff's department. Let me do some digging."

Relieved, she nodded. "Okay. My brother Reid used to be a detective and he promised to check around, too." She took a deep breath. "Now that we've discussed my situation, why don't you tell me about your niece?"

"Renee?" A shadow darkened his features as he spoke the name. "Do you remember my older sister, Denice?"

"Vaguely. She wasn't around a lot. Wasn't she tall, and really pretty? I think she liked to party."

"She did. And with a father like ours, I couldn't blame her. At least, not at first. But once she got pregnant, she cleaned up her act. I really thought she'd be a great mother…" His voice trailed off.

As the silence stretched out, she exhaled and prompted. "But? There's always a *but*."

He shrugged, clearly pretending to be unaffected, though the pain in his eyes told another story. "She wasn't. She and Renee's father married. Joshua was an addict and in a band. She started traveling with him. I'm sure you can guess the rest."

She nodded. "What happened to them?"

"Denice was driving drunk. Her husband and Renee were in the car. She drove onto I-635 going the wrong way. The head-on collision killed Denice and him instantly. Renee was asleep in the backseat. She was lucky. She had numerous broken bones and had to be hospitalized for a couple of weeks while they tried to get the swelling around her brain to go down. When she finally healed enough to be released, I brought her home with me. She was sixteen."

Her heart wrenched. "Poor girl. That had to be hard."

Gazing off into the distance, he nodded. "It was. The worst part was the screaming. She kept reliving the moment when she woke up in the wrecked car. Luckily, she had her seat belt on, but she was hanging upside down. Her mother was dead in the front seat and her father..."

Dragging a hand across his mouth, he swallowed. "Needless to say, I've been sending her to therapy. I really thought it was beginning to help." His grimace told her what he thought about that.

"Enough about the past," he finally said. "I need to find her. I couldn't save my sister, but I refuse to give up on her daughter."

Despite barely knowing him, Piper battled the strongest urge to go to him and wrap her arms around him. For comfort, nothing more. Or so she told herself, trying to ignore the way her mouth went dry at the thought of touching him.

Instead, she forced herself to focus on his statement. "Tell me about her. What does she like to do for fun? Does she have any hobbies?"

His blank look told her he truly didn't know.

Briefly, she closed her eyes. "How involved in her life were you, exactly?"

He swore. Under his breath, but still loud enough for her to hear. "I tried." His grim voice contained both bewilderment and guilt. "She pushed me away at every turn. Renee couldn't come to grips with the thought of living with me, an uncle she barely knew. She constantly tried to re-create her parents' lifestyle. I guess she believed she could find comfort in the familiar."

Unable to find the right words, Piper said nothing.

She actually had to curl her fingers into her palms, nails digging into her skin, to keep from reaching out to him.

"Hey, I'm sorry." Pushing to his feet, he shook himself, like a dog shaking off water. "I don't mean to sound so pitiful."

"You don't. I get what you're telling me. It was a lot more difficult than you expected, trying to raise a teenager."

"Yes." Sounding relieved, he sat back down. "I probably was overprotective. I didn't want her to make the same mistakes her mother made."

"I bet the more you pushed, the worse she pulled in the other direction. Poor kid just wanted love and acceptance. She didn't understand you were loving her the only way you knew how."

"Exactly."

She thought for a second. "Okay, let's start with the basics. Did she graduate high school?"

"Yes."

"Good. What were her plans for after graduation? College? Junior college?"

He snorted, then looked ashamed. "She had no plans that I know of. I figured she liked to party. At least she had a job."

"Aha." Finally something concrete. "Where did she work?"

"Several places. All waitressing jobs. She liked waitressing. And she did well, until she got fired."

"Why? What'd she do to make them let her go?"

"Actually, I'm not sure. I figured partying, but for all I know she could have stolen something."

Shocked, Piper struggled with the idea that Cord hadn't bothered to find out. "Getting fired is a direct hit on anyone's self-confidence. You never asked her why?"

"Hey." He spread his hands in a defensive gesture. "Every time I tried to talk to her about anything, whether it was about the weather or something more personal, like school or her job, she'd shut down and refuse to answer."

"What about after graduation?"

"The only time I ever heard her mention any sort of aspiration was that she wanted to tend bar. She said she was tired of waitressing. I told her she wasn't old enough to be a bartender. She looked at me and told me there were ways around her age."

With a sigh, she tried to keep her tone light. "Her last job—did she quit or get fired?"

He took another swig of water before answering. "I guess you could say both. She stopped showing up for work and they fired her."

"I assume since you appear to have covered all the bases that you've already talked to her friends."

To her surprise, he grimaced. "I tried. But she never brought anyone to the house and her coworkers couldn't think of any friends—male or female—either."

Her heart squeezed. "Poor kid. She was trying to cope all on her own."

"Maybe." He didn't sound convinced. "But the more realistic possibility is that she does have friends. Friends that are the type to stay hidden. The kind she knew I wouldn't approve of. Drug dealers and addicts. People like the ones she must have grown up around, since her parents no doubt brought them home."

"I don't know." Piper shook her head. "Have you ever considered the possibility that she might want the opposite lifestyle? She's new here. Maybe she's shy. It's really hard on teenagers moving to a new place and school."

"She's been here two years. Even the biggest wall-flower in the world would have made a friend or two after all that time. Remember, she liked to party. No one does that alone."

Since she hadn't actually met his niece, Piper figured he'd be more equipped to know. "Okay. Did you talk to her school? The teachers, her guidance counselor, anyone like that?"

"Yes." Cord's expression might have been carved from stone. "Most of them barely remembered her. Except the art teacher. That woman couldn't stop talking about how talented Renee is."

"Art?" Now they were getting somewhere. Most likely, Renee had used her art to help her cope with her loneliness, the same way Piper did with her refinishing old furniture. "What kind of art? Does she paint or sculpt or…?"

He shrugged. "I'm not sure. But the art teacher seemed surprised to hear she'd run away. She said before graduation, she and Renee had been looking at art schools so Renee could apply."

"Did she? Apply to any schools?" Though Piper had often been accused of wearing rose-colored glasses, she felt a strange sort of kinship with this girl, despite never meeting her.

"Again, I don't know." A slight edge had crept into his voice, as if he realized this was the sort of information he should have been privy to.

She didn't know him well enough to take him to task for his lack of knowledge about someone he'd shared his home with for twenty-four months.

Cord knew what Piper thought. Truth be told, he couldn't actually blame her. He'd done a crappy job of trying to raise Renee for the past two years. Part of that was due to his complete and utter unpreparedness and lack of experience.

The other part, the one he had trouble admitting even to himself, was from the instant he'd met the troubled sixteen-year-old, she'd reminded him of his sister, Denice. If Renee went down the same path as Denice had, Cord knew it would kill him.

He'd tried. By all that was holy, he'd tried. Every mistake he'd made—and there'd been plenty—he'd tried to rectify.

While he knew Piper wasn't judging him, hearing his own answers to her innocuous questions had made him inwardly cringe.

"Let's focus on you now," he said, aware changing the subject wouldn't make his errors go away. "You say you were framed?"

"Yes."

"Do you have many enemies?"

Startled, she considered. "I never thought about that before. It's possible. I do tend to be outspoken about what I feel is right. Not everyone agrees with me."

"Let's narrow that down. Anyone get angry with you recently?"

"Fowler and Marceline, but that's nothing unusual, I can barely breathe without annoying one or the other, Marceline especially. She likes to harp on the fact that I'm not a real Colton." She spoke matter-of-factly, simply because that's the way it had always been for as long as she could remember.

"I remember," he said, his expression inscrutable. "She did that even when we were all kids. What I never could figure out is why. It's not like she was born a Colton, either."

Secretly pleased, Piper looked down at her hands to

hide her smile. "Yeah, the logic she used never failed to amaze me."

"Anyone else?" he pressed. "Figuring out who tried to frame you would be a step in making sure you're acquitted."

"I'll think about it and make you a list." Though she'd only been half-serious, he nodded.

"You do that. Knowing who to investigate will put us that much closer to finding out who's trying to frame you."

The simple statement, made in such a matter-of-fact tone, floored her. Probably because after Fowler and Marceline's accusations, the idea that this man, whom she barely knew, actually believed her, made her feel weepy and joyful all at once.

"Thank you," she told him. "I'll get busy on that right away."

"Here." Handing her a pad of paper and a pen, he smiled. The masculine sensuality of that smile made her heart skip. "While you do that, I've got some chores to complete."

"It shouldn't take too long. I don't think I have too many enemies."

He laughed. "Once you get to thinking about it, it might surprise you."

And he left. Leaving her staring at a blank piece of paper trying to figure out who might hate her enough to frame her.

Piper Colton had no idea of the power of her own beauty, Cord thought as he trudged out to the barn. He'd known other beautiful women before and without exception, every move, every smile or glance, had been carefully and artfully calculated to show their attributes off to the best advantage. Piper, on the other hand, appeared genuine. Sweet and kind. And sexy as hell.

He considered himself lucky he had chores to keep his mind off where it didn't belong.

The wind had shifted to the north, bringing a chill. He brought the horses into the barn first, making sure they were snug in their stalls. Then he rounded up his goats and put them all in one stall. After they'd all been fed, he refilled the watering troughs and left them bunkered down.

Before heading in, he grabbed a bundle of firewood to take inside with him.

Piper sat where he'd left her, legs tucked up under her, pad and pen in hand.

"No luck so far," she announced, then eyed him. "What do you have there?"

"A cold front is coming in. They're predicting the first freeze of the season," he said, dropping his load on the brick hearth. He went outside for one more. She watched him as he placed his load in the small stack.

"Are we going to have a fire?"

He had to grin at the hint of excitement in her voice. "Sure, why not? The forecast says it'll drop down to around 25 degrees. Definitely fire-in-the-fireplace weather."

She grinned back. "Can you light it now?"

Momentarily captivated by the way her smile lit up her heart-shaped face, it took him a second to formulate a single-word answer. "Sure."

Once he had a nice blaze going, he straightened. The orange glow from the fire bathed the entire room—and Piper—in a warm, mellow light.

He was suddenly aware of exactly how cozy—or to

borrow her word from before, *intimate*—a simple thing as a fire on a cold winter's night could be.

Only if he let it.

"Now, the only thing that could make this more perfect would be a cup of hot cocoa," she sighed. When she wrinkled her nose at him, he knew he was in trouble.

"I bet I have some instant cocoa somewhere," he managed. "Let me go see." And he beat a hasty retreat from the room.

Once in the brightly lit (and non-cozy) kitchen, he gulped in air. What the hell? It wasn't like he'd never had a woman over his house before. He'd had more than a few girlfriends here since he'd bought the place. Just none of them had ever affected him the way Piper did.

Which was not only weird, but worrisome. Very, very dangerous to his equilibrium. What was left of it. The last two years had been a roller coaster of ups and downs. He'd just gotten his act together when Sam died. After that he'd faced Denice's death and becoming the legal guardian of a rebellious sixteen-year-old.

It seemed he'd barely adjusted, his life finally evening out when Renee took off. The last thing he needed would be to form any kind of attachment to Piper Colton, whether emotional or sexual.

While he placed the teakettle on the stove top to heat the water and emptied the little packets of cocoa into mugs, he reminded himself that she was his bounty. Or a client. Actually, both. Either way, she was off-limits.

The kettle whistled and he poured the water into the cocoa powder, stirring. He didn't have any whipped cream on hand since the only time he bothered to buy that was for pies. Plain old cocoa would have to do.

He carried the mugs back into the living room and

placed one down on the table in front of her. "Cheers," he said, raising his in a mock salute.

Her smile caused something to twist in his gut. "Cheers," she replied. "Thank you for making the cocoa."

"You're welcome." Placing his mug on the hearth, he pretended to fiddle with the logs and the fire so he wouldn't start grinning like an idiot.

"I've been working on a plan," she said, offhandedly scratching a pleased Truman behind his ears.

Surprised, he glanced back at her over his shoulder. She lifted a spiral notebook to show him. "Just some ideas at this point."

"Ideas of who might have actually killed Eldridge or where he might be?"

"No." She shook her head. "About places we might look for Renee."

"Seriously?" To keep himself occupied, he grabbed his mug and chugged some of his cocoa. The instant he did, he realized his mistake. Too hot. Somehow he managed to swallow, inwardly cursing the burn on his tongue.

Piper didn't appear to notice. "Why do you sound so surprised?"

"I figured you'd want to work on your stuff first." He shrugged, and then took another, more careful, sip.

"I thought we could do both." Patting the coach cushion next to her, she opened her notebook. "Come sit. Let's go over these notes."

As he debated the dubious wisdom of sitting so close to her, the doorbell rang. Truman immediately leaped to his feet and charged the door, barking.

"Truman, come," Cord ordered. Once Truman had reluctantly complied, Cord gave him the hand signal for *sit* and then *stay*. Piper watched, her expression amazed.

Now that the barking had quieted, Cord checked the peephole. "Fowler," he said out loud.

Piper gasped, jumping from the couch so quickly she nearly spilled her cocoa. She fled, heading toward her room. Cord waited until he heard her door close before he opened the front door.

Chapter 4

"What are you doing here?" Cord demanded, blocking the entrance so Fowler would have no choice but to remain on the front stoop.

Fowler peered at him, swaying slightly. He wore his usual suit, though his tie had been loosened. "I thought I'd check to see if you'd made any progress."

Was that a slight slurring of his words? Not that it was any of his business, but as far as Cord knew, Fowler didn't drink.

"This is my home." Cord kept his tone firm. "It's after nine p.m. If you want to discuss business, you'll need to stop by my office during business hours. I'd suggest you call first and make an appointment since I'm often out on the road."

None of his words appeared to register. "I know." Fowler gave him a lopsided grin. "But we were passing right by here and I decided to stop in and check with you."

We?

"Have you been drinking?" Peering around the other man, Cord tried to find Fowler's car. There it was, blocking his driveway. He couldn't tell if there was someone else inside or not.

"I have. But I'm not driving. Tiffany is. And she doesn't drink."

The difference from the uptight, overbearing business-man to this inebriated, regular guy made Cord wonder if he'd misjudged the other man. Either way, he knew he couldn't let Fowler inside the house.

"Good. I'm glad to hear it." Cord began closing the door. To his annoyance, Fowler stuck one foot, clad in expensive Italian leather, in the way.

"I'd suggest you move that foot," Cord warned him. "It might hurt if I stomp on it or slam the door with it still inside. You might even sustain a broken bone or two."

"You wouldn't dare." There. That pompous tone was 100 percent the Fowler everyone loved to hate.

"Try me." Cord checked his watch. "I'm going to count to three and then the door is going to close. One."

"You work for me," Fowler declared, his expression a strange combination of pinched and sloppy. "I demand you give me a status update."

"Demand? Wrong choice of words. I'm not on the payroll 24/7. Two."

"Damn you."

"Three."

Fowler jerked his foot back so hard he stumbled. Cord slammed the door, secured the dead bolt and took a deep breath. He peered through the blinds, wanting to make sure the other man actually left.

Only once he'd witnessed Fowler climbing into the passenger side of the car did he go and fetch Piper, Tru-man tagging along behind him.

Tapping lightly on her bedroom door, he turned the knob and peered inside. "He's gone." She looked up at him, her eyes wide. She sat perched on the edge of the bed as if about to take flight, her face pale. "What did you tell him?"

"Nothing. I sent him away." As he took a step into the room, he realized she was trembling. Damn. "Are you all right?" This was so unlike the brash, confident Piper he'd begun to know, it worried him.

"Yes. I'm fine."

One more step closer. "You don't look fine."

At that, she jumped to her feet. "All right, I'm not. As soon as I realized Fowler was here, I figured you'd give me up."

"Why would I do that?"

"Because you work for him." The way she spoke made him realize she'd clenched her teeth.

"True. But I already told you I wasn't about to turn you over just yet, remember? Legally, since you haven't missed your court date yet, I don't have to. I don't go back on my word. I told Fowler you'd be back before your court date. You agreed to this. We're good."

She shook her head, hands clenched into fists at her ides. "Tell me the truth. Is Fowler out there waiting for me?"

Though he knew he should keep his distance, he took yet one final step, stopping a few feet from her. "Let's get one thing straight between us, Piper Colton. I'm a man of my word. I don't lie. If I tell you he's gone, he's gone."

At his words she made an angry puff of sound before she spun and stalked to the other side of the room, away from him. Truman the traitor followed her, tail wagging. She reached down and petted the dog, scratching just above his collar. "You've just contradicted yourself. If you don't lie, how'd you get Fowler to leave?"

Though damned if he didn't feel he were hunting her,

he followed. "He didn't ask if I'd found you or if you were here. He demanded a status report, which I refused to give him. Nothing but the truth. That's the one thing you can always count on from me."

"Braggart."

Not sure he'd heard correctly, he stared. "What?"

"I called you a braggart." She tilted her head as she eyed him, and he wondered if she truly was daring him to defend himself. Damn, she was beautiful, with that heart-shaped face, her emerald eyed fringed with thick black lashes and her spiky blond hair tinged with hot pink. Sexy, too.

Whatever her intention, her words coaxed a reluctant smile from him. "It's the truth," he insisted, merely because he wanted to see what she'd do next. "I never lie."

"Never?"

"Never."

She circled him, keeping several feet between them.

Truman sat, watching her curiously. "That must make life difficult for you sometimes."

Thoroughly entertained, he acknowledged her comment with a nod.

"Do you like me?" No coquettishness in either her voice or her expression, just simple curiosity.

"Yes. Actually, I'm beginning to," he amended, still smiling. "Why do you want to know?"

She shrugged. "Just testing to see if you really won't lie. Are you attracted to me?"

A jolt went through him. "Are you flirting?"

Though she colored, she didn't look away. "Maybe. Maybe not. I'm trying to find out where we stand with each other. I also noticed you didn't answer the question."

He laughed; he couldn't help it. "I'd have to be dead not to find you attractive," he told her. "But don't worry,

I won't let it get in the way of the job I have to do. Or finding Renee. Both are too important to me."

Color still high, she finally smiled back. "Fair enough. Now how about we call it a night and regroup in the morning."

Though it was still early, he nodded. "Okay. Good night."

She sighed. "I'm probably going to regret this, but…"

Before he could ask what she meant, she crossed the space between them, grabbed him and pulled him down for a kiss. Her mouth moved across his, nothing tentative about it. A wave of lust swamped him. Damn if it wasn't the most erotic kiss he'd ever shared.

Standing stock-still, he let her nibble and explore, until he couldn't take it any longer. Finally, he seized control, needing to claim her. He tasted her, skimmed his fingers over her soft, soft skin, outlining her lush curves. He couldn't get enough, craving more, breathing her in until the force of his arousal told him he needed to break it off right now or they'd be in trouble.

He'd be in trouble, he amended silently. Despite the fact that he physically shook with desire, he stepped back, trying to slow his heartbeat and the way he inhaled short gasps of air. Drowning, that's what this had been like. Drowning in her.

"Good night," he rasped, and turned to go. The way he left felt more like a retreat than anything else, but so be it. "Truman, come."

His loyal dog, man's best friend, didn't budge. So Cord left him there with Piper.

Once he made it all the way across the house, he headed toward his room, desperately trying to think of something—anything—other than how badly he wanted to be inside of her.

A cold shower later—which helped, at least for a few minutes—and he finally slipped beneath his sheets. He'd lived long enough to understand what had just occurred between him and Piper was a huge mistake. He needed to do his best to forget it had ever happened. If she brought it up again, he'd say the same thing to her.

And if she initiated another kiss?

Just the thought had him burning again. Even though he'd made a conscious decision to try and forget, he couldn't help but relive the moment.

He'd held her. Close. Felt every curve and hollow of her body pressed tightly against his. He'd tasted her—or rather—she'd tasted him. Her self-confidence and boldness intrigued and aroused him, which only made her even more dangerous.

The next morning Piper woke and stretched, taking a moment to contemplate before jumping out of bed. She must have been exhausted, since she'd apparently fallen deeply asleep the instant her head hit the pillow. She remembered nothing after that, not even a single dream.

All her life, she'd been a morning person, to most of the family's dismay. When she woke, she liked to face the day head-on, full of energy and optimism.

Today would be no exception, even if she'd gotten a little carried away last night.

But who could blame her? Being around gorgeous, sexy-as-hell Cord would tempt a saint. And Piper definitely wasn't a saint. She, like any other red-blooded female, could appreciate a perfect specimen of a man. Cord, with his thick mane of dark hair, chiseled features and muscular body, definitely qualified. Every time she looked at him her mouth went dry and her body tingled.

Just thinking about him made her want to kiss him

again. And more, if she was honest with herself, which she always tried to be.

The way she saw it, with the two of them in such enforced, close proximity, sex would be inevitable. Maybe she'd simply tell him that, so they could get past the tiptoeing around each other and get right to it. Honestly, she'd been celibate long enough. She didn't know how much longer she could wait.

If he asked her, she'd tell him the truth. She wanted him. She felt certain enough of that fact to be honest and upfront about it. Though she couldn't say she never lied. She didn't truly believe Cord when he said he didn't.

A soft whine came from beside her. From a large lump under the blanket. A second later, Truman poked his big head out. "What are you doing there?" she asked, scratching him in his favorite place just below the ears. He sighed and closed his eyes.

"You can sleep in, boy," she told the dog. "I've got to get up. Things to do and all that."

She pushed back the covers and headed toward the bathroom. Thirty minutes later, showered, makeup done and hair dry, she tugged on a pair of jeans and a long-sleeved shirt, chose sneakers over boots, and headed toward the kitchen.

Coffee. She smelled coffee, thank heavens. Some people claimed not to drink it, but she'd rather do without breakfast than her coffee.

Turning the corner, following the delicious scent, she ran smack-dab into Cord.

"Whoa," he said, steadying her with hands on her arms. Large, capable-looking hands, she thought, remembering the feel of them on her body with a delicious shiver.

Cord released her, stepping back, almost as if she'd voiced the thought out loud.

Unsure if she should be hurt or amused or both, she decided to ignore it, at least for now. "Coffee," she intoned, stepping around him as she made a beeline for the coffeepot.

"Mugs are in the cabinet right above it," Cord said. "Powdered creamer, sugar and artificial sweetener, too."

After snagging a mug, a heavy white one with a local breakfast restaurant logo on it, she filled it. Then, raising it to her nose, she inhaled deeply before taking a sip. "Mmm. I like mine black."

When she raised her gaze from contemplation of the delicious morning nectar, she saw him studying her, his expression unreadable. "What?" she asked. "Don't tell me none of your previous guests drank black coffee."

"None of the female ones, that's for sure," he said. "Are you always this...bouncy so early in the morning?"

"Yes." Unrepentant, she grinned and then took another sip of coffee. "It's my blessing, or curse, depending how you look at it. As to early..." She glanced around the kitchen for a clock, finally seeing a digital display on the microwave. "Since when is six thirty early? Getting up at four a.m. in the summer to work cattle is early."

"I forgot you live on a ranch."

Still grinning, she nodded. "I do. And Eldridge always made all of us help when we were young." Though her smile wavered as she remembered the man she thought of as her father, she forced herself to continue on. "Most of us still help out around the ranch, along with pursuing our other interests." Which, in her case, meant repurposing old furniture and curb-side treasures.

She took a deep breath. "Do you want me to make breakfast? I cook a mean omelet."

"You cook?"

Realizing he still stood in the spot where they'd collided, near the doorway as if he wanted to be able to bolt from the room, she smiled. "I do. And I'm pretty darn good at it, too. Our ranch cook taught me."

"Hmm."

"An enigmatic response if I ever heard one." She gestured toward one of the empty kitchen chairs. "Why don't you sit down? I promise I don't bite."

Of course, the statement sounded a lot more provocative than she'd intended, definitely because the instant she'd uttered it, she pictured where and how she'd love to bite him.

Closing her eyes, she briefly allowed herself to linger over the fantasy. Then, she shook her head, took a big gulp of coffee and eyed him, letting a half smile play on her lips.

He still stood in the same spot as if rooted in place. "Look, Piper..." Shifting his weight from foot to foot, he dragged a hand through his hair. To her amazement, this ruffled look made him even sexier.

"We need to set up some boundaries," he continued. "I don't sleep with my clients."

"I'm not your client," she promptly replied, still smiling. "Technically, Fowler is."

He sighed. "True. But I'm helping you try and find out what really happened to Eldridge and you're going to assist me in locating my niece. You really need to take this seriously. It's important."

"You're right." Sobering, she nodded. "Sorry. I do take this seriously. It's just you're so darn good-looking, it's distracting."

After a second of startled silence, he burst out laughing. "Thanks, I guess. You're not bad yourself. Now, that said, can we focus on business?"

"Of course." Debating, even as she tried not to be offended that she apparently didn't have the same effect on him as he did on her, she shot him a quick, narrow look. "After breakfast. If you have any eggs, I'm making an omelet. If you'd like one, you'd better speak up. Otherwise, I'll just make one for myself."

Just then, Truman came padding into the kitchen.

"There you are," Cord said, setting down a large dog bowl full of kibble. "You're late for breakfast."

"He slept with me," Piper volunteered. "He's really an awesome dog."

Cord nodded. "Yes, he is."

She ended up cooking two omelets. He made toast and poured them each a glass of orange juice. He took a seat across from her and they both ate quickly and in silence, though she had to curb the impulse to speak.

Once they'd finished, he grabbed the plates, rinsed them off and put them in the dishwasher, an act that made her smile. She enjoyed watching him move around the small kitchen. Even if they managed to act completely businesslike around each other, she figured that would never change.

"More coffee?" he asked. When she nodded, he poured them both a cup.

"What's on the agenda for today?" Eager to get going, she pushed to her feet. Since he hadn't taken a seat, she figured that meant he was ready to get started.

He glanced at his watch. "I've got a personal errand to run first thing. After I get back, I figured we could discuss Renee. I can show you some pictures—she's a big fan of selfies on her Facebook and Instagram pages. Maybe if you get a feel for what she's like, her personality and looks, you might have some new insights into where she might be hiding."

"How about we talk in the car?" she countered. "Once you tell me her info, I can pull up her social media accounts on my phone."

"I thought you could stay here until I get back."

"What?" She cocked her head. "You weren't going to take me with you? Why not?"

Though he tried hard to appear annoyed, she could see the way he tried to keep from smiling. "It's a personal errand," he reiterated. "Which means it's something I have to do alone."

Suddenly, with a gut-wrenching realization, she understood. "Damn." She only swore in certain situations. This definitely felt like one. "Why didn't you tell me you had a girlfriend? I wouldn't have come on to you if I'd known."

Hurriedly, he bowed his head. At first, she thought it was to hide his anger, but as soon as she saw his shoulders shaking she realized he was laughing.

"What's so funny?" she asked, her voice cross. "I'm not one to poach on another woman's man."

He apparently found her last sentence hilarious, because he busted out laughing. Arms crossed, she eyed him while he attempted to rein in his amusement.

"I don't have a girlfriend," he finally said. "And, Piper, you jump to conclusions quicker than anyone I've ever met. You take off at a tangent before I even get a chance to explain."

She nodded. "I've heard that before. I've been told I might be a bit…overly enthusiastic."

"That's an understatement." He spoke gently. "I'm going to pay a visit to an elderly widow who used to know my father."

Of course her mind whirled at that. She could think

of several different scenarios now, especially since she'd known his father. There were drunks and there were abusive drunks. Cord's father fell into the latter category.

She ventured a guess, choosing the imaginary scenario least likely to offend him. "Collecting rent?"

"No." Draining the last of his coffee, he set the mug down with a thump. "It's actually none of your business."

"Of course you realize your evasiveness only makes me want to know the truth, right?" She grinned. "Sorry, but I'm nosy like that. And if you didn't want me to be all up in your business, you shouldn't have insisted I stay with you."

He nodded, conceding her point. "Fine." Checking his watch once more, he faced her. "You can come with me. I'll explain in the car. But on one condition. No matter what you think or believe or how you feel about the situation, I'd appreciate if you'd keep your opinion to yourself. Can you do that?"

She had no idea. In fact, she rather doubted it. "Of course," she replied, intrigued. One thing she had begun to learn about Cord was that he certainly wasn't boring. Or dumb. She'd met other male bodybuilder types before who were equally great to look at until they opened their mouths. Not him. He was the most fascinating man she'd ever met.

"When do we leave?" she asked, since he'd glanced at his watch a third time.

"Whenever you're ready. It's about a forty-five-minute drive each way, without traffic."

"Okay." Placing her mug next to his, she smiled her brightest smile. "Give me a minute to freshen up. I'll be right back."

He nodded, his expression either downright unenthused or simply resigned.

"We'll also discuss your niece while we're driving." Glancing back over her shoulder, she raised her brows. "I promise I won't waste your time."

Back in her room, she checked her appearance in the mirror, then used her phone to see the outside temperature. November in Texas, even this late in the month, could run the gamut from freezing to downright balmy. Since today's high had been forecast in the low fifties, she grabbed a light jacket, just in case.

When she reemerged just a few minutes later, Cord waited in the living room, jiggling his car keys in his hand. The sunlight streaming in the eastern window turned his dark hair to gold. "Ready?"

Temporarily struck dumb, she pushed away the aching need to touch him and nodded.

She waited until they'd backed out of his driveway and turned off his street before speaking, even though she wanted to bounce up and down in her seat like an impatient child. "Okay, so where exactly are we going?"

Unsmiling, he shot her a glance. "Did you ever know Ms. Berens? Most people called her the Widow Berens. Her first name is Lorraine."

The name didn't ring a bell. Piper finally shook her head. "I'm afraid I don't."

"Her husband used to own the pharmacy on Main Street, though he passed away, probably before you were born. She sold it and banked the money, intending to use it to live on for the rest of her life. I believe she supplements her income by making and selling custom quilts."

Piper nodded. "I've seen some of her quilts. They're beautiful."

"Yes they are. Well, back when my daddy was alive, he ran a scam on her. This was before internet dating scams, but he did something similar to her. She was lonely, he was a good-looking man, and he convinced her that he loved her."

"Oh, no." Piper feared she knew what he'd say next.

"He bilked her out of her entire savings." His grim voice told her what he thought of that. "Ever since I learned about it, I've been trying to make restitution by paying her back a little at a time."

Moved, she nodded, looking away so he wouldn't see the rawness of her emotions in her eyes or face. She'd always felt things deeply, a trait she'd learned at an early age to keep hidden to avoid ridicule. "That's kind of you," she managed, glad her voice sounded even. "Not many people would feel responsible for their father's sins."

"Maybe. Maybe not." He shrugged. "All I know is that it's the right thing to do. She was gullible and trusted the wrong man. My father didn't spend one second regretting what he did to her, not even on the day he died."

Hearing the trace of bitterness in his voice, she nodded. "Is there anything I can do?"

"Like what?"

She shrugged. "I don't know. Anything to help her. Cooking, cleaning, laundry?"

"I guess you can ask her. As far as I can tell, she's still able to take pretty good care of herself."

By the time he turned off the paved farm-to-market road onto a rutted, dirt one, Piper felt more like herself than she had since she'd been arrested. She'd always said helping others was the best medicine. The very act took all the focus off one's troubles. Marceline had scoffed, as had Fowler, and Piper's adoptive mother, Whitney. Her adoptive brother Reid had always smiled with pride. He'd often whispered to Piper how proud he was of her.

Piper wondered what Reid thought about her now.

"Here we are," Cord said, turning into a long, gravel

drive. A black metal gate that needed paint guarded the entrance, though it sat open, the part that closed hung crookedly from one hinge.

Despite this, the place felt homey rather than decrepit. She felt a sense of peace here.

The white farmhouse sat back from the road, under the shade of five huge live oak trees. "It's nice. The wood siding appears to have been freshly painted, unlike that gate."

He grimaced. "Yeah, I should've fixed that last time I was out here. No time to do it today, so it'll have to wait."

"Does Ms. Berens have children to help her?"

"No. At least not as far as I know. She's never mentioned any kids and I certainly haven't seen any in all the years I've known her."

Once he killed the engine, he turned to look at her. "Do you want to wait out here?"

"Oh, heck no." She grinned to take the sting off her words. "I want to meet her. I'm guessing she loves to have company."

To her surprise, he grinned back at her. "That she does. Don't say I didn't warn you."

Chapter 5

Side by side, they headed up the sidewalk. Before they even reached the porch, the front door opened and a tiny, white-haired woman greeted them. Beaming, she hugged Cord tightly before turning to study Piper.

"This is the first time you've brought a lady friend to see me," she said, winking at Piper as she held out her hand. "Howdy do. I'm Lorraine Berens."

As Piper shook her hand, mildly amazed at her strong grip, she realized she'd need to give a name. "I'm Penelope," she said, using her actual given name. "It's nice to meet you."

"Likewise." Releasing Piper, Lorraine turned back to Cord. "Come on inside. I just finished making a big apple pie. The apple orchard had a huge crop this year."

"Apple orchard?" Piper could scarcely contain her excitement. "When I was a kid, I used to love going apple-picking!"

"Well, honey, after we visit a spell, you can go out back and pick until your heart's content. There were so many on the trees, I couldn't get them all. A lot of 'em probably spoiled, but I bet there's still enough for you to gather a bushel to take home."

"I'd love that," Piper said, meaning it.

Cord touched her shoulder. "You can go right now if you want. I need to discuss something with Ms. Berens."

"No." Lorraine protested, before Piper could answer. "It's not often I get company. She can get her apples later, after we visit awhile."

The determination in her faded blue eyes made Piper smile. "You're right, of course." Piper nodded. "Cord, if there's something private you need to discuss, can it wait until right before we go?"

Chin set, he didn't appear happy, but he finally nodded. He followed Ms. B into the kitchen, held the plates for her while she cut the pie, and carried both his and Piper's back into the living room.

Watching the gentleness with which Cord treated the elderly woman, Piper felt something unfurl in her chest. Respect, certainly, but this was something more, an emotion she couldn't exactly put a name to, though she realized it was dangerous to her currently fragile existence.

Too serious, which meant dangerous. To push this away, Piper considered impulsively kissing him, right there in front of the elderly woman, just to see what he'd do. Before she could act on it, he handed her a slice of pie.

"This looks amazing," she marveled, meaning it. And the first bite…she moaned, rolling her eyes with pleasure.

"I'm so glad you like it," Ms. Berens exclaimed, beaming at her.

"Obviously." Cord grimaced, apparently irritated.

Piper tried not to mind. Her outgoing enthusiasm sometimes got on other people's nerves. But the elderly woman deserved the compliment—and a hundred more.

A second bite. This time, Piper rolled the filling around on her tongue, trying to savor it. It wasn't just the apples and cinnamon and sugar, but the perfect crust. One more bite, and then another. Before she knew it, she'd polished off the entire piece. Eyeing her empty plate with more than a trace of regret, she looked up to see both Ms. B and Cord staring at her. "It was good." She sighed. "More than good. Great. This is one of the best apple pies I've ever had."

Ms. B chuckled. "Honey, you do know how to flatter a gal."

Which made Piper laugh. Meanwhile, Cord sat silently, eating his slice of pie with grim determination. Piper again fought the urge to tease him out of his sudden bad mood.

"Are you all right, son?" Ms. B asked, setting her empty plate aside. "You're shoveling that pie into your mouth like it's liver and onions."

Piper sputtered. "She's right, you know."

Though Cord lifted one brow, he continued his determined chewing.

"Or something equally distasteful," Ms. B continued. "Instead of my wonderful apple pie." Turning her head, she winked at Piper.

As soon as Cord had cleaned his plate, he jumped up and carried it into the kitchen. Piper couldn't help but admire the way his tight jeans showcased his backside.

"He is a mighty fine specimen," Ms. B remarked, her sharp glance missing nothing.

For some reason, this comment made Piper laugh again. "That he is," she concurred.

When Cord marched back into the room, he glanced from one to the other, still unsmiling. "Is something funny?" He glowered at the two women, an unhappy giant.

Piper decided she'd had enough. "What the heck is wrong with you?" she asked, standing. "Ever since we got here, you've been in a bad mood. Is it me? Because if you didn't want me to come along, you could have told me up front."

He sighed. "It's not you, believe it or not. Not everything is about you, okay?"

Stung, she swallowed. But she knew what he meant. Ever since her life had been turned upside down, she'd been a bit self-absorbed. "Sorry," she muttered. "But if it's not me, then what's wrong?"

"I need to talk to Ms. Berens. Alone."

"All righty, then." Glancing around the small house wildly, Piper tried to decide where she could go. Even if she went in the kitchen and started doing the dishes, she'd still be able to hear every word.

Then she remembered the apple orchard. "I guess now would be a great time to go pick apples," she said brightly.

Cord jerked his head in a nod.

"Go ahead and pick all the apples you want, honey," Ms. Berens said. Smiling, she pointed one gnarled finger toward the kitchen. "Go out the back door and head for the big red barn. The orchard is right behind that."

Tempted, Piper looked from her to Cord. "Are you sure?"

"Of course I am. They're just going to go to waste. Take a sack with you. There are a couple hanging inside the pantry."

Though she spoke like Piper should know her way around the kitchen, which she didn't, Piper figured she'd manage. "Okay." She jumped at the chance. Not only would she be out in the fresh air and get some exercise, but apples fresh from the tree? Say no more.

"Have fun." The lack of humor in Cord's quick smile gave her pause. She eyed him, noting his clenched jaw and the tenseness in his stiff posture.

"Are you sure you don't mind?" She directed her question at him.

"Of course I don't. Go. Have fun. I've really got something private I want to discuss with Ms. B and it can't wait."

Nodding, she hurried into the kitchen, then grabbed a sack on her way out the back door.

Once outside, she breathed in the fresh air and smiled. Though she enjoyed being in town, she was a country girl at heart. This farm reminded her of the Colton Valley Ranch, of home. She felt a twinge of sadness because she missed the ranch and her family. Even Fowler and Marceline, despite everything.

Pushing away unpleasant thoughts since she didn't want to ruin a perfectly beautiful day, she found the apple trees without any trouble. Once there, she saw what Ms. Berens had meant. There was still a lot of fruit up in the trees, but fallen apples littered the ground. Some had rotted, others had clearly been savaged by wild animals or insects. Dismayed at the waste, Piper began gathering any remaining intact apples from the tree branches.

Though she stopped once she'd filled her sack, she could easily have filled several more. She wondered if the elderly widow might need her to pick more, so she hurried back to the house. Surely she'd given Cord enough time to discuss whatever was bothering him. Maybe once he'd gotten whatever was bothering him off his chest, he'd be in a better mood. One thing Piper had learned with her large and unpredictable family was how mercurial moods could be. For that reason, she tried to keep herself on an even keel, happy and upbeat, no matter the circumstances.

The only time she'd failed in recent memory had been when she'd been arrested for the murder of her adoptive father.

The thought had the unfortunate effect of dimming her smile. Shaking her head, she tried to think about something else, like finding Cord's niece and learning the truth about what had really happened to Eldridge. Rose-colored glasses or not, she knew things were going to look up soon. They had to.

Meanwhile, she had fresh-picked apples and a dawning idea of what to do with the rest.

As she burst through the back door, barreling inside in her excitement, she realized both Cord and Ms. B looked up, utterly silent. A quick glance showed Cord's expression still grim and miserable, while Ms. Berens looked perplexed.

"Is everything all right?" Piper asked, looking from one to the other. "I'm sorry, but, Cord, you look like someone just died."

Ms. B snorted. "Doesn't he, though? I keep trying to tell him that everything is all right. We all fall on hard times every once in a while."

Hard times. About to ask, Piper noted the warning glare Cord shot her and kept her questions to herself. "I, uh, came back to see if you needed any more apples, Ms. Berens. I got an entire sack full, but there are plenty more. If I don't pick them, they'll just go to waste."

"No, thanks. I spent an entire day canning them. I have enough apples to last me through winter and spring. But if you want to take more, grab another sack and go get them."

"What would she do with more apples?" Cord asked, his tone mild, though his eyes were still hard.

"Actually, I have a plan. There's a homeless encampment in Dallas," Piper said. "A tent city under I-45. I saw it on the news. I was thinking maybe I could take them the apples."

"Oooh!" Faded eyes sparkling, Ms. B clapped. "They'll surely love that. Please do. I have a lot of plastic grocery bags in the garage. Why don't you fill as many of those as you can? That will make me so happy."

Nodding, Piper gave Cord one more quick glance before moving away. Clearly he didn't want to share whatever was bothering him and she was okay with that, for now. "I'll just go pick apples," she said, infusing her voice with cheerfulness. "Call me if you need me."

And she hightailed it back out the door, stopping in the garage to pick up the bags. Outside the door, she'd noticed a red metal wagon, ancient from the looks of it, but in good enough shape for Piper to cart the apples back to the house.

On the way to the orchard, Piper hummed under her breath. Once there, she immediately began picking apples.

Busywork, the simple task of filling plastic bags with fruit, felt like exactly what she needed. By keeping her hands occupied, she freed up her mind to think.

Her life had completely changed over the past week. She'd been arrested and spent the night in jail. Members of her own family had confronted her and let her know they considered her a killer.

And she'd run, taken off. The exact opposite of what she normally did. In the past, when she had a problem, she usually took the bull by the horns and waded right into trouble. She preferred face-to-face, honest confrontation to subterfuge and lies.

Now look at her. Hanging out with the sexiest bounty hunter and private investigator alive, on the run. Even if he had gone all dark and sardonic for no good reason, she knew if she were alone with him, she could coax him out of whatever funk he'd gotten in.

She needed him focused and confident. He could do the job, she knew, because reputations like his came only from success. For now, he was stuck with her. At least until she got some answers. Was Eldridge truly dead? If so, someone wanted to frame her for his death. But who? Piper couldn't imagine. Even Marceline, as bitter and hateful as she could be, wouldn't do something so evil.

Or would she?

Each time she filled a bag, she loosely tied it and placed it in the wagon. Once she had every bag full, she counted. Twelve. That ought to be enough.

Heading back to the house, she took care to make a lot of noise. Whistling, she wheeled the wagon to Cord's truck and loaded her bagged-up apples in the bed. Then she returned the wagon to the same spot where she'd found it.

Opening the back door and stepping into the kitchen, she peered into the den. Ms. B sat in the same upholstered chair and appeared to be knitting something. Piper didn't see Cord at all.

"I always wanted to learn to knit," Piper said softly, approaching the older woman to peer at her creation. "Is that a scarf?"

"Why yes it is." Ms. B's lined face creased into a smile. "When you mentioned those homeless people living in tents, I started thinking. Winter is coming and they're going to need to stay warm. I decided I'd better get busy knitting them scarves, hats and gloves."

"Wow." Piper gave in to impulse and kissed the older woman's cheek. "You're really something."

Beaming at her, Ms. Berens shook her head. "Pshaw. You're the one who gave me the idea."

Behind Piper, someone cleared his throat. Cord.

"If you two are done with your mutual admiration society," he drawled, "Pi—I mean, Penelope and I have to go."

Ms. Berens frowned. "So soon? Are you sure you don't want to stay and have supper? I can fry up some chicken."

Homemade fried chicken made Piper's mouth water, but a quick glance at Cord and she kept her mouth shut.

"I wish we could, but we've got a lot to do." Cord leaned in and kissed the older woman's other cheek. "I'll be back soon and maybe we can have that then."

"Okay." Smiling fondly, Ms. B patted his hand. "Bring Penelope with you, too, if she doesn't mind."

Surprised, Piper swallowed. "I'll try to come," she allowed. "As long as our schedules mesh." Or she wasn't in jail.

Outside, Cord glanced at the bags of apples in his truck bed. "When are you planning to deliver all that?"

"Today." Optimism firmly in place again, she grinned. "It's only about a forty-five-minute drive from here. How about we swing by before we head back to your place?"

Though he grimaced, he nodded as they climbed up into the cab of his truck. "Sure, why not?"

"You're a good man, Charlie Brown." This time, she gave in to impulse and kissed his cheek. He stiffened, but didn't comment. Instead, he started the truck and backed it around.

"You got her knitting again," he commented. "I haven't seen her knit in a long time."

"She's making hats, gloves and scarves to keep the homeless warm." Buoyed by her enthusiasm, she bounced a little in the seat, despite her seat belt. "Kindness is a wonderful thing."

Eyes dark, he held her gaze. "Yes. Yes it is."

When he turned his attention back to the road, she released a breath she hadn't even realized she'd been holding.

"That was pretty awesome," she said, her voice a little softer than she would have liked. "Back there, what you do for Ms. Berens. Not everyone would be so kind."

"Kind?" Expression still shuttered, he glanced at her again before turning his attention back to the road. "At first, I started visiting her out of a sense of duty, obligation and guilt. I felt it was my responsibility to make restitution for my father's crime. But now, I actually enjoy her company. I've begun to feel like she's my elderly aunt or something."

"How often do you go out to see her?"

"Once a month." Another sidelong glance. "Though I try to call her weekly. If she needs something, I go out there sooner."

"She's lucky she has you."

He shook his head. "I'm not the only one. There are a lot of people looking out for the Widow Berens. Some of the guys from the neighboring farms check on her every Saturday. And the high school shop teacher has his students come out and repair things around her place for a grade. She's well taken care of. Today was the first time I wasn't able to—"

Cutting off the words, he turned up the radio. Piper turned it right back down. "Wasn't able to what?"

"Never mind."

They didn't call her Persistent Piper for nothing. "No really, I want to know."

His sigh contained equal parts exasperation and resignation. "You're going to bug me until I tell you, aren't you?"

"Bug you? I'm highly offended." But she ruined her statement with a grin she couldn't hold back. "Come on, Cord. Spill. Since we're working so closely together, I'd rather you don't have secrets."

"This has nothing to do with your case." Though he protested, one corner of his sexy mouth curved up in the beginnings of a smile.

"But you're thinking about telling me anyway?" She ventured a guess. "Does it have something to do with you making monetary payments to Ms. Berens every month?"

"Damn."

"I pay attention."

"If you really want to know, yes. Because I've been focusing on searching for Renee, I haven't had any paying jobs, so I wasn't able to pay Ms. Berens last month. I'd hoped to catch up, but until I find Renee, I've got to hold back a reserve so I can keep more doors open."

"So you didn't give her anything? Even though I'm guessing Fowler paid you something up front?"

"He did." Rueful now, he turned his attention back to the road. "But I'm not taking any other jobs until I find Renee—and learn the truth about Eldridge. So I had to tell Ms. B that once again, I couldn't pay her in full this month, either, never mind catch back up."

"I'm sure she didn't mind. She looks like she's doing okay."

He snorted. "You sound like her. What neither of you can see is that it's the principle of the thing. She told me today she hasn't touched a dime of the money I've paid her—it's in a savings account in case she ever needs it."

Piper nodded. "There you go. So stop beating yourself up. Once you find your niece and help me figure out what happened to Eldridge, you can make it up to her."

Hands on the steering wheel, he stared straight ahead at the road while he considered. "You're right. You both are," he finally said. "Though I know you probably don't understand, failing to meet my obligations makes me feel like my father. And the one thing I've sworn not to be is anything like that man."

"Tell me about him," she said impulsively. "I barely remember him. Just that he was a ranch hand on the ranch. Oh, and that the ladies loved him. He was a handsome devil." Like Cord. Because Cord looked a lot like his father, which he probably hated.

"Tell you about him?" Bitterness tinged Cord's husky voice. "He was an abusive drunk who cared nothing about anyone but himself. He lied constantly and didn't care what happened to his daughter or his son. My sister, Denice, needed help. She started drinking at an early age and was a full-blown alcoholic by her sophomore year. Not to mention the drugs. I went to him, tried to get him to see, but he laughed at me and told me I needed to take lessons from her, to loosen up and enjoy life." His voice broke. "And now I've gone and told you way more than you wanted to know."

Though sympathy made the back of her throat ache, she sensed to show this would be the worst thing she could do. So she simply nodded, careful not to look at him lest she reveal the depth of her emotions. "That stinks," she finally said, keeping her tone mild. "It's amazing you managed to overcome that to get where you are today."

He shot her a sideways glance.

"Uh, right. Anyway," he sounded determined to finish. "Renee is all the family I have left. I didn't do a good enough job with her, and now she's heading in the same direction Denice did. I've got to find her and get her that help before it's too late."

Cord had no idea why he'd let loose on Piper like that. All the bottled-up emotions had come spilling out, and he could only imagine how messed up she now thought he was.

Sadly, she wouldn't be too far from the mark.

Of course, despite the Colton name and wealth, her life was no picnic, either. Or it hadn't been, back when they'd been kids.

What surprised him was how much he liked her. He'd liked her back then, but had figured time and money would have changed her. Her breezy self-confidence mingled with earnest sincerity attracted him like a dog to a T-bone steak.

"I'm going to locate your niece," Piper announced. The certainty in her voice made him want to believe her.

"How?" he asked, equally serious.

"I'm not sure yet, but I will."

Her brilliant smile hit him hard in the chest. Blinking, he returned his attention to the road, uncertain how she could affect him so strongly.

"I believe in being positive," she continued. "What you put out into the universe comes back to you, magnified."

Though he had no idea what she meant by this, he nodded anyway. "You're a glass-half-full kind of person, I take it."

"Yes." She grinned again, making him think he'd say just about anything to see that smile. "Some people find it annoying. But it works. Just wait and see."

He signaled, exiting the interstate to take the road toward the homeless shelter so they could drop off the apples. "I hope you're right. The weather's getting colder and I worry about Renee. I don't know if she has a warm, safe place to stay and enough to eat." Not to mention he hoped she was clean and sober, though he didn't say that out loud.

"I think she is. If she had to fend for herself a lot growing up, and it kind of sounds like she did, she's got mad coping skills."

It struck him that he really had no idea. "You may be right. I don't really know."

Now Piper studied him, her clear green gaze sliding over him like water flowing over rock. "You said she's lived with you for two years, right?"

"Yes."

"Did you ever see her stoned or drunk?"

Slowly, he shook his head. "No. Not really."

"So you're basing your belief that she's a partier on her parents' past behavior?"

Stunned, he finally nodded. "Maybe I am. Again, I can't be too sure."

"Okay, then, tell me about her. What's she like?"

He thought of Renee, of the constant battles they'd had. "Angry," he finally said. "And sullen. Full of resentment and bitterness. I couldn't hardly speak to her without setting her off."

"She's hurting." Piper nodded, like it all made perfect sense. "And the emotions are confusing and overwhelming to her. That's what makes her behave that way."

"You sound as if you speak from experience," he said, his tone dry. "But you forget, I was there for part of your childhood. Your life wasn't bad at all."

She went quiet at that, silent for so long he thought he'd offended her.

Finally, she faced him, her expression once again perky and bright and, as he had begun to realize, completely and utterly fake. "You have no idea what my life was like growing up. We Coltons only let outsiders see what we want them to see."

Chapter 6

Of course Piper's cryptic statement only made Cord wonder what she meant. Eldridge had always been a pompous, arrogant ass, but Cord didn't see him ever abusing any of his children. He hadn't been affectionate or demonstrative, and maybe that's what Piper had meant. Of course, she also had to deal with Fowler and Marceline.

Deciding it prudent to change the subject, he nodded. "So what's your plan? How are you planning to find Renee?"

"Well, first I'm going to ask you a few questions about her. Hopefully, you'll know enough to be able to answer them." Her dry tone made him fight to suppress a smile.

"I'll do my best. Fire away."

"You said the only jobs she's ever had were waitressing. What kind of restaurants? Waffle House and Denny's or steak houses?"

"She worked at Chili's. She couldn't wait to be old enough to train to be a bartender. That was the height of ambition to her, tending bar."

"Well, a lot of people do that while working on something else." He caught the tactful note in her voice and smiled.

"You said her father was in a band? What kind of band and what instrument did he play?"

At least this one he knew the answer to. "Heavy metal. And he was lead singer and bass guitarist." Or screamer, as the case may be. Cord had attended a few of his concerts at his sister's request. He hadn't been able to even understand the words. Of course, his musical tastes tended more toward George Strait and Waylon Jennings.

"Does Renee play an instrument?" Piper asked.

He had to think about that. "I saw her a couple of times messing around with a beat-up old guitar. It was one of the few belongings she held on to after losing her parents. It belonged to her father."

"Electric guitar, then?"

"No. Oddly enough, it was a twelve-string acoustic guitar."

"Wow." Piper grimaced. "Much more difficult to play. I'm guessing she didn't like heavy metal music much, then."

"No. None of us did, except her parents. Even then, my sister wasn't into it except when she was with Joshua."

"Then what kind of music did Renee play?" Piper persisted.

"I'm guessing you have a reason for all these random questions?"

"You don't know, do you?" Piper shook her head. "Surely you heard her sitting around playing some sort of music, whether on the guitar or listening to the radio."

"I did," he said slowly, refusing to feel guilty. "You have to understand, it was difficult inserting myself into the life of someone who emphatically didn't want me in it."

She nodded. "I know. Believe me. But tell me anything you can remember. Anything at all. I'm going at this the way one attempts to put together a puzzle. All of the pieces eventually make a whole."

He had to admire her tenacity. "You'd make a good private investigator."

"Thank you. But I have my own plans for the future. Or at least I did. Once all of this craziness is over, I'm hoping I can get right back on course."

"Doing what?" He couldn't help but pounce on the chance to know her better.

"I like to find old furniture and restore it in a nontraditional way. Like fix up and paint a dining room hutch turquoise. People go crazy for that kind of thing. I'd actually saved up enough to open my own store, though I'm now using it to live on until this criminal case is sorted out." She took a deep breath. "Now, about the kind of music Renee liked…"

"The music. Right." Watching the road, he let his mind drift back. "Folk music," he said suddenly, slightly amazed. "Or country. She was playing some sort of ballad. I caught just a sliver of it before Renee saw me and stopped playing. She seemed ashamed, almost as if she didn't want me to know."

She tilted her head, considering him. "I wonder why?"

Hating that the question made him feel defensive, he shrugged. "I don't know."

"Did you ever ask her?"

"How could I, when even a 'good morning, did you sleep well' would piss her off?" He grimaced. "You have no idea what it's like living with a perpetually angry teenage girl."

"I…" Biting her lip, she looked down. "Sorry. You're right. I know you said you never saw her with friends, but surely there must have been someone. Who did she talk to—or text—on her phone?"

"I don't know. She took it with her. I was afraid to cancel the service in case she wanted to reach out to me. And yes, I tried to get the provider to help me track her with the phone's GPS. But she's eighteen and the phone is in her name. They refused." He took a deep breath. "She took her laptop, too."

"Wow. No wonder you've had difficulty finding her."

Relieved more than he should have been to hear her say that, he exhaled. "Yeah. Now you know what I'm facing. Still think you can locate her?"

"Not 'think.'" Again the dazzling smile. "I will find her. Just like you will find out not only who kidnapped Eldridge, but who hates me enough to try and frame me for a murder that might not have happened."

Glad to focus on something else, he nodded. "Let's start with the names of your enemies. How many names did you get on that list?"

Her frown nearly made him smile.

"I don't have any enemies, actually."

"That you know of."

"True." Twisting her hands in her lap, she fidgeted. "I mean, I'm sure there are people who don't like me. No one is popular with every single person. But framing someone for their own father's murder is a whole 'nother level of hatred. Like a sharp-edged sword of bitterness."

"Nice imagery," he congratulated her. "Okay, how about this. Who have you gotten into a disagreement with in the last month?"

"Fowler. Marceline."

"That's it?" He shouldn't have been surprised.

"Yeah." When she lifted her chin and met his gaze, the sparkle in her eyes made his gut twist. "And if you want to talk about angry, bitter people, those two win the prize."

"Did you argue with them at the same time? Or separately?"

"Oh, a little of both." Her breezy tone didn't match her serious expression. "They'd get together and gang up on me sometimes. Other times, it was just one or the other."

"Multiple disagreements?" This time he didn't bother to hide his shock. "How many would you say, if you had to estimate?"

"Why does this matter?" she asked. "You know as well as I do that neither of them framed me. Fowler might find me annoying, and Marceline just dislikes me, but they wouldn't do anything like this."

"You don't think?" He wasn't so sure.

She didn't answer. They'd reached the turnoff to the homeless shelter. When he pulled up in front of the dingy, cinder-block building, he glanced at her. "Wait in the car. Dropping these off will only take a minute."

After he'd handed the apples over to the grateful director, he got back in the truck and headed for home. As they neared the road that led to his place, he slowed to make the turn. The dirt and gravel were rough, which made him drive slowly.

"We're going to split up," she announced, holding on to the door handle. "Tomorrow. I'm going to go look for Renee, and you're going to investigate Eldridge's death. Do you know the police have never even found his body?"

Still stuck on the "split up" part, he slowly nodded. "Piper, I thought I made it clear I wasn't letting you out of my sight."

"That's ridiculous," she huffed. "And quite honestly, I refuse to allow it. I've given you my word not to run.

That should be enough for you. I've also promised to find your niece, and I will. Now you do what you agreed to do. Find out who really killed Eldridge—if he's even dead—so the police will drop the charges against me."

Once she'd said all that, she turned away to stare out the window. Since they were pulling into his driveway, he didn't respond. Instead, he parked and killed the engine. "Let's discuss this inside."

Pushing open her door, she jumped down from the pickup and strode up his sidewalk. Instead of anger, her entire bearing denoted confidence, as if she felt quite certain any reasonable person would be on her side.

He had to admire such an ability, even though the thought of sending her searching for Renee gave him a headache.

Truman came racing around the side of the house, shooting right past Cord as he made his way to Piper.

Cord watched while Truman enthusiastically greeted her. Even his own dog loved Piper.

After she'd finished loving on Truman, she waited for Cord to unlock the front door. When he did, he stepped aside to let her enter first, Truman trotting right behind her.

Barely had the heavy wood door closed behind them when she turned to face him. "If you can't treat me like you believe I'm really innocent, there's no point in you taking this case." She met and held his gaze, her quiet declaration tinged with disappointment.

The intensity of her stare made him dizzy. He thought of reminding her that technically he worked for Fowler, but since he'd also reached an agreement with her, he didn't.

Plus, damn it all to hell, she was right.

* * *

When Piper opened her eyes the next morning, the first thing that registered was the chill. Snuggling down under her blanket, she considered going back to sleep. But then she remembered she'd planned to begin her search for Renee today, no matter what Cord said. After declaring where she stood, she'd marched into her room with Truman hot on her heels and closed the door. She'd really hoped Cord would come after her but he had not. Apparently, he was just as stubborn as she was.

No matter. She wasn't his prisoner and she would do what she wanted. If he didn't like it, she'd leave.

"Isn't that right, Truman?" she crooned to the motionless lump under her blanket. For answer, the entire lump wiggled as Truman wagged his tail.

"You can stay here, boy. Sleep as long as you want." Taking a deep breath, she tossed back the covers and forced herself out of her bed.

Outside, a north wind buffeted the house. A quick glance at the weather app on her phone revealed a 30-degree drop in temperature from the day before.

Shivering, she hurried into her bathroom, turned on the shower—water temperature just this side of scalding—and got ready to face the day.

Half an hour later, hair dried and makeup applied, she headed to the kitchen for some coffee. She figured she'd whip up some scrambled eggs or maybe oatmeal, if Cord had it. Anything hot, to counteract the chill.

"Cold front blew in," Cord commented when she walked in. He wore a flannel shirt untucked, faded jeans and boots. With his shaggy dark hair still damp from the shower, she felt an intimacy she had no business feeling. Especially after their standoff the night before.

"I see that." Crossing her arms, she eyed him. Deciding to wait to continue the argument until after she'd been fortified by coffee and food, she let her gaze roam over him and then shook her head. "Do you have to look so good this early in the morning?" she grumbled, snagging a mug from the cupboard and pouring herself some strong coffee. "Unfair advantage."

"Do I?" He grinned. "And here I was thinking I looked like a farmer about to go feed his livestock."

Stunned—both at the sexiness of that smile and the concept of him actually being a farmer, which he was even if his place was small—she took too big of a sip and burned her tongue. When she swallowed out of desperation, she burned her throat, too.

Eyes watering, she nodded and tried to act like everything was normal, just like Cord had that time he'd chugged his hot cocoa. "Do you?" she asked. This time she blew on her cup before attempting another sip, much smaller this time. "Have livestock, I mean?"

He nodded, the amused glint in his eyes making her wonder if he knew how hard she was trying to act unaffected. "Aside from Truman?" He indicated the dog, now lying curled up in a dog bed near his empty food bowl. "Just a few chickens, a couple of goats, some cattle and a few horses."

"Are you kidding?" Suddenly suspicious, she went to the kitchen window. Outside, the sky had begun to lighten, though the sun wasn't fully risen. "How could I not have noticed animals?"

"Maybe you just weren't paying attention," he said. But his smile widened and she again had to wonder if he was pulling her leg.

"So is that what you're about to do?" she asked. "Go feed your livestock?"

"No. I already did." He turned and grabbed a white

box off the counter, placing it on the table. "Go ahead, help yourself. I went to town and got doughnuts."

She groaned. "My personal Kryptonite. I adore the darn things. Especially the crème-filled ones."

"I remember." He opened the box, snagging a bear claw. "That's why I got them."

He remembered? Stunned, she took a step closer, as if propelled by the fattening deliciousness in front of her. How many years ago had that been? "I wasn't aware you'd paid such close attention to me back then," she said, taking a plump doughnut and swearing to herself that she'd have just one.

Still smiling, he shrugged. "Yeah, well I kind of had a crush on you. Plus, to a kid whose life is hell on earth, the life lived by the rich daughter of the ranch owner is fascinating. I used to sit outside your house at night, watching the warm yellow light shining from the windows, and wonder what it must be like to live inside."

The hint of mockery in his voice contradicted his words. "That sounds sad," she said, watching him closely.

"It was. Then. But as you mentioned earlier, that was a long time ago." He helped himself to a second doughnut while she finished her first. She even licked the powdered sugar from her fingers.

"Let me close that lid," she said, doing exactly that. "They're calling my name and I don't want to have a second."

"Why not? They're good. I've had three so far."

Eyeing him, she shook her head. "I'm trying to watch my weight."

"You?" he snorted. "If you were to go outside and stand sideways, the wind would pick you up and carry you away."

She wanted to hug him. "Thanks," she said instead. "I think."

Even with the box closed, her mouth watered. Unable to resist shooting a couple of glances at the box, she swore she could smell the fresh dough and powdered sugar. Cord muttered something under his breath. In one swift move, he opened the top, snagged another one of her crème-filled delights, placed it on a paper napkin and handed it to her. "Here. You look like you're about to eat that box, cardboard and all."

What else could she do but devour the second pastry? He'd handed it to her; she was practically drooling on it. Resisting the urge to cram it into her mouth, she finished it in a few quick bites.

"Done," she exclaimed, washing it down with coffee. "That was good. Thank you so much for thinking of me."

His laugh, deep and relaxed and coming from the belly, created an entirely different craving inside of her. "You're welcome," he said.

"In case you're trying to butter me up, it won't work. You do remember what we discussed last night. Today's the day," she said. "I'm going to begin my search for your missing niece."

Just like that, his smile vanished. "I didn't forget," he said. "I'm still thinking I should come with you."

"No, you really need to be thinking of ways to investigate Eldridge's disappearance and possible murder." She smiled at him, hoping to take the sting off her words. "Remember, you agreed."

"You didn't exactly give me a choice," he grumbled. "And I still don't like the idea."

"It'll work out fine. You know as well as I do that I'll have a better chance since I'm a stranger."

"If you're planning to check out every Chili's restaurant on this side of Dallas, don't bother. I've already done that."

"I wasn't." She thought she knew exactly where Renee would go.

"Fine, do your thing." He refilled his cup and eyed her over the rim. "We'll meet up here tonight and compare notes over dinner."

For whatever reason, his words made her feel ridiculously happy. "Sounds like a plan. Um, do you happen to have a picture of her you could text me?"

"Sure." He got out his phone and scrolled through his pictures. "Give me your number."

Once she did, he punched it in. "There. You're now in my contacts. When you get my text, save my number in case you have to call me."

"Aye-aye, Captain." She gave him a mock salute. A second later, her phone chimed. She studied the picture and then saved his info. "Got it. I'm good to go. I'll see you later."

Wiping her hands on her napkin, she tossed it in the trash and turned to head back to her room to grab her purse.

"Wait."

Stopping, she turned slowly, raising one brow in inquiry.

"Remember, you gave me your word you'd be back."

At this, she gave into impulse and went to him, stood on her toes and placed a quick kiss on his cheek. "Yes, I did," she purred. "And I always keep my promises."

Then, leaving him staring at her with a stunned look on his handsome face, she sauntered out of the kitchen. In her room, she grabbed her purse and her car keys, then slipped on a jacket before heading toward the front door. "I'm gone," she hollered.

"You don't have to yell." His voice, a few feet to her left, made her start. "About that kiss…"

She'd just started to grin when he hauled her up against him and planted one on her. His mouth moved over hers, nothing tentative or casual about this kiss. Her knees went weak and she sagged against him. Just when she thought her entire body might combust, he released her.

"That's how you kiss goodbye," he declared, his dark gaze smoky. "I'll see you tonight."

A declaration rather than a question. Dimly she registered that, while she tried to catch her breath and regain her equilibrium.

Then, before she got herself in more trouble than she could handle, she spun on her heel and marched out the door.

Only once in her car, doors locked, engine running, did she allow herself to exhale. A quick glance in the rearview mirror revealed a face flushed with desire, and swollen lips that proclaimed she'd been thoroughly kissed.

Damn the man. Putting her car in Reverse, she turned around and then headed down his winding driveway. Since she'd done the exact same thing to him, she figured that kiss had been payback. Cord would have no way of knowing how much he affected her. And he wouldn't, she vowed. She'd have to be extra careful, because she could see how kissing him could be like doughnuts— something she couldn't resist.

Damn. Calling himself all kinds of names, Cord listened to the sound of Piper's car leave. Tires on gravel, his own early warning system for unwanted visitors. Though this time he heard his visitor drive away.

Could he trust her? While everyone that knew him

could count on Cord Maxwell's word being as good as gold, he wasn't sure they'd say the same thing about Piper Colton.

He shook his head, aware he'd be royally pissed if he had to hunt her down again.

But for whatever reason, he felt somewhat better knowing she was out there looking for Renee. Especially since he needed to head up to the sheriff's department and see if one of his pals there could tell him exactly what evidence they had on Piper.

Truman whined, a forlorn sound.

"Sorry, boy, she couldn't take you with her. But she'll be back. In the meantime, you want to go check on the other animals with me?"

The dog jumped to his feet, wagging his tail.

"Come on, then." Cord grabbed his coat and headed back out into the cold. He hadn't been kidding about his livestock, though he only maintained a few token animals, the ones he'd inherited from Sam. They were all in the barn now, warm and fed, since the weather forecasters had been warning of an impending ice storm coming in on yet another cold front. In North Texas, Novembers could go either way. Some years they were balmy and spring-like, others ushered in weather more suited to January and winter than autumn.

Keys in hand, he hurried to his truck, the frigid wind stinging his face. The sun had come up, though total cloud cover hid its warmth. Even the slate-gray sky warned of a worse chill.

Once inside, he let the engine run for a moment to warm up while he tried to get a grip on his raging libido. He didn't waste time wondering how he could want her at a time like this—no, he had a pretty good handle on how that worked. She was beautiful and hot and he'd always had a crush on her. Her confidence and direct nature only made her even more desirable. If he wasn't careful, he was going to get himself in a rattlesnake's nest of trouble.

As he pulled up to the cinder block building that housed the sheriff's office, he saw the bitter, cold wind hadn't deterred Nick Prado from having his morning smoke. Ever since they'd banned smoking inside the building, Nick and any of the other smokers had stood on the southern side of the building, and puffed away. Today this provided the added blessing of sheltering Nick from the wind.

Cord and Nick went way back. They'd become best buddies in kindergarten and their friendship had stood the test of time.

"Hey, Cord." Taking one last drag, Nick dropped his cigarette to the concrete and ground it under his heel. He then carefully picked it up and deposited the butt in the freestanding ashtray. "What brings you in this morning?" he asked.

"Let's get out of this cold," Cord suggested, jerking his chin toward the door.

"Gladly." Nick led the way. Once inside, both men shrugged out of their coats.

"Gotta love heat," Cord commented.

"True. You sure are early. Do you want a cup of coffee?" Nick headed toward the back. Though there were six desks in a bullpen area, none of them were occupied at the moment. Most of the other deputies either hadn't come in yet or were out on patrol.

Even Rochelle Ashely, the day receptionist, hadn't yet arrived. Which actually helped. The fewer people who heard Cord's questions, the better.

"I've got a few questions about Eldridge Colton," Cord began.

Instantly, Nick's posture tightened. He even looked around, as if he expected the sheriff to be listening in. "What about him?" Nick asked, his tone cautious.

"I understand y'all think Eldridge Colton is dead. Have you ever come up with a body?"

"No." Nick snorted. "You know as well as I do those rich people will make sure his body is never found."

Cord played along. "Yeah, you're probably right. I heard you arrested Piper Colton for the murder. For the DA to think you have a case, you must have some really compelling evidence against her, right?"

Nick shifted his weight from foot to foot, clearly uneasy. He considered Cord's question, gulping down his coffee. "What's this really about, Cord?" he finally asked.

"Piper's a friend," Cord admitted. "I'm checking into this on her behalf. I really don't think she did it."

"Oh, yeah? Well, we have an eyewitness and enough evidence to charge her with the crime."

Cord's heart sunk. "An eyewitness to what? Surely you're not saying you have someone who claims they saw Piper commit the murder?"

Jaw tight, Nick looked away. "I really shouldn't be discussing this case with you," he said. "I'm sorry, Cord, but I can't comment further."

"I understand," Cord said. And he did.

Taking his leave, Cord next headed over to the courthouse.

At the courthouse, Cord was well-known and he greeted everyone by name. Lots of the lawyers and bail bondsmen around here had, at one time or another, used Cord's services. Cord had done favors for many of them and he figured now would be a good time to call in those favors.

He located Jimbo Ryan, a personal injury attorney

known for his loud advertisements and cheap suits. "Hey, Jimbo," he greeted the man with a clap on the back. "How's business?"

They chatted for a few minutes before Jimbo made a show of glancing at his watch, an imitation Rolex. "Well, I've got to head to court. Time to get my client some cash." He grinned.

"Sounds good. You know, I need to find someone from the public defender's office. I heard Piper Colton was using them for her legal defense."

Jimbo's eyes went wide. "No way. With all the Colton money, I'd have thought they'd bring in some bigwig, celebrity attorney from up north or the west coast."

Cord shrugged. "I don't know. I'm just curious. Thought I'd see what I could dig up."

"Why?" Jimbo's gaze narrowed. For all his obnoxiousness, he had a pretty sharp brain in that big head. "I know you, Cord. You're the least nosy person I know. So either Piper has skipped bail or someone hired you to prove she wasn't guilty. Aha! That's it, isn't it?"

About to make a show out of recoiling in mock horror, Cord reconsidered. "Maybe," he allowed. "Maybe I have been asked to look into the evidence that led to her being charged. Keep that between us, all right? That's why I need to find out who is her attorney."

Scratching his comb-over, Jimbo shook his head. "If her family isn't willing to pay for a top-notch attorney, they must think she's guilty, too."

"I don't know." Cord shrugged. "I've just got to find out what evidence they have on her. I stopped off at the sheriff's office, but no one would talk."

"Between you and me..." Jimbo glanced to the left and to the right "... I think ole Piper Colton has some powerful enemies. There's no way a sweet gal like her could kill a tough old coot like Eldridge."

"I agree."

"But," Jimbo added, leaning in close, so close Cord could smell the whiskey he'd used to spike his coffee, "I've heard they had a witness. Someone who claimed to actually see Piper beating the old man." With that, Jimbo sauntered off, leaving Cord staring after him.

All the way home, Cord berated himself. Had he been taken in by her long-lashed green eyes and innocent expression? Was it possible he was actually harboring a murderess?

Chapter 7

Piper knew exactly where to start looking for Renee. Any little run-down bar or club between Terrell and Dallas. She figured the eighteen-year-old would want to work with a younger crowd. A quick search on her phone—a new, prepaid, no-contract one that she'd purchased with cash—revealed that, according to the Texas Alcoholic Beverage Commission, eighteen was the minimum age to be able to legally serve alcohol. She'd bet Cord didn't realize this, assuming as so many did, that since one had to be twenty-one to legally drink, that same age would apply to serving.

Renee, though, no doubt knew this. If tending bar somewhere, anywhere, was her dream, then that's what she'd be doing. Now all Piper had to do was find her.

Cord had said he'd searched, but a big man like him was bound to draw attention. She'd bet if he'd happened to wander into Renee's place of employment, she would have had plenty of time to hide. And her coworkers had no doubt been warned not to talk to a big, burly guy with shaggy dark hair.

Which was why Piper anticipated finding Renee without too much difficulty. No one would see a woman as any kind of threat.

Her main problem was the hour. This early in the morning most of the sort of places she needed to visit wouldn't yet be open.

So she didn't completely waste her time, Piper checked out all the breakfast places in between three of the most popular bars. Just in case Renee might have taken a little extra waitressing work to survive.

No luck there.

At lunchtime she passed a strip club advertising a five-dollar buffet. The parking lot was full. On impulse, she pulled in and parked.

Did she have enough nerve to go inside? From what little she knew of these places, the clientele would be all men.

Still, she wouldn't get what she wanted unless she was fearless. Piper took a deep breath and got out of her car.

The huge bald guy guarding the door waved her in without hesitation. He didn't stamp her hand or anything, so she guessed cover charges only were at night. When she asked, the door guy flashed a toothy grin. "No charge. Women are free. Women are always free."

Well, there you go.

Once inside, Piper kept her head held high while she tried to see in the smoke-filled, dim light. As she'd expected, men packed the place, their attention focused on a half-naked woman gyrating around a pole. Scantily clad waitresses circled the room, bringing overpriced drinks and private dances to those willing to pay.

Refusing to show her discomfort or embarrassment, Piper continued to scan the room. While she really hoped she wouldn't find Renee working in a place like this, one never knew. She'd heard the dancers made really good money.

"What can I get you, honey?" One of the waitresses, a tiny woman with a long, black braid, came up.

"Oh, nothing right now." Piper pulled out her phone and brought up the photo. "I'm trying to find my friend. Have you seen this girl?"

To her credit, the waitress actually studied the photo. "No, I haven't seen her," she said. "She doesn't work here, either, as a dancer or server."

Relieved, Piper smiled. "Thanks for your help."

"No problem." The waitress smiled back. "I hope you find your friend."

Aware of several men tracking her with their gazes, Piper hurried outside to her car. As soon as she got inside, she locked the doors. She wasn't sure she could go inside another "gentlemen's club," but if Renee didn't turn up at any of the bars, she might have to.

Glancing at her watch, Piper saw it was still way too early to hit up some of the other trendy bars. Earlier she'd used Yelp to find places an eighteen-year-old might think cool.

She decided to head back to Cord's house and take a nap. After dinner, she'd go back out. Maybe she'd even get lucky and find Renee tonight.

On the drive back, she admired the landscape. The leaves had started falling from the trees, but there was still enough color to make her smile. This time of year—Thanksgiving—had always been one of her favorites. She loved the huge family gathering, tasting everyone's dishes, and the mouthwatering meal. Whitney had always made sure they had both smoked turkey and ham, and last year Piper had counted at least ten different pies.

Thanksgiving was next week.

Realizing she wouldn't be there this year made her throat close up and her eyes sting. Despite everything, she loved her large family and she knew they—or at least most of them—loved her.

Well, this year would just be different. Raising her chin, Piper kept her gaze on the road. Since everyone had their own traditions, she wondered what Cord usually did for his holiday. Surely Renee had to be missing that.

She started daydreaming, another one of her flaws, at least according to Marceline. Maybe she and Cord's niece would hit it off. They could plan their Thanksgiving menu together—just because it would be a small gathering didn't mean they had to skimp on food.

Buoyed by her happy thoughts, when she reached Cord's place, she bounded from the car. His truck was gone, which she took as a good sign. If he was still working on finding out the true story with Eldridge, today would be a great day.

He'd shown her where he hid his spare key, so she located that and let herself in. Once inside, she debated going to her room for a quick nap but decided she'd turn on the TV and doze on the couch. Truman seemed to think that was a great idea and jumped up right beside her.

She'd just gotten all comfy, remote in hand, when she heard his truck pulling in.

Nap forgotten, she jumped up, ready to question him the instant he came in the door. Truman eyed her, but didn't budge from his spot.

Cord entered through the garage, removing his Stetson and hanging it on a peg by the laundry room door. She'd had the foresight to grab him a can of Dr Pepper, which she held out as an offering.

He eyed it—and then her—his expression completely

shuttered. "Thanks." He took the drink, popped the top and slugged down a third of the can.

She braced herself, fully expecting a loud belch. Once again, he surprised her with silence.

"What'd you find out?" she finally asked. "Judging from the look on your face, I'm not going to like whatever it is."

"Well…" He dragged one hand through his hair. "Maybe you'd better sit down."

She didn't move. "That bad?"

"I'm afraid so. Sit."

Just to hasten the process, she hopped up on one of the bar stools. "Tell me."

"Rumor has it that the police have an eyewitness who claims to have seen you beating on Eldridge."

She snorted. "That's the most ridiculous thing I've ever heard."

He didn't smile back or laugh with her. "Is it? Any idea who's the eyewitness?"

"Nope. None whatsoever." Equilibrium regained, she took a sip of her own Dr Pepper. "But it's BS. Complete and utter nonsense. I've never raised a hand against my father in my life."

"The police didn't tell you who it was?"

"No. All they would say is that someone had come forward. They spent ten hours trying to get me to confess to something I didn't do." Despite her bold tone, her lower lip wobbled a bit at the memory. "It was horrible."

"But they charged you anyway?"

She nodded. "When I asked for an attorney, they said they'd call one, but no one ever came."

She couldn't tell if the muscle working in his jaw meant he was angry with her or with them.

"Are you telling me the truth?" he demanded. "Because for me to help you, I've got to have that."

Her quiet and dignified response hid her hurt that he still questioned her integrity. "All I've given you is the truth."

"Okay, then." He took another drink. "So then do you mind telling me why you were at a tittie bar out off I-20?"

Flushing, she gaped at him. "How do you... Someone recognized me."

"Yep. Were you looking for a way to supplement your income?"

Shocked, she gasped. "No. Don't be ridiculous." Then her sense of humor reasserted itself. "Plus, I don't have the body to be a stripper."

His gaze raked over her, leaving little tendrils of fire. "Oh, I don't know about that. I think you'd be very successful."

Even though her entire body flushed, she managed to push through and focus. "Who called you? Is there any chance he's going to let Fowler know?"

"Nope. It was Daryl Stroud, a friend of mine. He's a probate attorney and I saw him briefly at the courthouse this morning. He'd heard I was asking around about you, so he thought he'd let me know he'd seen you on his lunch break."

She winced. "How'd he recognize me? I cut and colored my hair."

"You still look like you." He came closer. "With a sexier haircut."

Damn. Her entire body quivered and quaked. She had to fight the urge to step away. She wouldn't, because she had no reason to back down.

"So what were you doing there?" Of course, he persisted in his questioning. "You still haven't told me."

"Looking for Renee." The shocked expression on his face would have been priceless under different circumstances. "I mean," she rushed on, "it occurred to me she might have figured out that kind of job would be a good way to make a lot of cash quickly."

"She wouldn't do that."

"You never know." As his expression hardened, she explained. "She wasn't there and the waitress said she hadn't seen her. Tonight I'm going to check out some of the trendier bars on the outskirts of Dallas."

"Not alone, you're not."

Now she did move away. Restless, both with pent-up desire and nervous energy, she moved from one end of the room to the other. "Do you want me to find your niece or not?"

"Not at the cost of your safety."

Slowly, she shook her head. "You're not my bodyguard."

"I am right now."

She tried another way of reasoning with him. "The reason I want to go alone is because she won't recognize me, or have any reason to consider me a threat. With your size, she'd see you coming. I think that's probably why you haven't had any luck."

"Women who go alone to a bar are perceived by unscrupulous men as being there for one reason," he said, his voice as dark as his gaze. "Unless you can honestly tell me you're trained in self-defense or you have your concealed handgun permit, I'm going with you."

Stalemate. "I'm beginning to regret coming back here. I could have simply hung out in a mall or something until later."

"And risk someone recognizing you again?"

He had a point. Still, she wasn't accustomed to being

told what she could and couldn't do. For that reason alone, she was inclined to argue.

"How about we compromise," he finally said. "I'll go with you, but wait in the car. That way if you get into any trouble, I can rescue you."

Though she appreciated his attempt to meet her halfway, she wasn't sure how she felt about his insistence in wanting to take care of her. Part warm and fuzzy glow, and part oh hell no.

"You and your brothers T.C. and Reid are close, aren't you?" he asked, his voice quiet.

"Yes, but I don't see what that has to do with—"

"Would either of them let you go to a bar alone?"

"*Let me?* They're not like that."

"Okay, maybe I need to rephrase. Would T.C. or Reid be comfortable with you going to a bar alone?"

Her brothers? Was Cord actually comparing himself to her brothers? Was that how he saw her, like a younger sister?

She pushed away her outrage at the idea and focused on his question. "No," she finally, reluctantly, admitted. "But the two of them would have known better than to try and outright forbid me to do something. They know how stubborn I am. They would have suggested we organize a group of friends and all go together."

He took a step closer. "Is that what you want me to do?"

If she reached out, she could trail her fingers over his firm jaw. Or wind them in his shaggy hair and tug him closer for a kiss. Distracted by her thoughts, at first she couldn't formulate an answer.

"Is that what you want me to do?" he repeated, his voice a silky low growl.

Suddenly every part of her body tingled. If she dared, she'd tell him exactly what she really wanted him to do.

No. Turning around, she stalked to the window. They'd been talking about going to check out the bars. "I don't think that's necessary." Her comment came out a little more prim than she'd intended. Oh, well. She forged on. "This isn't a fun night on the town, Cord. I'm looking for your niece. If I find her, how do you think she'd react if she saw you?"

"She won't." The pure masculine confidence in his voice made her smile.

"Fine," she conceded, though less than gracefully. "You can come with me as long as you promise to stay in the car."

"Agreed."

"Good." Her earlier weariness had returned, so she headed toward her room. "I'm going to go take a nap for an hour or two. I'll see you later."

He nodded, not commenting, though she felt his gaze on her until she turned the corner in the hall. This time, Truman didn't follow her. She considered calling him, but knew Cord had been missing his dog.

Once inside her room, she hurried to the mirror, her cheeks hot and her body aching. For Cord. How wrong was that? Because what could be worse in the middle of this than to start a sexual relationship with the bounty hunter who'd been hired to bring her back?

The knowledge that Piper lay sprawled out in her bed unsettled Cord more than it should have. Restless, he puttered around the house, finally parking himself in front of his computer and checking email.

There was one from Fowler, asking for an update. Cord typed out a quick reply, simply stating things were going well. Which was the truth, although slightly evasive.

Once all his email had been read, he shut down the desktop and wandered into the kitchen. Glancing at the wall clock, he saw over ninety minutes had passed.

Still no sign of Piper. Briefly, he allowed himself to entertain the idea of going to wake her, but the way he instantly got hard told him it wouldn't be a good idea. They'd both end up tangled in her sheets, assuming she wanted him as badly as he did her. Something told him she did.

Needing a task to keep him occupied, he began rummaging through his cupboards. He figured he might as well make dinner since they wouldn't be going to check out bars until at least eight or nine.

He had the necessary ingredients to make one of his favorites—chicken stir-fry, so he put some jasmine rice in the rice cooker and got busy.

Half an hour later, the kitchen smelled wonderful, the dog had been fed and the homemade meal was ready. Eyeing the wok full of food, Cord's stomach growled. Still no Piper.

Turning back to give the chicken one last turn, he debated. Maybe if he just knocked on her door and didn't go inside...

"That smells amazing." Piper's voice, husky with sleep. "I didn't know you could cook."

"There's a lot you don't know about me," he said, turning. He kept his tone light while he took in the sight of her, spiky blond hair even more mussed and tousled, her green eyes still drowsy with sleep.

Sexy as hell. His body reacted with a vengeance.

"Sorry about the long nap," she said, yawning and stretching, which only served to draw his gaze to her perfect breasts. With a jolt of lust, he realized she wore no bra underneath her oversize T-shirt. His body responded, of course. Tightened and swelled. So much so, it was painful.

"Are you hungry?" he managed, well aware he needed to stick to the mundane. "I hope so, because dinner's ready and I'm starving."

"I could eat," she said, grinning. As she moved toward the table, he couldn't help admiring her cute, heart-shaped backside. Damn. If he got any harder, he would shatter. Clenching his teeth, he averted his eyes. "Let me dish you up a plate."

Without waiting for a response, he did just that. Made two plates and, even though he could barely walk, carried them over to the table.

He plunked hers down in front of her, along with a fork and paper napkin. Then he slid into a chair, praying she hadn't noticed the massive bulge in the front of his jeans.

A quick glance showed she seemed entranced by the food. She inhaled deeply before picking up her fork. "Amazing." Stabbing a piece of chicken, along with a sliver of carrot and a snow pea, she took a bite. Chewing slowly, the little moan of pleasure she made did nothing to help dampen his arousal.

"That is so good." Completely unaware of his state, she smiled at him. "You make a mean stir-fry, Cord Maxwell."

Hell. Even the way she drawled his name turned him on. What the hell was the matter with him? In a few hours, they were going in search of his missing niece, and he needed to keep his act together.

He grabbed his fork and started shoveling food into his mouth, barely tasting it.

"Are you okay?" she asked, making him realize she'd

stopped eating and, fork in hand, eyed his nearly empty plate.

"I'm really hungry." He'd gotten skilled at answering truthfully without giving everything away. "As a matter of fact, I'm going for seconds. How about you?"

"No, thank you." At least she'd turned her attention back to her meal. And his arousal had subsided somewhat. Thankfully.

He ate the second helping slower while standing up. Though she glanced at him, she didn't comment until he'd finished.

"That was really great." Pushing to her feet, she brought her now empty plate over to the sink.

"I'll wash up," he told her, leaning in to take her plate and getting a whiff of some kind of body lotion that smelled like strawberries instead of peaches. Of course his body reacted instantly.

"Great." She ruffled her still-mussed hair. "I'm going to go get cleaned up and dressed for checking out bars. I thought we'd leave around eight."

He answered in the affirmative and got busy rinsing dishes. A few minutes later he heard the shower start up and tortured himself with visuals.

This had to stop. He didn't know how much more he could take. Maybe if the two of them actually gave in to the desire that blazed to life every time they got close to each other, they could get it out of their systems.

He decided he'd mention that to her after they got back from searching for Renee. While he hated to be pessimistic, he seriously doubted they'd have much luck. Wherever his niece had taken off to, he'd begun to believe it was far, far away from here.

Dishes put away, dishwasher running, he wiped down the countertops and eyed the damn clock again. He wasn't one for waiting around to take action. Time actually had begun crawling.

At least he only had fewer than thirty minutes before they left.

Wandering into the living room, he clicked on the TV. A mindless sitcom might be the perfect distraction.

And then Piper strode into the room wearing a short skirt, sexy high heels and a tight, plunging shirt that left little to the imagination.

His heart stopped, right before a bolt of pure lust restarted it. And then he pictured her walking into a bar—alone—dressed like that. Every man in the place would have exactly the same reaction.

"That bad, huh?" she asked drily.

"What?" He blinked, needing to clear the red fog of desire.

"My outfit. I take it you don't like it. You look like you swallowed something bitter."

He cleared his throat. "Uh, no. It's nice. Too nice. Is it really necessary to dress like that?"

"Oh." Tugging her blouse up, she gave him a wry smile. "Too low cut?"

Just like that, he snapped out of it. "You're a grown woman," he said with a shrug. "If you feel it's appropriate, who am I to disagree?"

"Okay, fine." She flicked a little clutch purse at him. "If you're ready, let's go." She waited, watching him expectantly, though her happy smile had vanished and he felt like a jerk for killing it.

"I'm ready." Still way too aroused, he stood. "Piper?"

"Yes?" She turned her head, glancing at him over her shoulder.

"There's nothing wrong with your outfit."

A flicker of that smile, quickly gone. "That's it? That's the best you can do?"

He took a step closer, then another. "No. I can do this." Reaching out, he grabbed her shoulder and pulled her to him. She didn't resist, though she stumbled in her sky-high heels.

"What are you doing?" Her voice had gone faint, desire glazing her eyes.

"Showing you exactly how you're going to affect men when you walk into a bar looking as sexy as you do right now," he growled.

"Now, that's a compliment," she began. She never got to finish, because he pulled her to him, claiming her mouth with a desperate sort of possession he didn't want to think too much about. Not right now.

Her mouth opened as she yielded to him. He deepened the kiss, tangling his hand in her short, sexy hair as he inhaled her scent—still strawberries, and fought to keep from pushing her up against the wall and burying himself deep inside her.

"Okay, stop." Breathing hard, she pushed him away, her expression dazed but determined. "Your attempt to distract me, for whatever reason, won't work. I just put lipstick on. We've got a full night ahead of us. I'd like to get started."

Fighting to get his body under control, all he could manage was a nod. He followed her out the door to her car and climbed in the passenger seat.

The first bar they went to was a bust. The instant Piper stepped inside, she knew she wouldn't find Renee here. In fact, when she looked around, she was probably the youngest person there. Hard-core drinkers and loners dotted the smoky interior. Even the guy working behind the bar appeared to be drunk or stoned.

She supposed she was lucky that no one even looked up when she came in. Except the bartender, who cocked one eyebrow at her but didn't speak.

Back in the car, she drove to the second spot she'd mapped out. The crowded parking lot told her this place would be a better choice. "Fingers crossed," she said.

Cord nodded. "I'll be right here. Let me know if you need me."

"I will." She took a deep breath and headed in.

The instant she stepped inside, she got a good vibe. The DJ played current hits and the small dance floor was packed. Despite the deafening music, everyone appeared happy. No one even gave her a second glance as she scanned the room.

There. The young woman behind the bar. Pulling out her phone, Piper checked the photo she'd had Cord text her. Yep. She'd found Renee.

Chapter 8

Now what? As Piper made her way toward the bar, a determined man in a suit stepped in front of her. "Let me buy you a drink," he said, leering down her blouse.

She wished she could swat him away like a mosquito. Since she couldn't, she simply smiled sweetly and said no. When he persisted, she told him she needed to tell him a secret and to lean in. Then, mouth close to his ear, she said, "When I yell run, you'd better do it. Because in about ten seconds, my linebacker boyfriend is going to come out of the men's room and see you bothering me. It won't be pretty. The last guy who wouldn't take no for an answer is still in the hospital."

Eyes wide, he backed away so quickly she had to stifle a laugh. "Sorry," he mumbled, disappearing into the crowd.

Moving as quickly as she could, Piper wound through the press of people and made it to the bar. She climbed up on the single remaining stool and smiled at Renee.

Renee smiled back. "Love your hair," she said. She had one piercing on the side of her nose with a diamond in it and the deep red of her hair was streaked with blue and blonde. This unusual color combination actually worked, bringing out the brightness of her hazel eyes.

"Thanks." Due to the volume of the noise, Piper had to practically shout. "I like yours, too."

"What can I get you?" Renee asked. "I make a mean margarita. I promise it'll be one of the best you've ever had."

"Great. I'll take one."

While Renee went to make the drink, Piper eyed her, trying to figure out what to say or do now. She knew instinctively if she told the younger girl the truth, that her uncle waited in the car, Renee would get spooked and take off.

A moment later, Renee brought the margarita. "Here you go. Listen, if you want to start a tab, that'll be fine. Todd over there will be taking over for me."

"Is your shift over?"

Renee nodded.

"I don't want a tab. Can we settle up before you leave?"

"Sure, no problem. Give me a second." At least that would stall her for a minute. While Renee worked on a computerized machine, Piper sent Cord a text.

She's here. About to get off work. Watch for her to leave in a few minutes.

He texted back one word—Okay.

Heart pounding, Piper prayed her hands didn't shake as she handed over cash, plus tip. Renee smiled and thanked her.

"You haven't even tasted your drink," she chided.

"Oh, sorry." Hating that she felt so flustered, Piper took a gulp of her margarita. "Wow." She took another. "That is really good."

Renee beamed. "I can't explain, but tending bar is like a dream for me. I've wanted to do this ever since I was a little kid."

"A little kid?" Propping her chin in her hand, Piper studied her. Except for her height, Renee looked nothing like her uncle. With her bright red hair, fair skin and freckled nose, she must resemble her father.

"That seems an odd goal for a small child to have."

"Maybe." Renee shrugged. "But my mom used to take me to bars a lot. She'd leave me there while she flirted or danced with men and I always watched the bartender. They were everyone's friend. They listened, brought drinks and cleaned up messes. If we went to the same place a lot, they got to know me and kept an eye on me, too. I always felt like they were sort of guardian angels."

Moved, Piper reached across the bar and lightly touched the back of Renee's hand. "That's kind of sad, you know. But heartwarming, too."

"Do you think?" Clearly done talking, Renee moved away. "You have a good rest of your night, all right? If you need another drink, Todd will fix you up."

Piper watched until Renee disappeared, going through double doors to an area marked Employees Only.

"So that's why you dissed me." The guy in the suit was back, sneering. "You like the ladies. I don't see a boyfriend."

Piper got up, drank the rest of her margarita in a few gulps—no sense in wasting a good drink—and turned to go. Hopefully if she ignored him, he'd leave her alone.

Instead, he grabbed her arm. Hard. "Don't walk away when I'm taking to you."

She jerked herself free. "Leave me alone. I've already made it clear I'm not interested. Don't make me scream."

He appeared startled that she'd even consider doing

such a thing. But at least he didn't try to stop her as she made her way toward the door.

Outside, she hurried over toward her car. She made it just about halfway when her rejected suitor rushed up to her and shoved her, knocking her to the ground.

Stunned, knees and hands bleeding, she struggled to get up. Before she could, she saw Cord out of the car and barreling toward the suit guy.

By the time she'd made it back to her feet, Cord had punched the other man in the jaw, sending him to the asphalt. He yanked him back up, propelling him over to Piper. "I think you owe her an apology," he snarled.

"Sorry." Surly, but more than she'd expected. A guy like him seemed the type to keep fighting, even when outmatched.

"Apology accepted." She—they—needed him to go away. From the corner of her eye, she saw Renee exiting the building.

"I've got to go," she said, limping over toward the younger woman as fast as she could.

Behind her, suit guy called her an unflattering name. Though she didn't look back, she'd just bet that next sound was Cord's fist connecting with dumb-ass's jaw again.

"Excuse me," Piper called out. "Some guy just attacked me in the parking lot. I'm not sure what to do." She stopped under a light pole, so Renee could see the full extent of her damage.

Renee turned, her eyes widening as she took in Piper's bloody knees, torn skirt and scraped palms. "Where is he?" she asked, pulling out her phone as she scanned the parking lot. "I'll call the police."

Piper saw the second Renee recognized Cord. She stiffened, looking from Piper to the scuffle that still went on. "Which one?" she asked. "Which of those two guys attacked you?"

"The one in the suit," Piper said.

"It doesn't matter," Renee spoke into her phone, giving the address. "I've just called 9-1-1. The police are on their way. I'll have both of them arrested."

The police? Piper panicked. If they recognized her—and they probably would, since Eldridge's disappearance and suspected murder had resulted in multiple APB's being issued—they'd probably haul her in for questioning.

She couldn't have that.

Turning to run, her ankle gave out and she fell again, this time with a loud cry of pain and frustration.

Instantly, Cord ran over. Renee stiffened, but she didn't bolt.

"Are you all right?" he asked, gently helping Piper get up.

"I think so." Piper lifted her chin. "The only thing that's hurt is my pride."

"How can you joke at a time like this," Cord chided, his expression tight. His gaze slid past her to Renee. "Hello, Renee."

Shock, worry and then anger flitted across the younger woman's face. "What are you doing here?" she demanded. Then, as she took in the way he supported Piper, holding her close to him, she swallowed hard. "Do you two know each other?"

As Piper was about to speak, she caught movement from the corner of her eye. Her attacker had taken off running.

Cord tensed, about to go after him.

"Let him go," Piper said. "We have more important things to deal with." Ankle throbbing, she clutched Cord's arm to keep from falling as she turned to face Renee. "Yes, we do know each other. I came looking for you."

"Why?" Renee looked from one to the other.

"Your uncle has been worried sick about you. I've been helping him locate you."

"Worried?" Renee's eyes widened in astonishment. "Cord couldn't care less what I do."

"That's not true," Cord put in, his voice a deep rumble. "I've been searching for you ever since you took off."

"Really?" Now Renee didn't bother to hide her disbelief. "I've been here since day one. This isn't that far from home. Not once have you shown up."

"I didn't know where you were."

Piper looked from one to the other. Though she could tell Cord was trying, he'd assumed an adversarial stance, like a boxer gearing up for a fight. Picking up on this, Renee crossed her arms and lifted her chin.

A few people exited the front door, eyeing them curiously as they headed toward their vehicles.

"How about we go someplace private to talk?" Piper entreated. She tried to take a step toward Renee, but pain shot up her leg and she bit back a cry. If Cord hadn't been holding her up, she would have fallen.

"Maybe you should get your ankle looked at," Renee suggested. "My uncle and I can have our discussion another time."

Next to her, Piper felt Cord stiffen. "I'm fine," she lied. "When we get back to the house, I can ice it. I'd really like you two to get a chance to have a heart-to-heart."

"The house?" Renee looked from one to the other. "Are you two living together?" She fixed Cord with a narrow-eyed gaze. "That was quick. I didn't even know you were seeing someone. Of course, why would I, considering we never really talked?"

He cleared his throat. "I'd like to try and change that. Please. Come back to the house."

Clearly still indecisive, Renee looked from one to the other. "For a little while," she finally agreed. "But I'm taking my own car and I plan to leave once we're finished."

Cord stiffened. For a second Piper was afraid he'd say the wrong thing and drive Renee away. But finally, he nodded. "Sure thing."

Sirens sounded in the distance.

Piper panicked. "We've got to go."

"You can't," Renee said. "You've got to stay and tell the police how that guy assaulted you."

"I can't." She lunged forward, meaning to go for Cord's truck. Luckily, he still held on to her or she would have fallen again. The ankle had really started to hurt.

"Since her assailant is gone, and I got in a few good punches, I'm sure he has plenty of regrets. I don't see the point of Piper reporting anything." That said, he lifted Piper and carried her over to his truck. Briefly setting her down so he could open the door, he saw her wince. "Do you think you should go to the ER?"

"No. Though it hurts like the dickens, it's a sprain, I'm sure. And there's nothing they can do for that except tell me to put ice on it." She glanced back at Renee. "I really hope you two can work things out."

"Me, too."

The sirens grew louder. In a minute they'd be turning down the street and into the parking lot.

Cord placed Piper inside the truck and closed the door. "We have to go," he told Renee. "Now. Please. We'll explain later."

Finally, Renee spun on her heel and went to her car, something small and silver with multiple dents. "I'll follow you," she shouted. "Let's go!"

And they were off.

"Do you think she's really going to follow us?" Cord asked Piper.

"Why wouldn't she? She said she would." Piper spoke through clenched teeth. The pain from her ankle made her feel nauseous.

They passed the police cars, two of them, going in the opposite direction.

"That was close."

All Piper could do in response was nod.

"Are you okay?" He glanced at her. "I really think we should stop at an ER and get that checked out."

"First off, we can't. They'll want ID and insurance, and since my family is pretty well-known around here, they'd call Fowler. Second, I'll be fine once I get a hold of some ice."

Though he didn't appear convinced, he nodded and concentrated on the road.

Piper leaned back in the seat and wished she could fall asleep.

When they pulled up in Cord's driveway, she tensed, dreading getting out of the truck.

"I'll get you," Cord said, correctly interpreting her expression. "Once I have the door open, I'll carry you inside and put you on the couch."

"What if you drop me?" She ruined her weak attempt at humor with a muffled cry when she tried to move. "I'm not all that light, you know."

"Really," he scoffed. "I bet you don't weigh over a hundred pounds soaking wet."

Headlights pulled in behind them. "Renee's here," Piper pointed out. "Please be kind to her."

But he'd already gotten out of the truck so she wasn't sure if he'd heard her, which was probably for the best.

Biting her lip to stifle a moan of pain, the next few minutes felt like an eternity. Renee still had her key and hurried up the sidewalk to unlock the front door.

"Ready?" Cord asked.

Piper inhaled and then nodded. "As much as I'm ever going to be."

Then he lifted Piper out of the truck and set her down gently. "Lean on me," he said as he did. "Keep that ankle off the ground."

"What, decided I'm too heavy, after all?" she managed to quip, despite breaking into a sweat due to pain.

Instead of responding, he lifted her up and carried her inside.

"Wow." Renee watched, her heavily made-up eyes wide. "Like carrying your bride over the threshold."

Piper couldn't help but snort. "Right. He wishes."

"Do I?" Despite the gleam in his eye, he set her down gently on the sofa. Truman greeted them with a happy bark and wiggled his entire body.

Bride. Huh. She wondered why Renee would even think such a thing. Maybe a wishful longing for a family. Piper attempted to flash a friendly smile but it ended up feeling more like a grimace.

The ankle hurt. Cord made an ice pack and Renee gave her two Advil and a glass of water.

"Maybe she should have something stronger," Cord suggested. "I've got whiskey."

Renee nodded. "Would you rather have that?"

At that moment, the pain was so intense that Piper would have taken an elephant tranquilizer if offered. "Please," she managed, after downing the two pills with water.

But Renee stood stock-still, staring. "I recognize you now," she said slowly. "You're Piper Colton."

All Piper could do was glance at Cord before nodding. "Yes, I am."

She frowned. "Aren't you like, rich or something? What are you doing here with my uncle?"

Shifting the ice pack around, Piper took a minute to answer. "He's helping me. I got in a bit of trouble and—"

"You were arrested for murdering your father," Renee interrupted. "Now I remember. I saw it on the news."

If she hadn't been in so much pain, Piper would have been embarrassed. All she could do right now was nod toward Cord. "I'm sure Cord will be happy to explain."

She hoped he'd get the hint. He'd been sitting like a brooding lump for the entire time Renee had been there. If he really wanted her back, he needed to show it.

"Well?" Renee faced Cord. "What the heck is going on?"

"Does she look like a murderer?" Cord asked, a slight smile playing at the corner of his mouth. "She didn't kill anyone. In fact, we don't even know if Eldridge is dead. Someone planted evidence on her and we're trying to find out who."

"I see." Renee's expression cleared. "So her staying here is a...business arrangement, then?" The sarcasm in her voice made Piper smile.

"It is," she said. "One of my brothers hired him to find me and bring me home."

"Well, that obviously didn't work out." Clearly interested, Renee tapped one foot. "So what happened?"

"She agreed to help me look for you in exchange for me trying to figure out who framed her and why," Cord said.

"Did you?"

"Not yet." Cord got out his best bottle of whiskey and poured several fingers' worth into a glass. He brought it to Piper. "This is actually sippin' whiskey, but in your case I think it might be better if you do it like a shot. Just toss your head back and shoot it."

She stared at him before accepting the drink. "That's a pretty big shot."

"Believe me, you'll feel better after you drink it. You might even be able to sleep."

Privately she doubted that, but why not. She had nothing to lose. Plus, she wanted the focus off her and back to the two of them. If they were ever going to resolve their differences, they couldn't keep pretending the other one wasn't in the room.

Raising the glass to her mouth, she took a sip. "Not bad," she lied. "Since the two of you have a lot to discuss, I'll just lie here and drink my whiskey. Slowly."

Cord shot her a look before turning to face his niece. "Renee, why'd you run off?"

"I…" Renee's expression, an interesting combination of rebellious and holding back tears, matched her shaky voice. "You were angry all the time. And busy. Two years ago, when my parents died, I knew you weren't planning on taking care of a sixteen-year-old girl. We both toughed it out as long as we could. Once I turned eighteen, I didn't see the need to stay someplace where I wasn't wanted."

"I wanted you, Renee." His steady gaze and sure voice weren't angry or judgmental. "I just had a piss-poor way of showing that I cared. You're right, I didn't expect any of what happened. You lost your mom and your dad and I lost my sister. I was grieving, and then Sam, the man who was more like a father to me than my own, died. Not only did I have to navigate his estate, but I had to learn how to run my own business." He swallowed. "I know I was busy, but I honestly was trying to keep us afloat. Plus, the truth is, I didn't really know how to interact with a furious sixteen-year-old girl." He cut her a look. "And you have to admit, your attitude didn't make it any easier."

Renee's expression didn't change. "I was angry, in the beginning. The grief was so overwhelming, rage felt better."

Pretending strong interest in her drink, Piper continued to sip, trying not to gag at the taste, and adjusting the ice on her swollen and sore ankle. She couldn't help wishing the two of them would just hug and make up. Renee might think she was grown, but Piper could tell she still longed for a family connection.

"I'm not angry anymore, though," Renee continued. "I haven't been for a while. I did my best to change, to do well in school. I wanted you to notice. Yet you stayed the same—remote and uninterested."

"That's not true." Cord's stricken expression made Piper ache. "I went to your graduation, bought you a gift. I know I wasn't very good as a father figure, but I didn't know how."

Renee nodded, her expression unconvinced. As if he sensed she needed him, Truman went over and put his head on her leg. She pet him, almost absentmindedly, while considering Cord's words.

"I'd like a second chance." Cord moved closer. "It can't be easy, the life you're living now. Come back home. Let's try again to be a family."

Hesitating, Renee looked at Piper, who hurriedly averted her eyes.

"I like my job," Renee said. "But I have no real place to live. I've been crashing at various friends' houses. I'd like to have my room back. Or is she—" Renee pointed at Piper "—staying in my room?"

"She's in the guest room. The one I was using as an

office." Relief colored his voice. Now he finally hugged her, a one-armed, quick embrace that both seemed to find uncomfortable. "Yes, I'd love for you to have your room back."

"I'm not quitting my job," Renee said, as if she expected him to demand it. "I make decent money tending bar and I really like it. I'm saving up to get my own apartment."

Piper could see Cord visually bite back whatever he wanted to say. "That's cool," he agreed.

"Okay." Finally, Renee smiled.

"Then it's settled. We can go and get your things."

"No need." Renee held up her backpack. "Everything I own is in here." She took a deep breath. "It's late and I'm really tired. If you don't mind, I'm going to go to my room now and close the door."

"Sure." Cord cleared his throat, apparently struggling to find the right words. "Thank you," he said. "I'm glad to have you back home where you belong."

Head down, Renee nodded before hurrying off down the hallway.

By some miracle, Piper had managed to empty her glass. "You were right," she told Cord. "The whiskey helped."

"Good." Her drowsy smile made him ache to hold her. Instead, he grabbed the glass. "Want more?"

Briefly she considered. Then closing her eyes, she nodded. "I think so. Just a little. I have a feeling I'm going to need all the help I can get to sleep."

He did, too, judging from the force of his arousal. How he could want her now, injured and in pain, boggled his mind. But he did.

After pouring a little more whiskey, he placed her

glass on the coffee table. "Why don't I help you get to your room? I can bring you the whiskey there and you can drink it in bed, if you want."

Of course, thinking of her tangled in her sheets didn't help his libido any.

She nodded, coloring. "That sounds great. But first, do you mind helping me get to the bathroom? I need to freshen up and stuff before I go to bed."

The intimacy had just ratcheted up to an entirely different level.

"No problem." Though he replied automatically, he couldn't help but imagine undressing her, her silky skin bare.

"Great." She held out her hands. He gripped them, trying to keep as much space as possible between them while still supporting her.

As she struggled to stand while keeping her ankle up, he got a good look at it. Swollen to the size of a grapefruit, bruised in various shades of blue and purple, he realized she should have had it professionally looked at. Too bad he didn't know a doctor. Or even a nurse.

"I think you might have broken that," he said.

"Do you?" She sounded supremely unconcerned. Or maybe she was just focused on getting to her feet.

Somehow, he got her standing and, with her leaning heavily on him, they made it to her bathroom. Once she was able to stand, holding on to the counter, he made a hasty exit. At least it was a small room, and she'd be able to move between sink and commode without taking too many steps.

"I'll be right out here if you need me," he said, closing the door to give her privacy. He went down the hall to get their drinks and then headed to her room. He took a seat on the edge of her bed, listening while the water ran and she washed up and brushed her teeth.

"I'm ready," she called out.

First taking one more quick gulp of his own whiskey, he went to retrieve her and get her settled for the night. Once he had, he took his drink and beat a quick retreat, wondering if he'd get any sleep at all that night unless he took an icy shower.

Chapter 9

The next morning, Cord went down to the kitchen and drank a cup of coffee while both Piper and Renee slept. He'd tossed and turned all night, torn between desire for Piper and relief that he'd finally found Renee. Having his niece back home felt like a block of concrete had been lifted off his chest.

While he didn't like—at all—the idea of her working in a bar, he'd realized this was her way of declaring her independence while at the same time needing her family. Though he'd used a lot of Fowler's money paying bills, he wanted to make sure Renee had a chance at another kind of life. Bartending was fun and he could see how it would appeal to an eighteen-year-old girl who wasn't yet able to legally drink. But he wanted her to have a chance at more. He wondered if she'd consider enrolling in a junior college in the spring. Though he knew a question like that would have to wait, he'd ask her after the holidays.

The holidays. He thought of Piper, wondering what she planned to do. From what he remembered of his time living on the ranch, the Colton family had a huge shindig for Thanksgiving.

While he…usually he went out to eat at the local Waffle House, if anything.

This caused a pang. Even though he'd always made sure to take Renee with him, for the first time he wondered if she'd like something more traditional, like turkey.

Before Sam had died, he used to smoke a turkey in his smoker and invite Cord over. The two of them would drink beer and feast on the bird with maybe a side of Stove Top Stuffing. The first year after losing Sam, despite inheriting the smoker, Cord hadn't felt like continuing the tradition. The second, he'd refused to think about it. Maybe this year, he should.

Pouring another cup of coffee, he went down the hall to check on Piper. He found her sitting up in her bed, hair tousled, dark shadows under her eyes. Truman lay curled up beside her, barely raising his head when Cord entered.

"Here." He handed her the mug. "You look like you had a rough night."

Her half smile lasted only a second. "I didn't sleep much, despite the whiskey. But the ice might have helped, at least until it melted." Wincing as she moved, she slid her foot out from under her sheet. "I think the swelling might have gone down."

"Doubtful," he said. "Still looks pretty swollen to me. I know you don't want a doctor, but how about we drive into Dallas. It's more anonymous."

"I was on the local news. Once they get my name, they'll know who I am. No doctor. Anyway, I looked it up on my phone. I need to ice it for up to three days and stay off of it as much as possible. My ankle feels pretty stable—not wobbly—so that's good. It's not a severe sprain. And it's definitely not broken. The pain has eased off a lot."

"You fell when you tried to walk on it," he pointed out. "That's wobbly, as far as I'm concerned."

"It's better now," she insisted. "Help me get out of this bed and I'll show you."

Placing his coffee cup on the nightstand next to hers, he contemplated the best way to assist her without getting too intimate. Except now that she'd moved the sheet, he could see she wore the same T-shirt without a bra.

Of course, his entire body sprang to instant attention. As he pondered how to lift her without giving away his arousal, his cell rang.

Relieved, he answered. He'd barely said hello, when Fowler started talking. As he listened, his disbelief grew. "Wait, hold on," he began, but the other man wouldn't let him get a word in.

As Fowler started to wind down, Cord tried again. "Let me ask—" *Click.* Fowler hung up without letting Cord get a word in.

He shook his head and met Piper's gaze. "That was Fowler. He was pretty agitated."

"About what?"

No wonder Fowler had been rambling. What he'd done defied rational explanation, and made Cord wonder what Fowler's true motives were for wanting Piper back in the fold.

"I've got bad news," he said, anger clawing at his gut. "Fowler thought it might put more heat on you, so he went to the judge—who apparently golfs with him— and told him you'd disappeared and he believes you've skipped bail."

All the color blanched from Piper's face. "What does that mean for me? Since my court date hasn't arrived yet, surely they won't go on Fowler's speculation, will they?"

He nodded. "Unfortunately, they already have. Fowler

just told me the judge had the police put out a warrant for your arrest."

Green eyes huge, she stared at him. He braced himself for her to argue and complain, grimly aware that he wouldn't blame her, but also knowing that no amount of emotional outburst would change the situation.

She swore. He eyed her, aware he'd never heard her use profanity before. Then her chin came up and she looked him in the eye. "Fine. We'll deal with it. What now?"

"You can go to the courthouse, tell them the truth."

"What, that I'm shacked up with the bounty hunter sent to find me?" The hint of mockery in her tone took some of the sting off the words.

"No, that you have every intention of appearing in court and you've broken no laws. You haven't left the county."

She nodded. "I like that."

"Of course, Fowler will demand that you return home. Not that you have any legal obligation to do so."

"Fowler won't have to know."

He sighed. "I'm sure someone will contact him the instant you show up."

"How sure?"

With the way Fowler threw money around to get what he wanted, Cord felt quite certain there'd be a competition in the courthouse to see who could reach Fowler first. "Beyond a shadow of a doubt."

Tilting her head, she considered him. "What would you suggest I do?"

"For now? Nothing. Stay here. Rest your ankle and hang out with Renee. And me." He'd added the last as if he'd hastily tacked it on, when he really needed her help to navigate the rocky relationship with Renee.

Giving him a look full of skepticism, she crossed her

arms. "Is this good advice? Won't I get in more trouble for ignoring a warrant for my arrest?"

"No. Not until they serve you. The warrant's bogus anyway."

"You want me to hang out, nothing more?"

"Oh, I could think of a hell of a lot more," he drawled, aware the heat between them would effectively distract her.

Though she blushed, her direct gaze never wavered. "You said you never lied."

"And I haven't."

"Right. So give me the real reason you don't want me to leave and try to set the record straight."

"I already have."

"Maybe so, but there's more, isn't there?"

"All right. *Reasons*, plural." He sighed. "But yes, you're correct. While you should stay here for your safety and also because I do enjoy your company, I have no idea how to deal with Renee and keep her from blowing up at me. Plus," he tacked on the last, eyeing his dog, snoozing on her bed, "there's Truman. He'd be lost without you."

Piper laughed. An honest, from-the-belly laugh. One he found so sexy his entire body clenched. "You have a deal," she said, smiling up at him. "But first I need you to help me get up out of this bed."

Somehow he managed to do this. If she noticed how badly he wanted her, she didn't comment. He wondered if this would be his fate as long as she stayed here. Constant arousal, with no hope of fulfillment. Even if she gave him the slightest chance, he couldn't take it. Sam had drilled into him a sort of bounty hunter's code. One of the items on the list was never take advantage of a client or a fugitive. Thus far, Cord hadn't had a single problem adhering to this rule. Of course, Piper hadn't been around until now. He'd have to keep his craving for her in check. No matter what it took.

Over the next couple of days, Piper became skilled at maneuvering around using the set of crutches Cord had found for her. Truman stayed by her side, leaving only to go out and do his business and to eat his meals. She'd never had a dog of her own and she found she really enjoyed the canine's closeness. She'd taken to talking to him like he could understand, and she'd swear he tried, tilting his head as he listened. Piper also spent a lot of time hanging out with Renee, and learned the teenager had a real talent for drawing and painting.

"Art," Renee said, grinning. "That's what I'd really like to do someday. Like a graphic designer, or something. Bartending is fun, but it's not a forever job, you know?"

"I do. Maybe you should go to an art school and get your degree," Piper pointed out. "There are several good ones that aren't too far away. I can help you look into them, if you'd like."

Immediately the joy vanished from Renee's face. "Oh. No, thanks. I don't have the money to pay for that, and neither does Cord."

"There are grants and scholarships," Piper began. But Renee's closed-off expression told her to stop.

"I'm sorry," Piper murmured. "Maybe we'll discuss this another time."

"I'd rather not." Renee turned away. "If you don't mind, I'd like to be alone."

"Of course." Piper rose clumsily, still not skilled at using the crutches. She hobbled from the room, shaking her head as Renee closed the door behind her. "Did you see that, Truman?" she asked the dog, who stayed close to her left leg. "We'll have to work on that one, won't we?"

When she reached the kitchen, she realized if she was going to do something for Thanksgiving, she'd need to get going. The holiday was only a few days away.

At the thought, her heart ached. She missed her chaotic family and the large gathering at the dining room table. But, she told herself with determination, she was going to do her best to prepare a meal similar to what she would have had at home.

"Where's Renee?" Cord asked as he came through the garage door. "I thought you and she were going to practice cooking stuff tonight."

Piper sighed. "It didn't work out. I said the wrong thing and now she's mad at me."

Grimacing, he nodded. "I know the feeling."

"Hey, do you think you can pick up a few things at the grocery store for me?"

"Sure?" He glanced at his watch. "I can go now. That way I'll have it wrapped up before supper."

Locating a small pad of paper and a pen, she scribbled a list and handed it to him. "Here you go."

"Turkey, preferably fresh, cornbread mix, fresh green beans, chicken broth, sweet potatoes…" He looked up from the list. "What is this?"

"Thanksgiving dinner," she told him, using her best this-is-not-debatable tone. "I just realized it's in a couple days."

He hesitated for so long she wondered if she'd made yet another mistake.

"Okay," he finally said. "I actually have an electric smoker. I make a mean smoked turkey. I'd be happy to do that if you're planning on making all the sides."

She grinned. "That sounds perfect. I love smoked turkey. Where'd you learn to do that?"

"Sam taught me. I sure miss that guy. He was more of a father to me than my own father."

"I met him once," she remembered. "He seemed like a nice guy."

He nodded, not smiling. "He was. I'll be back in a few."

Though she wasn't sure she should ask, she did anyway. "Is something wrong? Maybe I shouldn't have suggested making the dinner, but it's a huge deal at Colton Valley Ranch. I think Renee might enjoy it."

"I understand. Sam and I used to always smoke a turkey and make a meal. It might not have been fancy, but at least it was homemade. I feel bad because I never did that for Renee. By the time she got here, I usually went to eat at the Waffle House."

Intrigued, she studied him. "Turkey waffles?"

This time her words coaxed a smile. "No. I feel bad that I didn't try harder."

Aware she had to tread carefully, she lifted one shoulder in a casual shrug. "I don't know. At least you shared the meal together. Some kids don't even have that."

Though he nodded, she could tell he wasn't entirely convinced. He glanced at the list again, then at her. "Thank you for doing this," he said softly. "I can't tell you how much I appreciate it."

"I'm looking forward to making my first Thanksgiving dinner," she said.

He nodded, then took the few steps that separated them and kissed her cheek. "I'll be back," he said again, and went out the door.

Stunned, she touched her cheek. Then, more uncertain of her own emotions than she'd ever admit, Piper went to the front window and watched him drive away, heart both aching and so full she wanted to cry. Truman seemed to sense her emotional turmoil. He whined and butted her leg with his massive head so she'd pet him.

Cord returned with the groceries ninety minutes later. Carrying in numerous plastic bags, he placed them on the kitchen counter before returning to his truck to get more.

Renee wandered into the kitchen as he brought in the last load and began unpacking. When Piper pushed to her feet using her crutch and hobbled over to try to help, both Cord and Renee looked at her and said, "No," at the exact same time. After, they shared a companionable grin.

"Fine," Piper said, her smile letting him know she'd caught the positive interaction between him and Renee. She sat back down.

"What is all this stuff?" Renee asked, her gaze fixed on the turkey.

"Thanksgiving dinner," Cord replied, helping Renee put some of the groceries away. "Piper has generously agreed to cook us a traditional meal."

"With that foot?" Renee appeared torn between wistfulness and a sort of resigned acceptance. "Piper, I know you probably meant well and the idea might have sounded good at the time, but I understand."

"You understand what?" Piper tilted her head, clearly perplexed.

"That you're not actually going to do it. It's okay." Renee's slight smile had all the heartache of someone who's had her hopes crashed one too many times. "But you might as well admit it now, so we don't actually believe we're going to have a turkey dinner on Thanksgiving Day."

"What, you don't like turkey?"

Renee shrugged. "I wouldn't know. I haven't actually ever had it, except for the kind in lunch meat."

"What?" This time both Piper and Cord spoke at once. "How is that possible?"

"Well, you know how Mom was." Renee looked down. "She wasn't big on anything even remotely traditional. Though we did have a canned ham one time for Christmas."

"Canned ham?" Clearly appalled, Piper stared. Then, as she realized she might sound insensitive, she nodded. "I've never had that. How was it?"

"Okay. Kind of rubbery, like Spam." Renee looked back at the turkey. "So are you really going to cook that thing?"

"Cord is," Piper answered. "I'm making the sides. Though it'd be a lot easier with your help."

"Me? I don't know how to cook."

"Would you like to learn?"

Renee considered the question. "Maybe," she allowed. "Having another skill might help me feel like I actually could fit in somewhere."

To Cord's surprise, Piper smiled. "Honey, I've felt like I don't belong for almost all of my life."

"Really?" Though Renee continued putting away the groceries, she glanced at Piper over her shoulder. "How do you deal with all the emotions? It's been really hard, moving around so much. Even here, though I've been here two years, I don't feel like I belong."

"I found a hobby that I love. I've learned if I keep busy, do the things I love to do, what other people think doesn't matter."

Renee lifted the turkey and went to put it in the freezer.

"Not there," Piper said. "We don't want it frozen. It needs to go in the fridge."

"Okay."

To Cord's surprise, Renee sounded agreeable. Less… angry. Turning so neither woman would see his expression, he finished putting up the groceries and gathered up the plastic bags to use again later.

"What's your hobby?" Renee asked, going over to sit next to Piper. "Of course, I always just sketch, and that helps, but I think I'd like something that makes me move around more."

"I repurpose old furniture. I know it doesn't sound exciting, but it's a blast. If my ankle wasn't messed up, I'd take you to a secondhand store and we'd buy something, like a dresser, and strip and paint it."

"I have an old dresser that I hate," Renee immediately said. "Do you think we could work on that?"

"Maybe we could." Piper looked thoughtful. "I'd have to send you to the hardware store to pick up supplies."

"How about after Thanksgiving?" Cord put in. "Piper's going to have enough to do with all that."

Piper's chin came up, making him remember what she'd said. "I think I can manage to fit both in," she drawled, her green gaze flashing. "What about you, Renee? Are you in?"

"Yes!" Renee grinned. "Let me show you the dresser first, though. It's pretty ugly. You might not be able to do anything with it."

Cord knew exactly which dresser she meant. It had been built in the seventies, and had been the one thing he had left from his childhood with his father. He'd kept it, though why he wasn't sure. When he'd learned he'd be raising a niece, he'd figured he might as well get some use out of the thing.

Since he'd never told Renee where it came from, finding out she hated it stunned him. But then, he grinned ruefully, it was an ugly dresser.

"Give me a second to get up." Once again, Piper attempted to struggle to her feet. This time, Cord rushed over in time to help her.

"Lean on me," he said, putting his arm around her slender waist. As she leaned into him, a sense of contentment and peace flowed over him. Rather than be alarmed, he went with the flow, amused to think he might be getting Zen or whatever.

Moving slowly, they went down the hall to Renee's room.

"Here it is." With a dramatic flourish, Renee gestured at the four-drawer monstrosity. "Do you think you can do anything with this?"

"Definitely," Piper responded immediately. "What's your favorite color?"

"Purple or lavender."

"How about we paint it that color?" Piper asked. "Though I honestly think it would look better turquoise."

"Really?" Clearly intrigued, Renee turned to study the dresser. "You know, I kind of like that idea. When can we do it?"

"Any time. As soon as we get the supplies." She looked at Cord. "I assume you have an electric sander?"

"Sure." Though he had no idea where it might be. "But are you sure you're up to tackling a job like that with your ankle messed up?"

Her brilliant smile made his heart skip a beat. "Oh, I'm only supervising. Renee here is doing most of the work."

Renee grinned, apparently nearly as besotted as he was with Piper. "Make me a list and I'll go get whatever you need."

"Great. And I'll pay for it, of course. As a small gift to you for being so sweet to me."

Cord watched as tough, belligerent Renee blushed. He knew she couldn't afford to buy anything but necessities. No doubt Piper had figured that out, too.

Watching her and his niece made his chest feel tight and his throat clog. For the first time he could imagine what it must be like to have a proper family, a longing he thought he'd outgrown but now realized he still wanted.

Someday. Not now. Definitely not now.

Being around Piper could be dangerous. She made him hope for the impossible. He could easily fall in love with her if he wasn't on guard, which would be a guarantee of pain and heartbreak. Women like her didn't settle for men like him.

Renee and Piper had their heads together, bent over a sheet of paper as they made their list. Truman, also clearly in love with Piper, lay at her feet. Cord cleared his throat, hoping he could sound normal. "I'll go dig out that sander," he said. And disappeared into the garage, glad to have something else to focus on.

Seeing Renee so genuinely happy gave Piper hope. The poor girl just needed some attention and direction, and she'd be fine. As for Piper, as usual, the simple act of planning how she'd refurbish the dresser raised her spirits, taking her mind off her sadness at not being with her family for Thanksgiving.

Handing the list to Renee, Piper dug fifty dollars out of her purse and handed it to her. "This should cover it."

"Okay." Renee appeared eager to be off.

"Go." Piper shooed her away. "When you get back, you can empty your stuff out and we'll have your uncle take it out into the garage."

"I'll be back." Renee spun on her heel and prepared to take off. When she reached the door, she turned and looked at Piper. "Thank you. I'm really glad you're staying with us."

After the door closed behind her, Piper made her way to the front window and watched her drive away. Truman woofed softly, as if he understood. "You're a good boy," she told him. "Let's go get ready for bed."

She found she slept better with a dog curled up at her side. And not just any dog. This dog. Truman. *Great.* She'd fallen in love with Cord's dog.

The next morning after breakfast, Piper and Renee started on the dresser. Since Renee had to go back to work that night, she wanted to get as much done in the day as she could. Piper told her not to rush, that it would be better to take her time so she didn't have to redo things, and to her surprise Renee listened.

Despite the attention to detail, the sanding went relatively quickly. After all the old stain had been removed, the primer went on. Since the hardware wasn't bad, they kept it to put back on once they'd finished.

The next day, the paint. Two coats.

"The color is lovely," Renee's hushed voice conveyed her awe. "I can't believe how such a small thing could transform something so hideous into something beautiful."

Piper grinned. "Addictive, isn't it? Now you see why I enjoy my hobby so much."

"Why don't you do more with it? Instead of a hobby, turn it into a business?"

Piper stopped smiling. "Actually, that was my plan. I'd been saving to open my own shop and nearly had enough. But then all this happened, and I had to withdraw my savings to survive." She sighed. "I'm being very careful with my money, but I don't know how long it will take to get back to where I was." Not to mention her reputation. Even though she had to believe she'd eventually be cleared, she wasn't sure her reputation would survive.

"I'm sorry." Renee looked like she'd give anything to take back her casual statement. "I didn't know."

"Of course you didn't, how could you?" Leaning on her crutch, Piper put one arm around the teenager and gave her an awkward hug. "Don't worry about it. None of that is your fault. Now, let's just get this dresser finished so you can display your showpiece in your bedroom."

Though it had been years since he'd used his smoker, once Cord got it cleaned up and plugged in, it worked like a charm. He and Piper had decided not to stuff the bird, so he'd simply seasoned it with a nice rub and put it in the smoker at 5 a.m, since it took eight to twelve hours. He had a four-hour window to get the internal temperature up from forty to one-forty. If that didn't happen, they'd have to take it out and cook it in the oven.

Since he'd done this before, he knew he'd finish it in the smoker. His mouth watered thinking about the delicious taste. For once, Truman stayed with Cord instead of Piper, no doubt attracted by the scent of the turkey.

Once he went inside, of course Truman parked his butt in the kitchen. Despite the early hour, Piper bustled around, only occasionally using her crutches. She sat a lot, though, slicing celery and onions while the cornbread baked. "I've never made the dressing before, but I've watched Whitney's cook Bettina do it a bunch of times," she confided.

He'd smiled and nodded, his heart full. Though the kitchen atmosphere felt strangely domestic, he didn't mind. In fact, he liked it. He'd always thought a man and his dog would be enough. Then his niece had come and he'd had hopes he could make a go of their odd little family. Now he knew better. Piper gave him a glimpse of how great life could be. She gave him hope for a much brighter future. The only thing that would have made this day even better would have been if Ms. Berens could have been here. When he'd invited her, she'd declined, stating she'd already accepted an invitation from one of her neighbors.

Renee came wandering in after he'd poured his second cup of coffee. "You're up early," he greeted her.

She glanced around with wide eyes. "Well, it's a special day and I wanted to help."

"You've come to the right place, then," Piper put in cheerfully. "I've got potatoes to be peeled, if you don't mind. Or you can do the prep work on the green beans. I'm going to be busy making my family's homemade cornbread dressing. It's complicated and takes the longest to make."

"That's what I smell." Renee sniffed the air appreciatively. "Cornbread. I'm guessing this must be hard on you, missing your family and all."

Piper's cheerful smile briefly faltered, but Cord admired the way she pulled herself together. "I won't lie. I am missing my family. But I'm also excited to be making new memories with the two of you."

Chapter 10

The turkey was ready around one o'clock. "We'll let it rest," Cord said. "That way you ladies will have time to get everything else ready." He eyed Truman, sitting near the counter, drooling. "Just make sure the dog doesn't counter surf and get it."

Piper laughed. "I'm watching him. And we're pretty much done," she told him. "The dressing, sweet potato casserole and corn casserole are all in the oven. The green beans are in the skillet on low. All I need to do is cook the dinner rolls."

"I can do that!" Renee offered, nearly dancing with excitement.

The next few minutes were busy. He sliced the turkey while Piper watched Renee arrange the side dishes on the kitchen counter. Renee got the rolls—perfectly browned—out of the oven. Through it all, Truman watched intently, still hoping for a morsel.

"Don't worry, buddy," Cord told him. "I'll make you a small plate of white meat."

As if he understood, Truman barked once.

"He's saying 'thank you,'" Renee said, making them all laugh.

Cord finished slicing and set down the platter of sliced turkey. "Ya'll ready?"

"Oh, yes!" Renee said, rubbing her hands together in anticipation. "Let's make our plates and then we can dig in!"

With the food set out buffet style, they took turns serving themselves. Looking exhausted, Piper asked Renee to make hers. Then, with their plates heaping, Cord and Renee took seats at the kitchen table next to Piper. She'd spruced it up a little with a homemade pumpkin and gourd centerpiece. Cord couldn't help but wonder if she missed her no doubt much fancier table at Colton Valley Ranch.

"I can't wait to taste the smoked turkey," Piper said, smiling. "I'm loving this. It's so much more relaxed than what I'm used to."

Momentarily dazzled by her smile, he could only nod and pick up his fork.

"Wait," Renee said. "This is my first traditional Thanksgiving meal and I want to say grace." She held out her hands. Cord took one and Piper the other.

"Thank You, God, for this food. A special meal, cooked with love. But most of all, thank You for these people." Renee's voice broke, but she bravely continued on. "Growing up the way I did, there are a lot of things I never got to do. I have a feeling that this is only one of the many firsts ahead of me." She blinked back tears, still holding his hand tightly. "Thank you, Cord, and you, Piper, for giving me something to start filling the hole inside of me. Love."

His heart expanding inside his chest, Cord gripped her hand as fiercely as she held on to his. Tears streamed down her young face, but despite it all, she smiled. So much hope shone in that smile that his own eyes misted. He glanced at Piper and she quickly looked down at her plate, but not before he noticed how her green eyes glistened with her own emotion.

He thought this just might be the best Thanksgiving he'd ever had.

"Now we can eat!" Pulling her hands free, Renee wiped at her eyes with her napkin, picked up her fork and dug in.

Truman barked, reminding them of his promise to make him a plate.

"I'll do it." Piper jumped up, wincing as she put too much weight too fast on her still-sore ankle.

"Piper—" Cord began.

"It's better, I promise," she said. "I actually forgot about it for a minute. I really want to feed Truman his Thanksgiving dinner myself, if you don't mind."

Her enthusiasm made him smile. "Not too much—he's not used to such rich food and it could make him sick," Cord warned her. "Just a few slices of white meat, no fat. He can also have a couple of green beans, if you rinse them off."

Piper nodded. Once she'd finished, she turned and nearly tripped over the enthusiastic pup. "Here you go, boy." She set the plate down. "Dig in."

Needing no urging, Truman devoured his food. Grinning, Piper sat back down, moving more gingerly than she had before.

Renee hadn't wasted any time digging in, either. "This is fantastic," she exclaimed between mouthfuls. "No wonder everyone always talks about how much they look forward to this day."

Cord and Piper exchanged amused glances before starting in on their own plates.

The smoked turkey had turned out perfectly. Everything had, actually. It had been a long time since he'd eaten a traditional Thanksgiving dinner and he relished every bite.

Once he'd cleaned his plate, he looked up to find both Piper and Renee watching him with identical expressions of amusement. "Do you want seconds?" Piper asked. "Or are you ready for dessert? We've made both pumpkin and pecan pies."

Though he preferred pecan, he didn't know who'd made which pie and didn't want to offend anyone. "I'd like both, please." Sitting back in his chair, he grinned. "You two are amazing cooks. I loved every bit of this meal. This is the best Thanksgiving I've ever had."

Renee ducked her head, her expression pleased.

"Thank you," Piper replied. "But we have to admire your culinary skills, as well. That smoked turkey was the bomb."

At the expression, Renee high-fived her. This made both of them giggle. Cord loved how well the two of them got along. The camaraderie made the atmosphere even more perfect.

Renee jumped up, waving Piper back into her seat. She brought him his pie, two slices on one plate along with a heaping scoop of Blue Bell vanilla ice cream. She brought the same to Piper, though her pieces were much skinnier. Finally, Renee cut her own piece, and she only got pumpkin, confirming his suspicions that she'd baked that one.

Even the pies tasted like ambrosia.

When he'd finished, Cord looked up from his plate and groaned. "I'm so full."

"Food coma," Renee agreed. "I could sleep."

"But it's nearly time for the Cowboys game," Piper announced. "Though a nap sounds lovely, you have to stay awake for that. They play at three."

"Is football part of your Thanksgiving traditions?" Renee asked.

"Yes." Piper's eyes sparkled. "Since the Cowboys always play on Thanksgiving, my family schedules the big meal around the game. Some years, we even go and watch it in person. Of course that means our dinner is either really early or really late. We haven't done that in several years, though."

Needing to move, Cord pushed himself up and started gathering the dishes. "What are you doing?" Piper asked, sounding alarmed.

"Washing up," he told her, resisting the urge to give her a quick kiss. "You go ahead and watch the pregame show. I've got this."

Tilting her head, her expression bemused, Piper hesitated. "Are you sure?"

"Very. You cooked, I'll clean."

"And I can help," Renee chimed in. "We can get these dishes rinsed off and in the dishwasher in plenty of time to watch the game with you."

Still, Piper didn't move. "I need to wrap up the leftovers," she began.

"We can do that." He made a shooing motion with his hand. "Now go on. Git. Let us get to work."

"You convinced me." Piper threw up her hands. "Come on, Truman. Let's go chill on the sofa."

A short while later, they were all seated in the living room, waiting for the game to start. Renee had taken the armchair, so Cord had to sit next to Piper on the couch. Truman lay on one side of her, his big head resting on her knee. Slightly envious of his dog, Cord considered sitting as far away from her as possible, then decided to do what he really wanted. So he took a spot right next to her, so close their thighs bumped. Then, with Renee pretending not to watch them, he casually draped his arm over her shoulders.

To his relief, rather than stiffening or looking at him, she sighed and snuggled in. Head against his shoulder, she kept her gaze on the TV. Truman raised his head, eyed Cord and then settled back down with a sigh.

"I know what we need," Renee said, jumping up. "Or rather, what you two need. Beer. What's football without a cold brew?"

"I'd love one," he said.

"Me, too," Piper said.

A minute later, Renee returned, carrying two bottles of beer and a can of Dr. Pepper.

Happily, he accepted his beer, aware he was grinning like a fool. Renee grinned back and he knew exactly what she had to be thinking. His heart was full and life was good. He wished it could be like this forever.

The day after, Piper still carried a bit of Thanksgiving contentment. Now that the actual day had passed, she knew exactly what would be going on back at Colton Valley Ranch. The day after Turkey Day, Whitney, rather than fighting crowds to catch sale prices at the mall, orchestrated a huge Christmas decorating event. The house would be decked out and if each year appeared more extravagant than the last, so much the better.

Briefly, Piper wondered if Whitney would continue on with Eldridge missing. But then, she realized of course she would. Her adoptive mother had always maintained that she wanted to keep everything as normal as possible so when Eldridge returned, nothing would be out of place. Whitney had never lost faith that her husband was alive.

Of course, Piper knew that most people outside the family thought Whitney had only married the much older Eldridge for his money. Piper didn't believe it after seeing how Whitney had reacted to Eldridge's disappearance. She truly loved her husband and was fiercely loyal not only to him, but to everyone in the family. Including Piper.

Which made Piper feel even guiltier for not contacting her. She would, she told herself. As soon as she figured out her own situation.

About that. The other day, when she and Cord had been discussing the bloody shirt that the police were using to pin the murder on her, Piper had told him she couldn't think of any enemies. Now she had to wonder. Fowler seemed more and more determined to bring her back home. He'd already told her to her face that he believed she was guilty. Maybe she needed to consider the possibility that he'd been the one to frame her.

As soon as she had the thought, she wanted to discard it. Despite his overbearing personality, Fowler was her brother. Or adoptive brother, as he liked to remind her. Either way, they were related. She couldn't imagine him having any reason for wanting to frame her for their father's murder.

Pulling out her cell phone, one of several disposable phones she'd purchased—hey, she watched TV crime shows—she punched in Reid's number. This brother had believed in her innocence even after her arrest. Since she used to be a police detective, maybe he could pull some strings to clear this mess up. If not, at the very least, he might be able to gather some information that would help her find out who had done this to her.

Taking a deep breath, she hit Send. The phone rang once, twice, three times. About to end the call on the fifth ring, partly relieved, Reid answered.

"About time you called," he said instead of hello once she'd identified herself. "How is everything?"

"Okay. Do you happen to know if I have a court date yet?"

"I don't know. There's still an active warrant though."

She swore under her breath. "How bad does it look for me?"

"Not good," he said, his voice grim. "Where are you?"

"I can't tell you that right now. But I can assure you I had nothing to do with Eldridge's disappearance. If he's dead, I certainly didn't kill him. Like I told Fowler and Marceline, someone is framing me."

"We all figured that out, Pipe. Whitney has been a huge champion of yours. She knows—as we all do—that there's no way you'd have done such a thing. She's even announced publicly that you're innocent."

Touched, she closed her eyes. Though Whitney had taken her in as more of a project than because of any deep feeling, she and Eldridge had always treated her like she was their daughter. "I miss her. Please tell her I'm safe and I'll see her as soon as I can."

"I will, but I need more. Explain to me why you've decided to go into hiding?"

"Because both Fowler and Marceline made it clear that they believe I'm the killer."

"What?"

She explained what had happened the day she got home from jail.

Reid swore again. "I'll talk to them. That's absolutely ridiculous."

"Oh, there's more." Briefly, she outlined what Fowler had told Cord that he'd done.

Hearing this, Reid swore again. "That explains the warrant. I wondered. What the hell is wrong with him? He's been going around agreeing with everyone about your innocence and then he pulls something like this?"

"That's why I'm beginning to wonder if he—and maybe Marceline—are the ones who framed me."

"Nope. Believe it or not, I actually considered that. I've been working behind the scenes to clear your name. I quietly investigated both Fowler and Marceline and they don't seem to be responsible. It's got to be someone else. Give me some other names."

"I'm working on it," she said. "As soon as I come up with something concrete, I promise I'll let you know. How was your Thanksgiving?"

He snorted. "Strained. We missed you, Pipe."

"I missed ya'll, too."

"What about you? How'd you spend the holiday?"

She smiled when she thought about it. "I ate with friends. Smoked turkey and all the fixin's. It was small, but nice."

"I'm glad. Whitney was beside herself, missing not only her Dridgey-pooh, but you, too."

No one had ever figured out why Eldridge had allowed Whitney to call him such a horrible endearment, but the old man actually seemed to like it.

Piper laughed. "So has the Christmas decorating commenced?"

"Of course." Reid sounded grim. "She's got more decorators than usual and it's looking more over-the-top than ever this year."

"Yikes."

"Yeah. Whitney keeps telling everyone who will listen that she wants this Christmas to be extra special because her husband will definitely be home."

Piper winced. "I hope so. I'll keep in touch, okay?"

"You do that." Reid paused. "And stay safe, okay?"

After promising she would, she ended the call.

"Hey, are you ready to paint?" Renee popped her head around the corner. She'd gone to the flea market and picked up an armoire and asked Piper to help her refinish it. Since Renee had spent all morning sanding it, it ought to be ready for primer soon. She'd even purchased the paint. This time, instead of turquoise, Renee had purchased her original color choice, purple.

"Yes, I am," Piper answered. Painting was the part she loved the best. She found the strokes of the paintbrush soothing. And watching the coats of color slowly transform the wood into something else made her happy.

Renee had everything ready to go in the garage. The double garage door was up so a fresh breeze brought needed ventilation. She'd placed the armoire on newspaper. Paintbrushes and paint sat next to it. Hunched over one of the legs with a piece of sandpaper, Renee didn't hear Piper approach, Truman by her side as usual.

Watching her, Piper was struck by how young she looked. Cord had speculated earlier that he thought Renee liked to party, as if she'd taken after her deceased mother. Piper knew the idea had caused him a lot of worry.

But she now believed it to be unfounded. Renee's idea of partying appeared to be staying up too late watching TV with popcorn. Though she loved tending bar and seemed to be a people person, Piper had yet to see Renee with anyone who might be considered a close friend. Since Renee definitely couldn't be considered shy, Piper couldn't help but wonder what was up with that.

What the heck. Piper figured she'd take a stab at solving the mystery.

"You must make lots of friends there at your bartending job, right?"

Renee barely looked up. "I'm almost done. Friends? I guess you could say that. But I don't believe in mixing work and pleasure, so any friends from the bar, stay at the bar."

"That makes sense," Piper replied. And it did. Sort of. "What about your other friends?" she persisted. "The high school ones. Why don't you go out with them once in a while?"

"Because there aren't any." Renee sounded supremely unconcerned. "I try not to make friends. That way it doesn't hurt as much when it's time to move away. I learned that at an early age." Renee's wry smile contained no humor. "Did you know I was in seven different elementary schools, four middle schools, and this high school was my fifth one?"

Piper's heart ached. "Wow." She did her best to match Renee's carefree tone. "That must have been hard."

"It was. What was even harder was trying to catch up. Not only did we move around a lot, but my parents didn't care too much if I went to school or not." Renee smiled. "But I did. I was determined to graduate, to make something of myself. And I will. I've been thinking about what you said. I'm tending bar and saving up so I can go to art school. It seemed like a lot of money before, but once I thought about it, I know if I work really hard, I can make this happen."

Impressed, Piper squeezed Renee's slender shoulder. "You're amazing, you know that?"

"I'm glad you think so," Renee quipped. "You can be my fan club. I sure need someone to cheer me on."

And that someone wasn't Cord. Piper heard the words as clearly as if Renee had spoken them out loud. "Your uncle cares about you, I promise."

"I know he does." Renee went back to sanding a minute area on the leg of the armoire.

"He just needs some help showing it. Like all men," Piper said, trying to lessen the seriousness of the moment yet still get her point across.

To her relief, Renee laughed. "You might be right."

"Oh, honey, I know I am. He was a mess when you were gone. He's just not sure how to go about this being a father figure thing. I think he's terrified of making a mistake. You have to help him along."

Now Renee's hazel eyes definitely had a sparkle. "I see," she said. "Just like you have to show him how to be a boyfriend. I've noticed he's not real good at that, either."

Though color flooded Piper's face, she attempted a smile. "We're both still feeling our way around in that area. I wouldn't exactly use the term *boyfriend* or *girl-friend*. More like friends."

Renee's brows rose. "With benefits?"

Could she get any more embarrassed? Piper didn't think she could. Now not only her face felt on fire, but her entire body. "That's none of your business, young lady," she said, her prim tone causing Renee's grin to widen.

"I thought so!" Renee crowed. "That's great. You'll be so good for him."

"Good for who?" Cord asked, wandering into the garage from outside.

Piper and Renee exchanged a quick glance, Piper silently imploring Renee not to say a single word.

Renee shook her head. "Girl talk," she said. "How do you like the armoire?"

Looking from one to the other, Cord dragged his attention from Piper back to the big piece of furniture. "It's nice. How'd you get that thing here, anyway? It's way too big to fit in your car."

Renee grinned. "I sweet-talked one of the guys that works there into delivering it after work."

Running a hand over the wood, Cord nodded. "It's solidly built. What color are you going to stain it?"

"No stain. We're using paint. Like we did with the dresser."

Now Cord glanced back at Piper, who managed a smile. "Yep. Paint."

"I see." Cord's tone indicated clearly that he didn't understand. "I honestly think you'd do better with stain. It'd bring out the texture of the wood."

"Painting this type of furniture is what I do. Did you even get a chance to look at the dresser Renee and I painted? The turquoise one in her bedroom?"

Cord nodded. "I did. And it looks great, though it's an odd color choice."

As compliments went, that stunk, but Piper knew not everyone appreciated the eclectic look of her stuff.

"Just wait until you see the color I chose for this one! Look." Renee opened the paint can. "Primrose purple."

Thankful for the time to finish composing herself, Piper enjoyed watching Cord's reaction. "Wow." He eyed the can. "That's certainly…bright."

Renee laughed out loud. "That it is. My bedroom could use some cheering up."

Cord nodded, but not before Piper saw the regret flash across his face.

"No worries." Renee jumped up and gave him a quick hug. "I'm just now figuring out my own style. This is fun."

"And relaxing," Piper put in.

"Do you have a minute to talk?" Cord asked Piper. "Alone? Maybe we could go for a walk or something, if your ankle is up for it."

Heaven help her, her heart leaped at the idea.

"I was just about to start painting with Renee," she began.

Renee glanced from Piper to Cord and back again. "You know what," she said slowly. "I think I'd like to go solo on this one. If you don't mind, that is."

"Of course I don't mind."

At her answer, Renee beamed, clearly thinking there was some romancing about to go on between the two of them.

Still Piper hesitated. When she told someone she'd help them, she never backed out without a good reason.

"Seriously." Renee gave her a little push. "Go walk. Talk. Enjoy each other's company. Take the crutches if you need them."

Cord didn't know why his niece apparently felt compelled to match-make, but judging from the way Piper valiantly attempted not to laugh, she wasn't taking it seriously. Which meant neither should he.

Even in torn, faded blue jeans and a T-shirt, Piper managed to look gorgeous. And sexy as hell. He considered reaching for her hand, but after all that nonsense with Renee, he didn't want to take a chance on his niece seeing. He didn't want to give her false hope for something that didn't stand a chance of happening.

"Do you want your crutches?" he asked.

She shook her head. "No. It's much better. I hardly even notice it unless I move too fast." As they walked, Truman trotted along at Piper's side.

"My dog now thinks he's yours," Cord commented.

"I love him," Piper said, grinning. Then she glanced from Truman to Cord and back again. "He seems to love me, doesn't he? Does that bother you? I promise, I'm not trying to steal your dog. I can try to discourage him if you want."

Incredulous, Cord shook his head. "Why would I want that? You seem to make him happy, and vice versa. I'm all for happiness. Don't worry about it. I've been enjoying watching the two of you have your mutual lovefest."

Relief shone in her face. "Okay. Thanks."

They'd barely walked past the first pasture when Piper stopped and turned to face him. "I know you had to wonder about all that back in the garage. It's just that Renee wants to experience a family so badly. That's why she's trying to push the two of us together."

His gut clenched. "Do you really think so? Even though she's eighteen?"

"I do." Green eyes serious, she met his gaze. "She might be older, but she's still young enough to want what she never had. She didn't have a normal life her entire childhood. Just now she's beginning to get a taste of what she missed and she wants more."

"I know." He tried to sound hopeful, even though he wasn't, at least not at that particular moment. He wished life actually could be that tidy and everyone could have a perfect, happy ending. "I'm going to do the best I can to make sure she's happy."

"Good. She deserves the best. She's a nice kid." Expression curious, she glanced at him. "What'd you need to talk to me about?"

"Your case. I've been avoiding my office lately, but I have to stop by and check on mail, pay some bills and generally straighten the place up. I also need to do more work on finding out what's going on with your charges."

"I'd like to go with you," Piper said.

Regretfully, he shook his head. "Too dangerous. It's in town and someone could see you. I won't be gone long."

"All right," she agreed, her disgruntled expression telling him she didn't like it. "Now that you have your niece back, I feel like I should be doing more to get answers on my own case. I can't do that if I'm hiding out at your place."

Damn, he wanted to kiss that frown away from her beautiful face. Somehow, he restrained himself and simply smiled instead. "Piper, I promised you I'll get to the bottom of this. While I'm at the office, I'll check in with a few more of my contacts. Also, I think we need to start talking to attorneys, don't you? Since they don't have a body, this should be easy to get dismissed."

"Do you think? Alanna was supposed to be hiring one, though I haven't heard anything."

"Yes, I do. In fact, I honestly believe whoever planted that bloody shirt is trying to stir things up and mess with you. They have to know that won't be enough to convict you."

She tilted her head, her expression serious. "Maybe, but what about the supposed eyewitness? Why won't anyone tell me who it is?"

"That's why you need a lawyer. They could be making that up hoping to scare you into a confession."

"Let me talk to Reid again," she finally said. "Knowing him, he, along with T.C. and Alanna, might have already hired one. If not, I'm sure they have someone in mind."

"You do that." He nodded. "We'll discuss our findings later, after I get home."

She nodded, holding his gaze, her color high. "Thank you, Cord."

Surprised, he eyed her. "For what?"

"For believing in me, when even some of my own relatives did not."

Then, before he could formulate a response, she turned and went back to the house, walking slowly but not hobbling, Truman at her side.

Instead of following her, Cord simply got into his truck and headed to town. He couldn't get Piper out of his head, though he wasn't sure how to deal with her ability to have such a strong effect on him. This could get plenty messy, with potential for all three of them to get hurt. He'd have to do his best to ensure that didn't happen. But how?

Chapter 11

When Cord reached his office and opened the door, he wasn't surprised to find a bunch of mail the postman had dropped in the door slot. Most of it appeared to be junk, though he spied what looked like a couple of bills. He gathered it all up, sorted through it and tossed the advertisements. Placing the bills on his desk, he checked his messages. There were three, two of them solicitors. The third was a hang up call. He could picture Sam chiding him about letting the business slide. Well, now that Renee was home, he could get to work again. He had connections. Several had let him know that there would be jobs waiting for him when he wanted them. Starting Monday, he'd begin placing phone calls and putting out feelers.

Right now, he needed to get to the bottom of this nonsense with Piper.

The door opened without a knock, and Fowler stepped inside, almost as if Cord's thoughts had summoned him.

"Any word?" he asked, by way of greeting.

"Afternoon, Fowler." Cord tried to keep the exasperation out of his voice. "Why don't you have a seat and we'll talk."

Fowler sat. "Do you have any bourbon?"

Careful not to show his surprise, Cord nodded. "I do." He reached behind him, opened his credenza and pulled out a bottle and one glass.

"Get two," Fowler ordered. "We're celebrating."

Celebrating? Had Fowler somehow learned the truth about Piper's whereabouts? His gut clenched, though he kept his face expressionless as he got out a second glass.

"All right," he said, pouring them each a drink. "I don't have ice, so this will have to do." He slid the glass across the desk to Fowler, who took it. "What are we drinking a toast to?" Cord asked, his tone casual.

"I'm engaged." Fowler beamed, an expression Cord had never seen before on the other man's patrician features. "I finally asked Tiffany to marry me. She said yes."

Since Fowler and Tiffany had been dating for years, Cord wasn't surprised. He did wonder why the other man chose to share this with him, since they barely knew each other.

"Congratulations," Cord said, clinking his glass to Fowler's, taking a small sip and waiting.

"Yes. This is supposed to be the happiest time in my life. But with not knowing if Piper is safe, it's not." He leaned forward in his chair, his gaze intense. "You've got to find her and bring her home. It's bad enough with Eldridge missing and possibly dead."

Cord noted Fowler didn't call Eldridge Dad or Father. In fact, neither did Piper, now that he thought about it.

"But with Piper gone, Whitney is hysterical," Fowler continued. "When Tiffany and I gave her the news of our engagement, all she could say was that I needed to bring my sister home." He sniffed.

"I'm working on it," Cord began.

"Are you?" Voice angry, Fowler drank deeply. "I've paid you a boatload of money and so far, gotten nothing back for my investment. Instead, you've been dodging my phone calls and refusing to give me anything."

Damn. Cord took another sip to stall things. He had to be careful because he didn't want to start outright lying. His father had turned telling falsehoods into an art form. Cord refused to be like him. While he'd never claimed to be a saint, he'd learned early on that there were ways around having to outright lie. Though this situation with Piper had him coming pretty damn close.

"Here's what I have done," Cord said, outlining both his visit to the sheriff and to the courthouse. "All they have on Piper is circumstantial. I imagine if your family were to hire a good attorney, they could make the charges go away."

"That's not what I'm paying you to do," Fowler declared, his narrow gaze radiating anger. "You're to bring Piper home, nothing more."

"You do know I can't legally make her do anything, right?"

Fowler narrowed his eyes. "You know as well as I do that there are ways to get such things done."

Was he suggesting Cord kidnap here? "I plan to stay inside the law," he began.

"I don't care what you have to do. Just get her back home."

"Yeah, well maybe if the charges were dropped, she'd show up on her own," Cord snapped back. "Ever think of that?"

Now would be the time for Fowler to agree, to state his belief in Piper's innocence.

Instead, Fowler shook his head. "The police have no idea who killed Eldridge."

"Of if he's even dead."

"True." Finishing his drink Fowler placed the empty glass down on the desk with a thunk. "All this uncertainty is hampering my ability to run the company."

Cord decided he'd had enough. "Let me ask you something, Fowler. Do you believe Piper killed Eldridge?"

Instead of being offended by the question, Fowler considered carefully. "Honestly, I don't know what to think. That bloody shirt was ancient, something Eldridge hadn't worn in years. And I can't really picture Piper whaling on the old man, never mind killing him. But what I believe doesn't matter. The police claim they have an eyewitness—"

"Who?" Cord interrupted. "No one will give me a name. I'm considering the possibility that it's all a lie, a trumped up way to attempt to make their bogus charge stick. What I don't understand is why."

Now Fowler stared, making Cord realize he'd probably said way too much.

Instead, Fowler simply nodded. "You're absolutely right. And we can figure that out—once we bring Piper back home. The entire family should be celebrating my engagement, not worrying about her. I'm afraid I'm going to have to set a deadline, Cord."

Not trusting himself to speak, Cord nodded.

"Two weeks," Fowler said. "After that, I'm not paying you another dime."

Two weeks? "Have you received notice of the court date, then?" Cord asked.

"I don't know." Fowler glowered at him. "What's that got to do with this?"

"You hired me to find a bail jumper. Technically, she hasn't jumped bail until she misses her court date."

"So?" Fowler pushed to his feet. "I'm disappointed in you, Cord. You came highly recommended, but I'm beginning to suspect I've been wasting my time and money."

"My deadline isn't up yet," Cord argued. "She'll be back to your ranch before her court date, you have my word on it."

"Good." Fowler shook his head. "But sooner would be better. I hope to hell your word is good. I'm sick and tired of playing games. I've got an engagement to celebrate."

With that, he left, closing the door softly behind him.

When her disposable cell phone rang about an hour after Cord left, Piper's heart did a funny little leap before she remembered she'd given Reid this number.

"What's up, brother dearest? Great minds think alike! I was just about to call you."

He snorted. "Right."

"No, really," she insisted. "Not just because I miss you, though."

"Right back at you, darling sister. What did you need to know?"

"You go ahead and tell me first," she said. "I was just going to call to check on things and ask you something, but I have a feeling I'm going to want to hear what you have to say."

"You're right. I think you are. You are not going to believe what Fowler did now."

Her heart sank. "Every time I hear his name, I feel sick. What'd he do?"

"Calm down, it's nothing to do with you. He finally proposed to Tiffany."

"What?" Piper couldn't have been more stunned if Reid had said Fowler quit Colton Incorporated. "But…"

"I know, right? They've been dating so long. No one thought they'd make it official, despite Tiffany wanting it so badly."

"Wow." Piper swallowed. "I don't know what to say."

"Then don't, because there's more. Some in the family, including me, wonder if Tiffany got rid of Eldridge to make Fowler an emotional wreck so he'd propose. Plus, she'd know he would end up as chairman of the company. She might have even been the one who set you up, Pipe."

"Tiffany?" Piper's head spun. "But she and I get along just fine, I think. At least, anytime we've had a family get-together, she was always pleasant and friendly."

"And ingratiating," Reid pointed out. "She never made any secret that she had her eye fixed firmly on the prize."

Now Piper snorted. "Fowler's no prize."

"He is to someone like her. Just think about it. Tiffany setting you up would be par for the course."

Piper wasn't so sure. "But she had an alibi for the night Eldridge disappeared," she pointed out. "I remember, because she made such a big deal out of her girls' trip to New Orleans. And the police verified it."

"True, but she still could have hired someone. A disgruntled maid or something."

"Possibly," Piper admitted, though she let her doubt show in her voice.

"Yeah. It's something, at least."

"Thanks, Reid. Keep me posted if anything else happens."

"I will," he promised. "Now, what did you want to ask me?"

She cleared her throat. "Do you think I need to hire an attorney?"

"You already have one," he said promptly. "Of course your loving siblings chipped in to hire a good one. Top-notch law firm, one of the better criminal defense attorneys in Dallas. He'll want a meeting with you soon, but right now his people are gathering evidence. He seems to think he won't have any problem getting the charges—and the warrant—dropped. That's why he doesn't want you to turn yourself in, at least not yet."

"Seriously?" Once, Piper would have shouted for joy. Now her happiness at the thought was tempered by a healthy dose of cynicism. The very chain of events recently had proved to her the time had come to put aside, even if only temporarily, her rose-colored glasses.

"Yes, seriously."

"That would be awesome. You'll call me if anything changes, right?"

"Of course." Reid paused. "Hey, Pipe? You might want to consider calling Whitney. She was so worried about you that I passed on to her that we've talked and you're all right. While she's glad about that, she's upset you haven't called her."

"I see." Piper's voice came out small. She could envision that conversation. Whitney would alternate between hysterics and recriminations, lobbing accusations left and right. Whitney had become a master at making her children, both adopted, step or birth, feel guilty.

"I can't do that just yet," Piper told Reid. "I'm not ready. I hate that my absence is hurting her, but I promise I'll make it up to her when I get back home."

Since she'd given him an opening, of course Reid pounced. "Any idea when that will be?"

"No. Just not yet. Unless you've received word on my court date."

"Not that I know of." Reid went silent for a moment.

When he spoke again, she could actually hear the frown in his voice. "Soon?"

"Hopefully. I really want to come home, Reid." She spoke earnestly. "But I can't. Not until I find out who's trying to set me up and why. Whoever it is clearly has connections to the police department, since they refuse to name the supposed eyewitness who saw me beating Eldridge."

"It is odd," Reid agreed. "That and the fact that Eldridge outweighs you by forty pounds. He might be old, but he's still strong. There's no way he'd let you beat him, even if you wanted to."

"Which I didn't. But I've been trying out the scenario in my mind, trying to see all angles. Someone smaller, if they came up from behind, they'd have the element of surprise. That'd be the only way they could take Eldridge down."

"Who do you think of as 'they'?" he asked. "When you're picturing that scenario, whose face do you see?"

Though she hated to admit it, she figured Reid already knew. "Marceline," she answered. "I see Marceline's face, Reid."

After Fowler left, Cord carried the glasses over to the sink, rinsed them out and placed them on the sideboard. The flash of anger he'd felt at the other man's deadline had dissipated, and worry had taken its place. On the one hand, he couldn't actually blame Fowler. As far as the other man could tell, Cord had accomplished exactly nothing. He'd taken Fowler's money, asked a few questions, but hadn't given Fowler a single hint about where Piper might be.

Piper. He didn't for a second believe the charges would stick. They had circumstantial evidence at best, and if they really did have some mysterious eyewitness, that person had to be someone with a grudge against Piper.

Finally, he didn't want Piper to go. The speed at which he'd gotten used to having her in his life astounded him.

All of this had him twisted up in knots. He preferred to keep things simple, uncomplicated. The job Fowler had hired him to do had been straightforward, yet he hadn't been able to bring himself to complete it. Which meant Cord was living one big, fat lie. Talk about bitter irony. Even the fact that he legally couldn't make Piper do anything unless she skipped her court date didn't make him feel any better. He'd become the one thing he'd vowed never to become. A liar.

He needed to focus on something else. Like something he could actually control. For as long as he could remember, when times were chaotic or confusing, he'd made lists. Lists helped clear the clutter from his mind and enabled him to focus.

Fowler had hired him to do a job. Personal feelings aside, he needed to do what he'd been hired to do. Of course, he'd wait until as close to the deadline as possible, but he'd need to remind Piper about her promise to return for her court date.

Which led to...

Find out who set Piper up. The sheriff could stonewall him, but not her defense attorney. He'd call the brother Piper had been talking to and see if Reid could arrange hiring a lawyer to defend her. Except then he'd have to explain more than he was sure he was ready to.

He let his pen hover over the paper. And then, because he had to continue, he filled in the blank.

Explore the combustible attraction between Piper and me.

There. Out in the open, finally. This thing that sparked

between them deserved a chance. More than sexual attraction, he liked her, honestly liked her. Thought they'd be great friends. And more.

Much, much more.

Closing his eyes, he could see her, her image branded into every fiber of his being. He wanted her, she wanted him, but he knew if they ever gave in to their blazing need, everything would forever change between them.

Oddly enough for a man who'd taken pride in being a free spirit, he believed he was ready for something like that. A serious relationship, possibly even permanent. Even his dog had done everything he could to show Cord how much he'd like that idea.

But...could his timing be any worse? Of course, this gave him even more incentive to find out who framed Piper and why. Once that got settled, then they could explore their relationship without anything hanging over them.

Decision made, he folded the list and put it inside his desk drawer. He knew, though he didn't want to face it, that there was one final item he hadn't written down.

But he thought it. He couldn't help but think it. Would Piper want anything to do with him once her name had been cleared and she'd gone back to live in the family mansion?

Instead of driving directly home, he took another spin by the sheriff's office. This time, the only person there was Briggs, a longtime deputy who'd become disenchanted with what he called "the process" and kept up a constant countdown until he could retire. Sheriff Watkins only tolerated him because he was a damn good deputy, even though his old-school methods sometimes got him in trouble.

"Hey, Maxwell." Briggs lumbered over to shake Cord's hand. "What's up? I haven't seen you around here lately."

Cord grinned. He liked the big guy. "Fowler Colton hired me to find his sister Piper," he said.

Briggs's grin widened. "Plus you're nosing around trying to get information on her arrest. I heard."

"That, too. She's a tiny little thing. I can't picture her even attempting to take on Eldridge. Not to mention, he's the only father she's ever known."

"I know, I know." Briggs grimaced. "And since they don't even have a body, I'm surprised they were able to make the charge stick." He wiggled his bushy eyebrows and rubbed his fingers together in the universal gesture for money, letting Cord know what he thought without actually saying it.

Someone in the DA's office had been bought off. Of course. Cord had suspected that all along.

"Did Fowler hire you to find out what happened to his old man?" Briggs asked. "Because if you have any information, please share it with this office. Eldridge Colton is such a high-profile big shot, two-thirds of the department is working that case."

"Do you think he's alive?" Cord kept his tone conversational.

"My gut feeling is that he is. But no one knows for sure. Even with so many valuable resources, our office hasn't found squat. That bloody shirt and an eyewitness is all we've got."

Aha. *Now* they were getting somewhere. "Why the secrecy about the eyewitness?" Cord asked. "Every time I try to get information on that person, I'm stonewalled."

"Because the witness feels that their life is in danger." Briggs shook his head. "Note my careful avoidance of using male or female pronoun."

"Noted and applauded," Cord replied. "So this witness is going to remain secret until the trial."

"Yes, sir." Briggs clapped his meaty hand on Cord's shoulder. "Sorry. But we've got to protect the witness. I know you understand."

"I do. Sort of. At least all the secrecy finally makes sense." Cord said his goodbyes and drove slowly home. When he walked in the front door, his dog raised his head and wagged his tail rather than jumping up and greeting him. Cord shook his head but went over and petted him anyway.

"Do what?" Piper asked when he told her what he'd learned. "The witness says he or she feels threatened? In danger? From who?"

"I guess you." Saying it out loud made the story sound even more ridiculous.

"Or whoever is framing me," Piper suggested, her arms crossed. "Maybe they paid this person off to be an eyewitness and then when they wanted to tell the truth, threatened them."

"Except wouldn't the police already know the story was an outright lie?" he pointed out.

She groaned. "All these convoluted machinations are giving me a headache. Oh, I almost forgot. My brother Reid called today and told me Fowler is now engaged."

"I know. He came by the office and relayed the news himself." He told her about Fowler's frustration with his lack of results and the deadline he'd been given. He almost told her how he felt about lying, but at the last minute kept that to himself.

"I'm not going back early," she said once he'd finished, just as he'd suspected she might. "Not until you prove I didn't kill Eldridge or my court date."

Which was exactly what he'd thought she would say.

"Then I guess I'd better get busy," he said.

"You'd miss me if I wasn't around, anyway," she teased. As she laughed up at him, something changed. The air between them, the light, the expression in her gorgeous emerald eyes. He felt the same stubborn tug of desire arcing between them.

He caught her arm. Her harsh intake of breath sounded like a hiss.

"You're right," he growled. "I would." And then he kissed her, helpless under the pull of attraction.

She met his kiss with one of her own. Openmouthed, the furthest thing from tentative. Confident and sexy and oh so damn desirable.

He lost himself in her. Her tongue, mating with his, her body, all curvy and soft, pressed up against his hardness.

That. The physical manifestation of his need, his craving.

As she pressed against him, the friction of her wordless want pushed him closer and closer to the brink. He tried to pull back, to put some distance between them, to let some air cool his overheated brain, but she was having none of that.

"Piper," he began, needing to ask.

Her gaze met his, emerald darkened to stormy sea. "Yes. And yes again."

They made it to his bedroom, mainly because it was closer than hers. Bodies wrapped around each other, they staggered toward his bed. He kicked the door closed behind him to shut Truman out, and then, as an afterthought, locked it. Just in case Renee returned home early.

When he turned, she caught him, pulling him down with her, her throaty laugh hitting him low and deep.

He yanked off his shirt, fingers fumbling with his belt

buckle, until she pushed his hands away and undid it for him. The feel of her small hands touching him was almost too much. Rigid, he clenched his jaw as she eased his jeans down over his turgid arousal. When she would have stroked him, he caught her wrists to stop her. "Not yet. I want to see you naked first."

The sensual, slow smile she gave him had the same effect as a caress. Suddenly, he couldn't bear to watch her remove her clothes, so he did it for her. Instinct and experience guided his fingers, as he stroked her soft skin while undressing her.

Finally, she stood naked in front of him, her lush body everything he could want in a woman…and more. When he slipped his finger between the folds of her womanhood, the slick nectar, proof of her readiness, beckoned him to taste her.

Together, they fell back onto the bed, and he used his tongue to gather the first of her honeyed liquid. Hair wild, she pushed herself to a half-sitting position, and watched him, her eyes glazed with desire. And then, when he let his tongue grow bolder, she lost her tenuous grip on self-control. Her back arched as spasms shook her, her body pulsing at him, begging him for more than just his tongue.

He nearly lost it right then. Might have, would have, if not for the overwhelming need to push himself inside her.

More than ready, she welcomed him. Harder than he'd ever been, he gasped out loud as he filled her. She sheathed him, the perfect combination of warmth and wet.

Any and all attempts to maintain self-control disappeared as he began to move. She rose to meet each thrust, her boldness and self-awareness so sexy he could barely refrain from climaxing. Only the certainty of how much he wanted to prolong this lovemaking kept him going.

He could have tried several tricks. Reach up and grab her waist to hold her still. Close his eyes and think of something else. But he wanted to watch her face as he pushed her back to the zenith, to see her eyes darken as she shattered around him.

"Don't stop," she gasped, her body shuddering as he pounded into her. She made a sound, a cross between a scream and a moan, and arched her back, squeezing him as she quivered and shuddered and pushed him into his own release.

They rocked together, bodies slick with sweat, her skin gleaming. He held her, realizing he never wanted to let her go. Which meant he was in big trouble indeed.

"Wow," she murmured, snuggling up against him. "Wow and wow."

He kissed the top of her head, his chest aching. "I second that."

After a quick glance at him through her long lashes, she went silent for so long he wondered if she'd fallen asleep.

Which was okay. He'd gladly spend another hour or two simply holding her while she slept.

He'd wanted to explore their mutual attraction. Now that he had, he knew this was something special, something once in a lifetime. Which could be dangerous. Or could be pure heaven.

"Well," she murmured, shifting so she could look up at him. "This changes things, doesn't it?"

Instead of questioning her statement—how could he, when she was right—he simply nodded.

Her grin startled him. "Now that we've got this first time over with, can we be official friends with benefits?"

Unbelievably, he felt a stab of hurt. But then again, what had he been expecting? Her to want to move in with him permanently? Again, she was right. If anything, they needed to keep it casual and see where it might lead. After all, it wasn't as if there were no obstacles between them.

"Yeah." Unable to help himself, he kissed her again, on the cheek this time. He knew if she turned her head, his lips would graze her mouth, and he'd lose himself in her again. In fact, he hoped she would.

Instead, she sighed. "I guess we need to get up. I want a shower. I'm sure you need to clean up, too. After all, you've got a lot to do."

Pushing up, her saucy grin made his blood heat. "What do I have to do," he asked slowly, a hundred carnal images filling his head.

"Find out who's framing me. I don't want that hanging over my head anymore," she declared, stepping into the bathroom and closing the door behind her.

He could only stare after her, pondering how her words echoed his own thoughts from earlier. She was right, he knew. They both wanted more. And this—whatever it was—relationship, or start of one—could only flourish without clouds darkening the horizon.

Chapter 12

It wasn't until she'd closed the door that Piper realized she'd gone into Cord's bathroom. If she wanted hers, she'd have to open the door, stride back through the bedroom and spoil her dramatic exit.

A quick glance at herself in the mirror revealed a woman who'd been thoroughly made love to. Shaking her head at her own conflicting emotions, she took a deep breath and opened the door. Head held high, she marched over to the bed and scooped her discarded clothing up off the floor. She pulled on her T-shirt and stepped into her panties before she looked at Cord. He still lay on his side, his magnificent body tempting even now, when she felt sore and sated beyond all belief.

Inside she trembled with longing. Outside, she knew she had to play it cool.

"Bye," she said sweetly, then hightailed it out of his room and down the hall, praying Renee hadn't come back home. Truman jumped up from his spot outside Cord's door and followed her. He leaped onto her bed while she continued on past.

Safely inside her own bathroom, she gripped the edge

of the counter. Her own sense of self-preservation and pride had forced her to be flippant with Cord, while inside she was a quivering mess.

She'd never had sex like that. More than just her body had been involved—Cord had managed to touch her heart and soul, too.

Foolishness, she chided herself. Turning the shower on hot, she stripped off her garments and stepped inside, hoping the water would wash away all the unwanted emotions that churned way too close to the surface.

Wow. Stunned, Cord watched her go. He wondered how it could be possible that Piper appeared to be unaware that she'd just rocked his world.

His cell chimed, indicating he'd missed a call. He grinned, aware he hadn't even heard it ring. Glancing at the screen, he recognized the number. Ms. Berens. Immediately concerned, he called her back.

"I hope I didn't bother you." The quiver in her voice was new. "But I've fallen and I can't pull myself back up. I've called all of my neighbors and no one seems to be home. Can you come out here? I promise to reward you with a slice of my fresh baked coconut cake."

"Are you hurt?"

"No, no. Just embarrassed. That's why I didn't want to call 9-1-1. Please, will you help me? Save a little old lady's pride?"

"Of course. I'm on my way." Hanging up the phone, he pulled on his clothes and started down the hallway to let Piper know. Before he turned the corner, he heard the shower start up.

Reversing direction, he snatched up his keys from the tray and headed out.

Breaking every speed limit, he considered himself

lucky he didn't blow past any police cars. Rocketing down the gravel road, he parked and jumped out, heading for the house at a dead run. All he could think of was the time he'd found his father on the floor, unconscious after hitting his head. Of course, dear old Dad had been drunk at the time.

"Ms. Berens?" he called, pushing open the back door which she always kept unlocked, despite his many warnings.

"In here." If anything, she sounded weaker. He'd probably need to take her up to the hospital to be checked out.

She lay on the carpet in the den, her back up against the sofa. Her sweet smile looked the same.

"Did you hit your head?" he asked. "Any broken bones?"

"Not at all. My legs just went out from under me and I went down like a sack of potatoes. Landed right on my behind, where I have more than enough cushion to break my fall."

He nodded, stepping closer. "All right. I'm going to pick you up and put you on the couch. After that, we'll try standing. With my help. Do you have a walker?" A quick glance around the room revealed nothing.

"Oh no, I don't need one," she responded instantly. "I have a cane, and that's always been more than enough."

Until now, he thought, but didn't say anything. He'd see how stable she was on her feet before making any decisions.

Putting his hands under her armpits, surprised at how frail she felt, he easily lifted her onto the couch.

"Thank you, dear." Licking her lips, she frowned. "I'm really thirsty. Would you mind getting me a glass of water?"

After he'd done so, she gulped the entire thing down and then asked him for another. The second glass, she drank much more slowly.

"How long were you on the floor?" he asked, his concern growing.

She shrugged. "A few hours. No big deal. However, I really need to visit the ladies' room."

"Do you want to see if you can stand on your own?"

"I'll need my cane." She pointed. "Can you bring it to me?"

He located the large, four-footed cane and handed it to her. Still smiling, she gripped it and struggled to her feet. "See?" She beamed. "I'm right as rain. I'll be right back and then we'll have some cake."

While he waited, he got out his wallet and counted out the money he'd brought for her. Five hundred dollars. Not enough to make up for last time, but all he could spare right now.

When Ms. Berens returned, she was leaning heavily on her cane.

"You'd better sit down," he said, taking her arm and guiding her to a chair.

"But the cake…" she protested.

"I'll slice the cake. And I'll bring you some more water." In the kitchen, he saw the white cake, a masterpiece of coconut, on her covered cake dish. Since he'd been there so many times, he knew exactly where she kept her plates and cutlery.

He fixed them both a nice-sized slice, refilled her water glass and left them on the counter while he located her TV tray. Once he'd placed that in front of her, he brought her the cake and drink, returned to grab his and sat down on the couch by her.

"Before I forget, I brought you this," he said, handing her the money. "I'm sorry about last time."

"No need." Staring at the bills, she seemed confused. "Will you put these in the kitchen? I have an extra cookie jar where I keep my spending money. That's where I put money until I can get it into the bank."

Of course he knew this, since he'd seen her place his payments there before. He took care of that, returned and began eating his cake, watching her to see if she really was okay.

She took a few bites, then set her plate down. "I'm not hungry."

Eyeing her, he realized she looked awfully pale. "Are you sure you're all right?" he asked. Before he'd even finished speaking, she slumped back, clearly unconscious.

Right away, he dialed 9-1-1, cursing himself for not doing so the minute he'd gotten there. Tersely, he explained the situation. The operator asked him to check for a pulse and he did so, relieved to find a weak one.

After learning an ambulance was on the way, he hung up. Now all he could do was pray Ms. Berens could hang on until they got there.

It was full dark when he got home. He'd been gone four hours. The hospital in Terrell had admitted Ms. Berens and placed her in ICU. The diagnosis was renal failure. They'd asked about next of kin and he'd had to tell them there was no one.

He'd also done a lot of thinking and soul-searching. What he and Piper had done was not only wrong, but violated the unspoken code he lived by as a fugitive recovery specialist. Not only that, but he could only imagine how furious the Coltons would be if they learned he'd taken advantage of Piper when she was her most vulnerable. Fowler might want his money back and Cord wouldn't exactly blame him. For all he knew, he thought glumly, the influential Colton family could blacklist him and he'd be ruined. Piper's brother Reid had lots of connections to the local sheriff's department and could easily make Cord's life hell.

Between worrying about that and about Ms. Berens's condition, he felt completely worn down. The only bright spot right now was how well he and Renee seemed to be getting along. Maybe he and his niece actually could become a family, after all.

Finding Cord gone after she got out of the shower felt a bit unsettling. But Piper figured he had a good reason for taking off and truth be told, she could use the time to think about what had just happened between them. Now was quite probably the worst possible time to start a relationship.

However, they'd only made love. No vows of undying devotion had been exchanged. The thought made her grin. Maybe she and Cord could continue to keep things casual, easy breezy, and see what happened. As long as they could keep having mind-blowing sex.

Her entire body tingled. While she'd definitely had a few lovers in her past, nothing she'd experienced with them had even come close to this.

Maybe it just seemed that way because of the heightened circumstances. Right now, her life was a mess of danger, intrigue and suspense. Combine those with enforced proximity to a handsome man and things were bound to combust.

She figured if she kept telling herself that, she wouldn't get hurt. In reality, the accusations leveled against her ensured she'd have to keep her life on hold. How could she move forward with such a thing hanging over her?

After the second hour had dragged past, she began to worry. Since his pickup wasn't there, she knew he'd left the premises. Not wanting to be too intrusive, she started three times to text him, but didn't, at least not then.

However, being indecisive wasn't in her makeup, and after three hours had passed, she finally sent a simple text asking if he was okay. He didn't respond.

Not that she was watching the clock—oh, who was she kidding, she totally stared at the clock—but as the time inched up on four hours, she found herself wishing she had found something of her own to occupy her time. Waiting and worrying for Cord to come back felt a bit obsessive.

Still...

Pacing—this was so not like him, but what if something awful had happened—she finally realized what had occurred between them earlier must have so freaked him out that he'd had to put distance and time between them.

Much calmer once she understood that, she began rummaging in the kitchen to see what she could put together for dinner. If he didn't show up to eat, at least she'd have herself a nice meal.

When he finally walked through the door, she had a fragrant chicken and bean soup simmering on the stove. One look at him and her heart sank. He looked like he'd been through hell and back.

Everything she'd told herself flew out the window. She moved across the room and pulled him close in a tight hug. "What happened?"

Holding himself stiffly, he pulled away. "Ms. Berens called. She fell. I went over there and helped her get up, but she became unconscious. I had to call 9-1-1."

Stunned, she swallowed hard. "Is she okay?"

"No. She's in ICU with acute renal failure. The doctors don't think she's going to make it. They asked me to contact her next of kin, but she doesn't have any. I stopped by the neighborhood and let all of her neighbors know." His voice broke and he covered his eyes and turned away.

Though she wasn't sure if he wanted comfort, she knew she had to give it. She went to him and wrapped her arms around him from behind.

"Don't," he said, the single word cutting through her like a knife.

"I'm sorry." She stepped away. "I know how much you care about Ms. Berens. Why don't you sit down and eat? I made some nice chicken soup."

"I didn't mean you shouldn't hug me because of what happened to Ms. Berens. That's under control. She's in good hands now. I'm talking about what happened between us." Expression hard, he eyed her. "Piper, there's something I need to make clear. What happened earlier shouldn't have. I took advantage of you when you were vulnerable."

"Took advantage?" Aware her mouth hung open, she closed it. "Do you really think I wasn't a full participant? Or maybe——" she narrowed her eyes "——maybe you think you somehow coerced me, that I'm so feeble-minded I couldn't make a choice whether or not to make love with you?"

"Stop," he snapped. "Regardless of your motivation or mine, I can promise you that won't happen again."

"Fine," she snapped right back. "I didn't want it to anyway." Tossing her head—short hair didn't have quite the effect long hair did—she stormed into the kitchen and ladled up a bowl of soup. "I don't know about you, but I'm going to eat. Join me or don't, that's up to you."

After staring at her for a few seconds, he shook his head. "I need to say I'm sorry," he began.

"Don't you dare apologize for the best damn sex I've ever had." Oops. Her eyes widened. She hadn't meant to give so much information away. Her face heated, but she held her ground.

Cord burst out laughing. "This argument is—"

"Completely unnecessary."

He nodded. "Right. And was it really the best—"

"Yes, it was. Bar none."

"I see." He flashed her a grin so sexy it made her knees go weak. "Are you ever going to let me finish a sentence?"

"Sorry." Filling a second bowl, she carried it over to the table. "Here. Food. Even you have to eat."

To her relief, he sat and dug in.

They were in companionable silence for a few minutes with Truman snoring from his dog bed. After Cord had emptied his bowl, he went back for seconds. "Thanks for making this," he began. "But we really do need to talk."

Her cell phone rang.

"Who else has that number?" Cord asked.

"It's Reid," Piper replied, feeling nervous for no good reason.

"Put it on speaker," Cord told her. "I want to hear if he's learned anything new."

Answering, before touching the speaker phone button, she asked Reid if it was okay.

"Sure," Reid said. "Though I have to ask why. Is there someone with you?"

"Yes." Meeting Cord's gaze, she squashed the impulse to childishly stick out her tongue. He wasn't the only one who knew how to be honest.

"Who?" Reid wanted to know.

"I'd rather not tell you. But this person is a friend and I promise you, is on my side."

"Some of what I want to tell you is family stuff." Reid sounded uncomfortable. "I'm not sure a stranger should hear this."

Piper glanced at Cord, who shrugged. "It's okay," she said. "I'm positive everything will be kept private."

"If you're sure." Reid took a deep breath. "It's about Marceline."

Even the name brought Piper a quick twist of uneasiness. "What'd she do now?"

"I found her out by the barn, sobbing like her heart had been broken. She refused to talk to me at first, but finally she said she's in love, and the man broke up with her because she won't go public with their relationship."

"Wow. Poor Marceline." Piper couldn't believe she actually felt sorry for the other woman. "Do you have any idea who her boyfriend is?"

"Dylan Harlow."

"The ranch hand?" Now Piper was shocked. "No wonder he refuses to continue dating her. She's always acted like all the hired hands were beneath her."

"Exactly. I only knew because I trailed her one time and saw them kissing. Anyhow, I pretended not to have any idea who she meant."

"What did you say?" Piper couldn't even begin to imagine having that sort of conversation with Marceline.

"I told her a story from my past." Reid sounded rueful. "Back when I was a golden boy at college, a fancy Colton. I fell for a beautiful girl who was working two jobs to put herself through school. One of those jobs was as a janitor. I blew it by being a snob."

"Wow. Is that true?"

Reid sighed. "Sadly, yes."

"How'd Marceline react? Do you think she got it?"

"Actually, she seemed to. She said she wants her love back."

Again Piper exchanged a glance with Cord. "That's great. But I don't understand why you felt that story, touching as it is, was important enough to call me."

At her words, Reid laughed. "Because there's more. Marceline and I rarely talk, but for whatever reason, once she heard my lost love tale, she got chatty. She mentioned you."

Piper braced herself. "Oh, yeah? What'd she say?"

"She felt she might have been too hard on you. She blamed herself—well, Fowler, too—for your disappearance. When we discussed that bloody shirt and who might want to frame you, Marceline said she had a good idea who."

Inhaling sharply, Piper swallowed. "Well? Who? Don't prolong the suspense, Reid. Not about something as important as this."

"Sorry," Reid responded, sounding anything but. "Anyway, Marceline said she has this maid named Sarah she sometimes uses to do her dirty work. Apparently this woman has known you for years, Pipe. Seems she's bitter."

"Sarah Sleighter," Piper said slowly. "She used to be really jealous of me. But why would Marceline give her up?"

"You know, I asked that same question. Marceline said she wanted to be helpful to her family. Sort of to prove she really is a big ole softy."

Piper snorted at that. "She's still a snot."

"I'd use a much stronger word," Reid said, laughing. "Anyway, I wanted to pass that on to you. I went to try and talk to Sarah, but it seems she's disappeared. No one's seen hide nor hair of her for weeks."

"Because the police probably have her in protective custody," Cord drawled, speaking up finally. "They told me—if she's their witness—that she fears her life is in danger."

Reid went silent. Piper knew why. He was trying to figure out if he could recognize Cord's voice.

"I didn't realize you were with a man," Reid finally said, sounding as if he'd just swallowed a lemon.

Piper grimaced and Cord mouthed the word *"Sorry."*

Since she didn't know what to say, Piper didn't speak. Reid apparently got the hint. "Sorry," he said. "I know it's none of my business. But, Pipe, I'll always be your big brother, so I'm going to have to say this—Guy with my baby sister, whoever you are, don't hurt her. Because if you do, I can guarantee I'm going to come looking for you. You got that?"

Appalled, Piper looked at Cord to see how he was taking Reid's threat. To her shock, a grim smile creased his face. "I got it," he said. "No worries there."

"As long as we're on the same page." Some of the tension had gone out of Reid's voice.

Piper and Cord exchanged a glance. "Good to know." Cord crossed his arms. Piper couldn't read his expression.

"What are you thinking?" Reid asked. "You understand you can't go to the police with this information, right? It's all in confidence."

"I made no promises," Cord said. "But I can reassure you I'm not going to the police."

"Don't be involving my sister in anything illegal, you hear?" Reid sounded pissed again. "She's got enough trouble as it is."

"I don't think I need you telling me—or Piper—what

I can and cannot do," Cord began, his expression hard. "I appreciate your concern, but your sister is an adult and—"

"Thanks for the information," Piper interjected. "We're going to let you go now. Keep in touch." And she ended the call before either man could escalate things.

"Please don't provoke my brother." Piper faced Cord and grimaced. "He's very protective of me."

"I got that." Cord's expression softened. "I'm sorry. What he said just hit me the wrong way."

She sighed.

"However, what he had to say underscored my point. I don't want to hurt you."

"Are you planning on hurting me?"

Her question appeared to surprise him. "Of course not."

"Then don't say we have to stop. Because that's what will really hurt me. I can't fathom the pain if you and I don't ever tangle up the sheets again."

He laughed. "You win. Now tell me about Sarah Sleighter. I remember her from when I lived on the ranch. Shy, quiet little thing. Her mother was a maid. Why does she hate you enough to do something like frame you for murder?"

"I didn't really get that she hated me," Piper said slowly. "She seemed bitter over what she called my good fortune when Whitney adopted me. She used to always make snide comments about that when we were kids."

"What about lately? Did she ever speak to you?"

"Not really. When her mother retired, Sarah took her place. She works as one of Marceline's personal maids. I didn't see much of her."

"Servants." Cord shook his head. "I can't even imagine what it's like to be that rich. I bet you miss it, don't you?"

"Not at all." Piper didn't even have to consider her answer. "Sure, it's nice to have someone cook and clean for you, but I never used the maids the way Marceline did."

"I wonder if she's really in protective custody, or if that's a lie," Cord said. "Such a thing seems extreme for something like this. It's not like you're a mobster or hardened criminal."

"Right?" Piper sighed. "It's entirely possible the other ranch staffers are keeping her hidden. If she convinced them she's really in danger, they'd close ranks around her. They're really loyal to each other."

"Interesting. If she's on the ranch, I want to talk to her." Cord stood and walked to the window, turning his back to her while he looked out into the darkness.

"How are you going to do that?"

He glanced over his shoulder at her. "I'm going out there in the morning, after I check on Ms. Berens. And you can go with me, if we can disguise you well enough so that no one recognizes you."

That night, even though Cord had much on his mind, exhaustion claimed his body and he slept soundly. To his relief, the phone didn't ring with bad news from the hospital, and he woke in the morning refreshed and re-energized.

And aroused, with Piper on his mind. Since this had become a regular occurrence these days, he hopped in the shower and got ready to face the day.

After dressing, he called the hospital to check on Ms. Berens. There had been no change, she was still unresponsive and in the ICU. He decided he'd pop in there personally and check on her later.

After breakfast, he ran to the discount superstore and purchased supplies for Piper's disguise. She disappeared to get ready, promising to be gone only a few minutes. When she reappeared, he could barely recognize her.

"Amazing," he drawled, eyeing the new Piper with a long, wavy wig of medium brown hair. With her thick, nonprescription glasses, she looked nothing like herself, yet Cord had to admit he still found her sexy. Of course, he had personal experience with those curves under her baggy tunic. The only part of her that remained unchanged were her bright green eyes.

"Let's go." They climbed in his truck and were off.

Though years had passed since he'd set foot on the Colton family ranch, Cord remembered the layout as if it had been yesterday. As a child, he'd explored every nook and cranny of the place; every barn and shed and pasture. He hadn't really been inside the mansion except for the kitchen. One of the Coltons' cooks had been fond of the various children running wild around the place and used to bake them cookies and allow them in the kitchen to eat. Mrs. P. He wondered if she still worked there.

"No, she retired a few years ago," Piper said in response to his question. "She was a nice lady and worked directly under the head cook, Bettina. All of us kids loved her. The cook that took her place isn't nearly as kind. Sometimes I think she and Marceline are long lost twins."

He laughed. A short silence fell. Next to him, Piper fidgeted in her seat.

"Are you nervous?" he found himself asking.

"A little." The tightness of her laugh gave her away. "I'm just worried about being recognized."

"Don't talk to anyone and you should be fine."

She nodded, her gaze once again faraway.

From memory, he followed the road to the drive. The huge black iron gates were open.

"They haven't been working right for weeks," Piper

said. "Whitney keeps saying she's going to have someone repair them, but it never happens."

"Good thing. If they'd been closed, you would have had to put in your code to open them. That might have drawn more interest than we want."

She nodded, sitting up straight as they drove slowly down the long driveway. "It's funny, but I feel like a tourist right now. Curious and slightly excited, but not like I'm at home."

"But this is still your home," he reminded her.

"Maybe." Her casual shrug didn't fool him. "I haven't felt comfortable here for quite some time, if you want to know the truth. I've never belonged. Especially after both Marceline and Fowler confronted me."

He doubted she was aware of the pain in her voice. Unable to help himself, he squeezed her shoulder.

Chapter 13

They rounded a curve and ahead, the ranch mansion came into view. Two stories, with columns, the structure resembled nothing so much as a Southern plantation from the old Deep South. Cord figured the Coltons had intentionally built it that way. As a small child, the house had seemed magical, like some sort of newer castle. He couldn't imagine what it must have been like growing up in such a place, especially since it had been made clear by Marceline that Piper didn't belong.

"Drive a little faster," Piper hissed. "You can park out in the lot near the covered arena." She held up those hideous thick glasses. "Once we're out of the car and walking around, I'll wear these, plus the Texas Rangers baseball cap."

Her jitters came through in both her voice and the way she bounced around in her seat. "With all that, no one will recognize you, I promise." He tried to reassure her. "Just remember not to talk to anyone."

"Except Sarah," she said darkly. "If we manage to locate her, I promise you, I'll have a lot to say."

"After," he cautioned. "Don't say anything until after we get her cornered so she has no choice but to talk to us."

"What are you planning to do?"

"I'm not sure. We'll play it by ear."

Piper exhaled sharply. "But no one gets hurt, right?"

"I'll do my best," he promised. "Now, are the staff quarters still inside the main house?"

"Not anymore. Eldridge built a huge dormitory-style building for them. We can walk to it from here."

"Good." He parked, wondering at his sudden, savage urge to protect her. "Stay close to me, okay?"

She regarded him curiously. "What are you worried might happen?"

Ignoring this, he took her arm. "Now remember our story."

"Yes. If we're stopped and questioned, we're there to visit our cousin who's a maid."

He nodded and they continued to walk, with him holding on to her arm like an old married couple. Across the large parking lot, she skirted the side of a huge indoor arena. "There." She pointed. "That's where most of the staff lives. At least, the ones who don't drive in from town."

As they approached the building, a short, slender man in stained coveralls came out. "Excuse me, sir?" Piper called out, earning an annoyed look from Cord. "Can you tell us where to find Sarah Sleighter? She's our cousin and we're hoping to surprise her."

"You're family?" He eyed them suspiciously. "I wasn't aware she had any people here in Texas."

"She doesn't," Piper replied. Even though she'd agreed not to talk, she felt she had to since she knew Cord wouldn't tell an outright lie. "We drove down from Oklahoma. She called us and said she was in trouble."

"That she is." He nodded, looking tired. "But truth be told, I wonder about her sometimes. She's fond of making up stories and several of us have come to believe her supposed danger is all in her mind."

"Is she here?" Cord asked, his voice casual.

The man shrugged. "I'm not sure she is, but she lives in room 223. I think her stuff is still there, but who knows. I haven't seen her in a good while. Second floor, turn right after you step out from the elevator."

Without waiting for their reply, he hurried off, leaving Piper and Cord to mull over his words.

"Room 223," Cord repeated. "I wonder if she's there. Even though Deputy Briggs said the witness was being protected, he never said where."

"Let's go find out." Leading the way, Piper strode up to the front door.

They located the room without difficulty. Of course, the door had been closed. Cord knocked. "Sarah? It's your cousin Sam, come up all the way from Tulsa."

The door opened, just a crack. "I don't have any cousins in Oklahoma," she said, her voice dripping scorn.

Cord shoved the door open, ignoring her strangled cry. "Sarah Sleighter? Cord Maxwell. I'm a private investigator. I'd like to have a word with you."

But Sarah's gaze had slipped right past him to find Piper. "Your eyes..." Sarah said. "I'd recognize that particular shade of green anywhere. You're Piper Colton." She shoved Cord. Hard. Not expecting the move, he stumbled slightly, but righted himself quickly.

Not fast enough. Pushing past Piper, Sarah took off down the hall, running.

Piper went after her, Cord close on Piper's heels.

They caught her before she reached the staircase, having bypassed the elevator. Cord twisted her around and handcuffed her.

"You can't do that," she protested. "If you're the police, you have to read me my rights and tell me what I'm being arrested for."

"Well, then, it's a good thing I'm not the police," Cord responded. "I'm a bounty hunter."

"He's helping me," Piper put in.

Panting, chest heaving, Sarah eyed Piper, her narrow gaze full of bitterness. "I can't believe you had the nerve to come back around here after what you've done."

"What I've done?" Piper got real close. Too close. "How about you? Putting that old bloody shirt in my closet and setting me up for something I didn't do."

Sarah curled her lip and spat.

"That's enough." Cord spun her around and nudged her forward. "I'm taking you to the police station. We're going to get this shirt thing straightened out once and for all. We know you planted it to frame Piper."

On the way to the car, with Sarah cuffed, Cord half expected her to scream for help. To his surprise, she didn't, just walked silently and sullenly, getting in the backseat of his truck without protest.

Cord signaled Piper to wait. Closing the doors so Sarah couldn't hear them, he touched her shoulder where Sarah had shoved her. "You okay?"

"I think so."

"Good. I want you to call Reid and have him meet us at the sheriff's office. Tell him to have your lawyer there as well, if possible. On the way there, I'm going to drop you off on Third and Main. You can wander down to that little coffee shop and have something to drink. I'll pick you up when we've finished."

She nodded.

Sarah endured the ride in silence, contenting herself with shooting hateful looks at the back of Piper's head. When Cord pulled over and dropped Piper off, Sarah protested. "She needs to go, too. She's the whole reason nothing's been right."

Deciding to let that statement go, Cord made a non-committal sound and drove on. When he reached the sheriff's department, a tall man waited in the parking lot, leaning against his truck. That had to be Reid.

Pulling up next to him and parking, Cord jumped out and greeted him. "Reid Colton?"

"I am." Reid eyed him dispassionately. "And you are?"

"Cord Maxwell." He held out his hand.

They shook. Cord appreciated Piper's brother's no-nonsense grip.

"You're that bounty hunter, aren't you?" Reid asked, following him around to the backseat passenger side.

"I prefer fugitive recovery specialist, but yes. I run Sam Ater's place. S.A. Enterprises. I own it now. I'm also a PI."

"Ah, now I understand." Reid's expression cleared. "Piper hired you, didn't she?"

"In a manner of speaking, yes." Opening the back door, Cord helped Sarah from the car. "Meet Sarah. She planted the bloody shirt and gave false testimony against Piper."

"You have no proof of that," Sarah protested.

Both men ignored her. Propelling her toward the doorway, they got her inside.

The instant he saw them, Deputy Briggs's gaze went to Sarah. "What are you doing here? You were supposed to go into protective custody."

Mouth sullen, she shrugged. "It was boring. So I left

and went home. I have a job and bills to pay. It seemed like a good idea."

"Until it wasn't," Briggs pointed out. "Now look what kind of mess you've gotten yourself into."

"I believe Ms. Sleighter has a statement to make," Reid put in.

"No, I don't."

Cord stepped forward and shot her a warning look. "Yes. You do."

Briggs looked from one man to the other. "Would you fellas mind telling me exactly what is going on?"

"I'd rather let her do that," Cord said.

Everyone stared at Sarah. She stared right back, defiant and stubborn.

"Come on, now," Reid interjected, his voice soft. "The game's up and you know it. You might as well just go ahead and tell them the truth."

Her eyes flashed anger, but finally she nodded. "Fine. I planted the damn shirt. Eldridge gave it to me to clean right before he disappeared. He'd had some sort of accident with a hunting knife and went to the hospital for stitches. That shirt couldn't be cleaned, but I hung on to it. When Eldridge vanished, and it seemed clear someone killed him, I saw my opportunity for revenge. Piper shouldn't have gotten the life she did. It just wasn't fair."

"Let me get this straight. You tried to frame an innocent woman for murder just because you were jealous?"

Her chin came up. "Yes. But you don't understand. She didn't deserve to be a Colton. She got Whitney to adopt her, when it should have been me."

Despite himself, Cord felt a pang of pity for the other woman.

"I have no choice but to arrest you for falsifying evidence," Briggs intoned. He read her rights out loud.

"Wait," Sarah interrupted. "You should know that Piper Colton was with us, right before we came here. Cord dropped her off in town. You need to go looking for her right now."

Reid shook his head. "That'd be weird," Reid drawled. "But I highly doubt it since Cord's a bounty hunter and could sure use the money. I think if he found her, he'd damn sure bring her in."

Grateful, Cord sent Reid a look of thanks. He held his breath. Sure enough, Briggs nodded. Since Sarah had been lying all along, no one believed her now.

"I take it this should be enough to drop all charges against my sister?" Reid asked. "And get rid of that warrant the sheriff has on her right now?"

"Yes." Briggs didn't sound too happy. "If you have a way of getting the word out to her, she'll be cleared by this time tomorrow. And give her my apology."

"Will do." Reid sounded positively cheerful. He grabbed Cord's arm. "I'd like a word with you before we leave."

Cord nodded, watching as Briggs took Sarah Sleighter toward the back to be booked. Once she'd disappeared from view, he walked out with Reid. "What's up?"

"Did you really drop off my sister right before you came here?"

"Yes. She's at the coffee shop on Third."

"Okay." Reid tugged his cowboy hat down lower. "I guess I'll meet you there."

He strode toward his truck before Cord could say anything. *Great.* Cord debated sending Piper a quick text, but there was way too much to say.

Sipping coffee and people watching was something Piper hadn't been able to do in far too long. Ever since this craziness with Eldridge had started. She hoped now that Cord had taken Sarah to the sheriff, he and Reid could get her to make a full confession which would exonerate Piper. Then she could have her life back.

But did she truly want that? Her life had become so much fuller now. Because of Cord? She took a quick sip of her latte, careful not to burn her tongue. It was her second one. She'd nursed her first one for so long that it had gotten cold.

Shifting in her seat, she watched as another couple walked hand and hand into the coffee shop. She felt jumpy, despite knowing her disguise was good enough that no one would recognize her. Still, the disguise came with a price. The wig itched and the long curls kept getting in her face. The oversize eyeglasses kept slipping to the end of her nose.

For what felt like the thirtieth time, she checked her phone. Only one hour and ten minutes had passed. And no texts from Cord or Reid. No missed calls, either. While she'd been able to calculate the drive time to and from the sheriff's department, she had no idea how long the meeting would take.

With a huge sigh, she tried to relax. Difficult, considering the massive amount of caffeine she'd ingested.

The front door opened again and she looked up. Reid walked in, his green gaze scanning the room. Despite her disguise, she knew he'd recognize her, but she held utterly still, just to see.

Spotting her, he strode over, unsmiling. Towering over her, he held out his hand. "It's over," he said. "Now it's time for you to come home."

Panic flashed through her. She didn't understand it, but she knew she had to stall, to give herself time to think.

Luckily, before she could articulate what she wanted, Cord came inside, heading straight for her.

"My sister and I need to talk," Reid said, glowering at the other man. "Could you at least give us some privacy?"

"No," Piper snapped, standing up. "Cord can hear whatever you have to say, but I'd rather talk somewhere else."

"How about my place," Cord said, his easy tone washing over her like warm honey. He placed his hand on her shoulder and, heaven help her, she leaned into his touch.

Reid glanced from one to the other. "That'll work," he finally allowed. "Piper, you can ride with me and we'll follow you there."

"I don't think so," Cord began.

Piper reached up and touched his hand. "I can fight my own battles," she told him softly, before turning to face her brother. "Reid, I know you're worried about me, but I can take care of myself. I'm not riding with you, I'm going with Cord." She smiled to take the sting from her words. "We can talk there."

"Follow us." Cord let Piper lead the way. They all trooped outside, Reid grumbling under his breath.

Once in Cord's truck and on the way, Piper sighed. "I'm sorry about my brother," she began.

"No need. I get it. He's just worried about you."

"And bossy and high-handed," she said, smiling. "He mustn't be thinking clearly because he knows better. Giving me an order is the surest way to get me to do the opposite."

Glancing at her, one side of his mouth twisted in a wry smile. "You don't say."

She laughed. "Sad, but true."

"You know the sheriff's going to drop all charges. You'll no longer have a warrant out for your arrest and they're canceling your court date. You're free, Piper. Free to go back to living the way you want to. No more hiding."

Her smile faded. "I know. That's what Reid said. He wants me to go back to the ranch immediately."

Watching the road, he nodded. "Makes sense."

Troubled, she tried to find the right words to ask him if he wanted her to go. "I imagine you're tired of me imposing on you."

"Not at all." His answer came easily. "You're welcome to stay as long as you want."

Warmth blossomed through her at his words. Until she remembered he'd asked her to help him with Renee.

"I think Renee might like that," she said carefully. "Don't you?"

"Sure." He kept driving, his face expressionless. "And I really think it'd be better if we agree to keep our hands off each other."

"Seriously?"

"Yes. I mean it. Let your life get back to normal before you do anything rash. You need time."

Though normally she would have teased him and maybe pressed for more, right now she felt too vulnerable. While Cord might really think they could stay together and keep their hands off each other, more power to him. Personally, she had her doubts.

But he was right about one thing. They both needed time. She wanted to explore this thing between them, see where it might go.

They reached Cord's place and parked. Reid pulled in right behind them.

"Nice farm," he said as he walked toward them.

"Thanks." Cord gave a guarded smile. "I realize it's

not on par with what you're used to, but it's mine and I'm damn proud of it."

"As you should be." Reid glanced at Piper, who flashed him a brilliant smile to hide her uncertainty. "After we talk, I'd like to see the rest of it, if you don't mind."

"Sounds great." Cord led them inside, dropped his keys into a tray by the phone. Spotting Piper, Truman ambled over, tail wagging.

"Hey, boy," Piper crooned, scratching him under the chin. "Who's a good boy, huh?"

Cord shook his head. "My dog has really taken to your sister," he told Reid. "In fact, when she's around, I cease to exist."

Straightening, Piper grinned. "That's not true. He still loves you. He and I just have a special bond."

Reid watched the two of them and then cleared his throat. "Piper, we still need to have a discussion."

Her grin faltered, but she lifted her chin. "All right. Talk. I'll listen."

Of course Reid shot Cord a glance indicating he should leave. Cord understood. A big brother naturally felt protective about his baby sister.

"Where's Renee?" Piper asked. "I didn't see her car."

"I don't know." Cord looked from her to Reid. "Listen, I'd be more than happy to give the two of you some privacy. I need to check on some livestock."

Piper opened her mouth to protest, then closed it. "Maybe that would be a good idea," she said. Reid's expression showed both relief and determination, but he didn't push his luck.

"I'll be back in a little bit." On his way out the kitchen door, Cord gave her shoulder another quick squeeze.

"Holler if you need me. I've got my phone." He whistled for Truman. Unsurprisingly, the dog pretended not to hear him.

The instant the door closed behind Cord, Reid crossed his arms. "Awfully cozy, there. What's going on between the two of you?"

Piper kept her chin up. Though she felt her face heat, she didn't look away. "Now, that's really none of your business, is it?"

His loud sigh told her what he thought about that. "Fair enough," he said. "You're a grown woman. But I want you to think about what Fowler's going to do once he finds out where you're staying. He paid Cord to find you. From what I understand, Cord accepted a partial payment. Fowler will demand a refund, and I can't say I blame him."

Troubled, she knew he was right. And she also knew how badly Cord needed the money. She thought of the Widow Berens, sick and in the hospital and knew Cord would do everything he could to help her. As her heart twisted, she realized she could be in real trouble. She could love a man like him. More easily than she'd realized.

"Earth to Piper," Reid said. "What are you going to do?"

"I don't know." But she did. She still had a good portion of her savings left. If Fowler demanded his money back from Cord, she'd replace it. No way would she let Cord suffer because of her actions.

"Don't take this on yourself," Reid continued. "I know how you are. You can't blame yourself for any of this. You're the one stuck in the middle. None of this is your fault."

Touched, she thanked him.

"You know, I always liked Cord Maxwell," Reid continued. "He's always seemed like a man of his word."

"He is. That's why I trust him to help me out."

"*Seemed* is the operative word. Now I'm thinking differently." Reid sat forward, reminding her of a jungle cat about to pounce. "He's like a double agent, working for both sides at once. He took Fowler's job, accepted payment, and then, when he found you, he lied to Fowler and agreed to help you."

"He didn't lie. He doesn't do that."

"Really? Sounds a lot like lying to me, even if it is only by omission. An honorable man would have owned up to Fowler what was going on."

"Really?" She crossed her arms. "If he'd done that, it would have been like throwing me to the wolves."

For the first time since they'd begun talking, Reid appeared uncertain. "Well…"

"Well what? How can you not admire someone who did what's best for your sister?"

He thought about it for a moment. "Point taken."

"Cord's a really good guy," she continued. She didn't know why she felt so desperate that her brother see him the way she did, but she did. Maybe because even if she and Cord never saw each other again after all this was over, she'd never forget him or what he'd done for her.

And *to* her. Glad Reid couldn't read her thoughts, she gave what she hoped was a casual shrug.

"You care about him, don't you?" Eyes narrowed, arms crossed, her brother waited for her reply.

Damn.

"Maybe," she allowed. "A little. He's been awfully kind to me." There. That made her sound more like she thought of him as a friend.

"I checked him out, you know." Reid continued to watch her. "To be a fugitive recovery agent here in Texas, he has to be either a peace officer, a level III—armed—security officer or a licensed private investigator. Since he's able to carry a firearm and have a concealed handgun permit, he can't have any felony convictions. Just to be sure, I checked that, too. The guy's never been arrested. His father, on the other hand—"

"You remember his father, don't you?" she interrupted. "He worked for us as a ranch hand. He had an alcohol problem and I think Cord spent a lot of time bailing him out of trouble."

"Correct." The tense line in Reid's jaw relaxed somewhat. "His sister, Denice, was also trouble."

"I know. She was killed a couple of years ago in a car accident. Cord is raising her teenage daughter, Renee."

He nodded. "So you know everything, then. He's shared this with you?"

"Yes." Laying her hand on his arm, she squeezed. "He's a good guy, Reid. I promise you."

Finally, Reid sighed. "I'll have to trust your judgment on that one. Hopefully he isn't making a bunch of promises to you. Despite what you might think, guys in his line of work have to learn to be pretty good liars."

"I just told you. He doesn't believe in lying."

Reid snorted. "Right. I bet. And has he also told you to trust him? Listen, Pipe, guys who say things like that are the ones you should run from."

Hurt, all she could do was shake her head. She knew if she protested, Reid would become even more convinced that she'd been taken in by a con artist.

But Reid hadn't seen Cord with his niece, or with the elderly Ms. Berens. He didn't know Cord like she did, and no amount of talking would change his mind.

"Piper, I have to look after you," Reid told her.

"Actually, you don't. But I appreciate the effort." She smiled to soften the sting of what she'd say next. "I'm going to stay with Cord for now." Chin up, she braced herself for an argument.

Instead, Reid regarded her thoughtfully and nodded. "Okay," he said. "Then I think I'll go find Cord and take a look around his place."

Rolling her eyes, she followed him to the door. "Don't pull any of that big-brother-issuing-a-dire-warning stuff on him, okay?"

Reid exited the house without making a single promise.

After feeding the three horses, Cord fed the goats and the chickens. While doing his chores, he kept an eye on the house because he knew once Reid had finished reading Piper the riot act, the older man would be coming for him.

That is, if Piper had truly decided to stay. It was entirely possible Reid could convince her to pack up and return home.

And then he caught site of Reid heading his way. He wouldn't ever admit it out loud, but a weight lifted off his heart. If Reid wanted to talk to him, he figured that meant Piper would be staying, at least a little longer.

"You keep a clean barn," Reid said, once he reached Cord.

"Thanks." Accepting the compliment with an easy smile, Reid continued mucking out the horse stall.

"About my sister," Reid began.

Here it came. Bracing himself, Cord nodded.

"Piper tells me you're a good guy. Says you don't believe in lying. I want to know what you're planning on telling Fowler."

"I think that's between Fowler and me." Cord kept his tone easy. "And Fowler's not the reason why you're out here."

"True. I've already warned you about hurting my sister."

"Yes, you have." Continuing to work, Cord finally finished and faced the other man. "I care about Piper," he said, choosing his words carefully. "Hurting her is the last thing I'd ever want to do."

"Still, it happens," Reid insisted. "But I just had this conversation with her and, as she pointed out, she's fully capable of making her own choices. I would like you to promise me one thing, though."

"What's that?"

"Don't stand in her way if she decides she wants to come home."

Surprised, Cord nodded and held out his hand. "I won't. I give you my word. If that's what Piper wants, then I'll step aside and let her go."

He said it like it'd be an easy thing, a simple act. And maybe, right now, it seemed like it might be. But somewhere deep inside him, way down inside his soul, he had a flash of insight and realized letting Piper go might be very difficult, indeed.

His words appeared to satisfy Reid. "All righty, then. Why don't you show me around your farm?"

Chapter 14

Later, after Reid had gone and Cord had showered, he wandered into the living room, enticed by the scent of something delicious cooking. Both Piper and Renee looked up when he entered. "Hey," Renee said, by way of greeting. Piper merely smiled.

"What's in there?" he asked, pointing to the newly acquired Crock-Pot Piper had insisted he buy.

"Beef stew," Renee piped up, grinning. "Piper showed me how to make it."

"Smells great," he said, walking over and ruffling her hair. "What are you doing home?"

"I have the night off."

"She asked me to help her organize her artwork into some kind of portfolio," Piper said. Glancing at the kitchen countertop, he saw they'd covered it with sketches of various sizes and mediums. Moving closer, he saw Renee had also taken photographs of the two furniture pieces she and Piper had remodeled. The two of them sat at the kitchen table, which was piled high with notebooks and sketch pads. Renee apparently had quite a large body of work, which made Cord realize she'd always walked around drawing pictures. He really should have paid better attention.

At least he could make up for it now.

"This one's really good," Piper said, her voice ringing with admiration.

"Do you mind if I see?" Cord asked, directing his question at his niece.

Though she raised her brow, Renee nodded. "Sure."

Piper passed him the sketch pad. There, on the cream paper, Renee had drawn a portrait of Cord, saddling up one of his horses. Every shadow, every pencil stroke, combined to create a realistic likeness, both of the man and the horse. He stared, amazed at her raw talent. "That's unbelievably good," he said, his voice hushed. "You are one talented artist, Renee."

She beamed. "Thank you."

"We're putting together a portfolio to help her get accepted into art school," Piper said. "She's already sent in a couple of applications. This is the next step. We only need to include the best work, but she has so many wonderful pieces that it's hard to choose."

"I can imagine." Art school. He wondered how much that cost, and realized no matter what, he'd find a way to pay it. Turning to go, he took a deep breath. "I'd like to see the portfolio once you decide on the final pictures. Then maybe we can look at the different schools' brochures together, if you want."

"I'd like that." Renee positively glowed. He felt a pang, realizing he could see the echo of his sister, Denice, in her face.

Clearing away the ache in his throat, he glanced at Piper, who watched him with a softness in her gaze that told him she suspected how he felt. "How long until the stew's ready?" he asked.

"We're cooking it on high, so maybe a couple of hours."

"Perfect." He glanced at his watch. "I've got to run a few errands. I'll be back in time for supper." He headed out, afraid to look at either of them in case he revealed the depth of his emotions. He wanted to run by the courthouse and see if there was anything new.

Even this late in the workday, the courthouse was busy. Most of the last hearings for the day were wrapping up, and the mood was harried, but more relaxed. Rumors were flying, though most of the lawyers clammed up when they saw him. The ones who would talk only knew bits and pieces. All he was able to learn was that something big had happened in Eldridge Colton's case. Details would be released on the early edition of the evening news.

"All four big networks," a bail bondsman named Cletus chortled. "This is gonna be interesting."

Since no one would repeat any actual facts, Cord headed home. If he hurried, he could make it in time before the news aired.

As soon as he pulled into his driveway and parked, he rushed inside the house, flashed a quick smile at Piper and Renee and grabbed the remote.

Both Piper and Renee looked at him, wearing identical expressions of startled bemusement. Truman even roused himself enough to let out a single woof.

"The news is on," he said by way of explanation. "I went up to the courthouse today. People were talking. There were all kinds of rumors flying around, but no one would give me specifics or confirm or deny anything. I think it might have something to do with your case, Piper. Everyone seemed to think whatever it was would be on the news."

To give her credit, Piper didn't question him. She simply crossed over and sat beside him. "I haven't heard from Reid yet, but he might be busy wrapping up whatever it might be."

He could smell her perfume, that strawberry floral scent that made him want to taste her. "Probably," he agreed.

· The anchorwoman came on, talking about a bad accident involving a tractor trailer and a train. Cord listened, his impatience tempered by the way Piper's thigh nudged against his, distracting him.

"There," Piper said. "Turn it up."

"Eldridge Colton is still missing," the dark-haired announcer said. "But today, his longtime attorney Hugh Barrington claims he saw Mr. Colton being forced into a dark sedan at gunpoint. The police are investigating. Next in the news…"

Cord turned the TV off. "Call Reid."

"My thoughts exactly." Piper pulled out her phone.

While she spoke with her brother, Renee wandered over. "So maybe her father is alive?"

"It would certainly seem that way." Still trying to listen, he couldn't get much from Piper's side of the conversation. She mostly made single-word comments.

Renee checked her watch. "I've got to go. I'm dying to try the stew, but I made plans with some friends. Piper promised to put a bowl in the fridge for me to nuke when I get home. I'll have my phone. Will you fill me in if something else happens?"

"Definitely." He tore his attention away from Piper to give his niece a quick hug. "Drive safely."

She smiled and waved before heading out the door.

"Thanks, Reid," Piper finally said. "I agree, this is great news. And yes, I promise I'll think about returning to the ranch. Soon. No, I can't give you a specific date. Okay, bye."

After ending the call, she slipped her phone back into her back pocket. "Reid says Hugh rushed over to the mansion with the same story. It apparently happened in downtown Dallas, right around the corner from Colton Incorporated. The police were called and they swarmed the area, but there's no evidence, no other witnesses, and Hugh says he couldn't read the license plates. All he could tell was that they were Texas plates."

"Does Reid believe him?"

"Well, Whitney became hysterical. Reid says Fowler pointed out it had to be wishful thinking. If Eldridge is alive and someone has him, why wouldn't the kidnappers have contacted the family wanting a ransom?" Piper sighed. "Hugh Barrington's been Eldridge's attorney—and friend—for years. He's upset, too. He told everyone none of this makes sense, but he saw what he saw and he just wants his best friend back."

Mind racing, Cord calculated and discarded several different scenarios. "One possibility is that Marceline and Fowler set up a fake sighting to have you rush home. With Marceline's maid being involved, it doesn't seem too much of a stretch to think she might have something else planned for you."

Piper frowned. "Do you really think so? Despite Marceline's animosity toward me, I can't believe she's truly that evil. Reid says he thinks she's trying to turn over a new leaf. It's been eating me up wondering what happened to Eldridge. For me, what's important is that he may actually be alive."

He didn't have the heart to dispute that possibility. "Until we learn otherwise, we're going to have to believe he is."

His stomach growled, reminding him he'd skipped lunch.

Piper laughed. "I can see you're hungry. The stew should be close to ready. Let me ladle us up a couple of bowls and we'll eat."

Amazed at how domestic—and right—this felt, he nodded. Before Piper, any time a woman had showed signs of wanting to play house, he'd panicked. Now, he felt like settling in and enjoying it.

The stew tasted as amazing as it smelled. "Renee really made this?" he asked, after emptying his bowl and going back for seconds.

"She sure did." Piper smiled. "I was disappointed that she didn't want to stay and eat with us."

"You know how teenagers are. Friends before family."

"True." With one final spoonful, Piper emptied her own bowl. "Except she told me she didn't have any friends."

He stared. "Seriously?"

"Yep. But when she casually announced she had made plans with friends, I didn't want to question her. I'm hoping since she feels more secure here at home, she's reaching out to others her own age."

"That would be awesome."

"It would," Piper agreed. "She's a good kid, so I think you can trust her. She did ask me to set aside a bowl for her. Since you weren't here, I told her she had to be home by midnight. I hope that's okay."

"Midnight?" He frowned. "I'm ashamed to say I hadn't even thought about giving her a curfew. Thanks for helping me out with that. Did she argue?"

"Nope." Standing, Piper carried her empty bowl to the sink. "In fact she actually seemed pleased that I cared enough to make rules."

Guilt stabbed him again and he groaned. "I suck at this parenting thing."

"No, you don't." Piper crossed over to the fridge and took out a cellophane-covered bowl. "You just need more practice."

"Thanks, but I still feel terrible."

"Well don't. I have just the dessert to make you feel better. I had Renee help me with it, too."

"What is it?"

"Wait and see." She filled two smaller bowls, got out a can of whipped topping and sprayed generously. "Here you go," she said, placing one in front of him and keeping the other, a much smaller portion of whatever it was.

He picked up his spoon and prepared to dig in. With all the whipped cream, he had no idea what he was about to eat.

The first creamy bite had him grinning like a fool. "Banana pudding! How'd you know that's my favorite?"

"Renee told me." She grinned back, before taking a spoonful and popping it into her mouth. "Mmm." She rolled her eyes.

"I have no idea how Renee would know such a thing, but I'm glad she did." Neither spoke again for a moment while they both enjoyed the treat.

They watched TV together, side by side on the couch. Only an hour into it and Piper couldn't seem to stop yawning. "I'm sorry." She flashed a sheepish grin. "It's been a long day. I think I'm going to go to bed."

More than anything, he wanted to join her. Instead, he nodded. "I'll see you in the morning. I'm going to get up early so I can check on Ms. Berens."

She nodded. "I hope I can sleep. I can't stop thinking about Eldridge."

Though he hated to worry her, he also couldn't let her

get her hopes up too much. "Just remember, right now it's only a rumor started by one man. Until there's more evidence, we need to take it with a grain of salt."

"That's kind of what Reid said," she told him. "But Whitney is hysterical and everything is in an uproar. I think my family is going with the opposite reaction—believing the story until it's proven false." She sighed. "I have to admit, I kind of prefer that, too."

He wanted to pull her close and hold her. Instead, he settled for a quick squeeze of her hand, holding it a second longer than necessary before reluctantly releasing her.

"I really hope he's alive," she said, the warmth in her eyes telling him she'd welcome the distraction of a kiss.

"Me, too." Regretfully, he knew if he kissed her, she'd never make it to her bed alone. "Good night."

Was that disappointment in her eyes? She nodded and headed off to her room. He heard the door close a second later.

That night, he tossed and turned, struck by a feeling that Piper was doing the same. He rose early and showered, heading into the kitchen with the intention of making a strong pot of coffee, only to find her already there.

Hair tousled, she had the sexy appearance of someone who'd just finished making love. Even though he knew that wasn't the case, his body reacted violently. She appeared preoccupied, staring at her coffee, lost in her thoughts.

"Are you all right?" he asked.

Barely glancing at him, she gave a slow nod. "I've just got a lot to think about. I know you have a lot to do. Don't worry about me. I'll be here when you return."

The casual promise made his chest tight.

"I'll be back," he promised, aching with the conflict

of his desire and his duty. Aware he needed to leave the room before desire won, he hurried through his chores. When he'd finished, he went to his room to call and check on Ms. Berens before heading there to visit her.

Piper didn't let on to Cord how much it upset her that he clearly didn't think Hugh Barrington's story was real. While Eldridge could be cold and distant sometimes, he'd been a decent father to her—the only father she'd ever had. All along she'd felt he wasn't dead. Hearing what Hugh had seen only confirmed that for her.

Unfortunately, this also meant that Eldridge was in some sort of danger. This idea made her feel crazy. She'd thought about various possibilities all night long, resulting in very little sleep.

Reid wanted her home. Part of her felt like packing up her bags and jumping in her car to do exactly that. But then she thought of how the atmosphere must be at Colton Valley Ranch right now, and knew she'd have a clearer head and more peaceful existence by remaining at Cord's. Whitney had been in hysterics ever since her Eldridge—her Dridgey-pooh—had gone missing. The pet name alone made Piper, along with everyone else, cringe. But Whitney seemed sincere in her need for her much-older husband. Marceline would be her usual overbearing and snooty self, and Fowler would be desperately trying to control everything.

Of course, she missed T.C. and Alanna and Reid, though she'd seen more of him than her other two siblings. She needed to get in touch with them all, once the furor died down, and thank them again for believing in her when it seemed like no one else had.

But to go home? She wasn't even sure where that was

anymore. Right now, Cord and Renee needed her more than her family did.

And truth be told, she needed them just as much. Right now, she needed a distraction, something to make her stop thinking about her family and Eldridge.

Cord strode past her, jingling his truck keys. "I'm off to the hospital. Ms. Berens is awake and they're moving her out of ICU into a regular room."

"I changed my mind about staying here. I'd like to go with you," she immediately said. "That is, if it's all right with you."

He gave an easy smile. "Sure. I'd enjoy the company. And I know Ms. Berens would be glad to see you. The two of you certainly seemed to hit it off."

"We did." Following him outside, she climbed up in his truck. "She's really sweet. I hate to think of such a horrible thing happening to her."

"Me, too. I'm not sure how old she is, exactly." He started the engine. "But I'm hoping they can get her well enough to be able to enjoy life a little bit longer at least."

While she didn't know much about kidney failure, she knew enough to realize the condition was serious. "Will she have to go on dialysis?" she asked as they pulled into the hospital parking lot.

"I don't know. I don't think her kidneys have completely failed yet. I'm hoping we can get an update once we get there."

Hospitals had always unsettled Piper—she guessed most people felt this way. Cord strode to the elevator and pressed the button. "We'll check in at the ICU first, in case she's still there."

At the ICU desk, Cord spoke briefly to a nurse. "Do you mind waiting just a moment?" she asked. "We'll put you in this private waiting room."

Cord and Piper exchanged a glance. Piper wasn't sure if he knew, but being sent to the private, counseling area usually wasn't a good sign.

The small, windowless room had a table, six chairs and a box of tissue on top of the table. Heart in her throat, Piper took a seat. Cord did not. He stood, hands jammed into his pockets, looking perplexed.

"I don't understand," he said. "When I called to check on her, they said her condition was much improved. Surely she didn't..." He left the rest of the sentence incomplete, but Piper knew what he meant.

A soft tap and the door opened. A slender man wearing a white coat entered. "Hello. I'm Dr. Han. Are you Ms. Berens's next of kin?"

Piper glanced at Cord, hoping he'd say yes.

"No, we're just good friends," he answered. "She has no family that we're aware of. Is she all right?"

The doctor looked from one to the other, clearly not certain how much to say now that he knew they weren't family. "She is as well as can be expected," he finally said cautiously. "For whatever reason, her kidney function has improved. I hesitate to use the term *miraculous*, but that's what it is. We're going to keep an eye on her, but if she continues to make progress, we'll release her to a rehabilitation facility in a few days."

Cord nodded. "Thank you. I can't tell you how relieved I am."

"Let me be clear, she's not out of the woods by any means. Honestly, with her condition, it's extremely likely she'll be back here again. Congestive heart failure and renal failure often go hand in hand."

"Congestive heart failure?" Cord asked. "I only knew about the kidney issues."

"She's apparently had CHF a long time. She's been

managing it with medication, but those same medications do a number on the kidneys." Dr. Han grasped the door handle. "Before I go, do you have any other questions?"

"No. Thank you very much for speaking with us." Cord shook the other man's hand. "Is she still in the same room?"

"Yes, for the moment. Room 8. I'm not sure when she'll be moved, but it'll most likely be today."

After the doctor left, Cord let out his breath in a loud sigh. Watching the emotions play over his handsome face, Piper went to him and wrapped her arms around him in a hug.

"She's become kind of like the mother I never had," he said, his voice shaky. "I actually can't envision what it'd be like without her around."

"You don't have to," Piper soothed. "You heard the doctor. She's improving. All you can do is take it one day at a time."

He nodded, stepping back. "You're right. Come on." Taking her hand, he led her to the door. "Let's go visit her."

Entering room 8, Ms. Berens was sitting up in bed eating. The instant she saw them, she beamed. "Welcome, you two. I tell you what, this hospital food is nothing to brag about. I can't wait to get home and cook my own meals again."

Cord dropped into the chair next to the bed. "That doesn't look so bad. Scrambled eggs and bacon, toast and grits."

Though she shook her head, she took another bite, her faded eyes twinkling. "Tastes like a TV dinner. But that's okay. I'm just glad they're feeding me."

Piper moved closer, stopping at the end of the bed.

"Hello, Ms. Berens. I'm glad to see you looking so chipper."

"Thank you, dear." The older woman dipped her chin. "I'm glad you could come with Cord. I enjoyed visiting with you the other day. I just wish this second visit was under better circumstances."

Piper moved up next to Cord and smiled. "I'm just happy you're feeling better."

"You gave me quite a scare," Cord put in.

Ms. Berens sighed. "I know. It frightened me, too, when I woke up here in this hospital. Listen, Cord. There's something you need to know. I have had a will made and you're my executor as well as beneficiary. The original is in a small safe I keep under my bed. I wanted you to know where to find it after I'm gone."

Cord swallowed hard. "None of that kind of talk," he managed. "You're going to get better and be back home before you know it."

"Oh, I hope so." She put her fork down. "I'd like that better than anything."

"Then you eat up and regain your strength." Cord stood. "You also need to get lots of rest. We'll be back to see you again tomorrow."

Glad he'd included her, Piper nodded. "Take care, Ms. Berens."

Head back against the pillow, the older woman smiled. She'd already closed her eyes.

"She's going to be fine," Cord said as they walked back to the elevator. "She might be old, but she's tough."

Slipping her arm around his waist, Piper nodded, her throat tight. In that instant she realized how close she was to falling deeply in love with Cord Maxwell.

Worse, she wasn't even sure she wanted to try and resist.

As they pulled up to the house and parked, Cord's cell phone rang. "Renee," he told Piper, answering it as he strode up the sidewalk. "Really? Okay, thanks. Will do."

"What's up?" Piper asked, closing the front door behind her.

"Renee says to turn on the television. Apparently there's breaking news in Eldridge's case." He grabbed the remote and turned it on.

They both listened in silence—and Piper in mounting horror—as the reporter asked the sheriff questions. "A body believed to be Eldridge Colton's has been found, burned beyond recognition in a fiery crash on the service road of I-30. The vehicle, a black Ford Crown Victoria, matches the description of the car Eldridge's attorney and family friend reported seeing Mr. Colton forced into at gunpoint."

Piper's cell rang just as the segment ended. Reid. Chest tight, still in shock, she answered. "I just heard."

"It's not looking good." Reid sounded defeated. "Hugh is here and insists that was the car he saw. He thinks Eldridge must have been trying to get away from the kidnapper and crashed. We're all shocked. Whitney fainted, and Marceline and Alanna are in there with her now. Fowler, being Fowler, is insisting we have a reading of the will."

Wiping at her streaming eyes, Piper couldn't articulate how she felt about that at first. "Everyone needs to tell Fowler to back off. We don't even know for sure that body was him."

Silence on Reid's end. "Good point, Pipe. Until the coroner's office gets back to us with confirmation, there's no need to read the will. Hugh told Fowler he's too grief stricken to do it yet, but I'll tell that SOB to calm down."

At least anger had replaced grief in her brother's

voice. Good. Piper wished she could believe her own words and feel hope. Or something other than this crushing sense of loss. "I'll be there in an hour," she said. "I just need time to pack."

When she turned around, Cord watched her silently.

"I've got to go home," she said. "My family needs me."

Without saying a word, he pulled her close in a quick, hard hug. "You've got to do what you've got to do," he said. "Call me if you need me or if there's anything I can do. Anything at all."

She nodded, holding herself stiffly. She knew if she gave in and accepted his comfort, she'd break. "Please explain to Renee for me," she asked. "I'm not sure if— or when—I'll be back."

"I will."

Half expecting him to follow her, she felt a mixture of relief and disappointment when he didn't. Packing quickly, she knew she'd have to move fast, so she didn't stumble over her goodbye.

"I'll call you," she said, hurrying past him. He stood in the exact same place where she'd left him a few minutes ago. She fumbled with the doorknob, but made it outside. She got in her car and drove off, refusing to look back. Her heart could only take so much hurt.

The physical act of driving felt cathartic. In just a few minutes, some of the tension drained from her sore shoulders and neck. When she finally pulled up in front of the mansion, she wasn't surprised to see several other cars, including the huge old Lincoln Continental Hugh Barrington drove. Though she wondered why the attorney was still here, she figured he had the right as Eldridge's oldest friend. Meanwhile, her entire family would be here to support one another in their time of grief. They were Coltons after all, and that's what Coltons did.

Refusing to let despair settle on her, she took a deep breath and got out of the car. If it were up to her, she'd avoid Fowler and Marceline, as this situation wasn't the right time to settle their differences. She only hoped someone had helped Whitney get and remain under control. Her legendary hysterics would be the last thing a group of people desperately trying to hold themselves together needed.

Though she'd started off moving with purpose, Piper's steps slowed as she climbed the stairs leading to the ornate double front door. As she turned the handle to let herself in, she nearly collided with a visibly shaken Hugh Carrington.

"Piper!" he exclaimed, grasping at her hands, as though she alone could keep him from falling over. "I'm so glad you're here. Fowler is insisting we have a reading of the will and I informed him we couldn't unless all of the family was present."

Piper swallowed hard. "Isn't that a bit premature? Eldridge hasn't even been declared..." Choking up, she couldn't finish.

"I agree. But Whitney backed Fowler up. That poor woman has been through enough." His dejected expression matched his voice. "I can't say no to her."

"I understand," Piper lied. "Is everyone already gathered in the study?"

"Yes. Reid said you were on your way."

Might as well get this over with, then. Keeping hold of Hugh's arm, Piper let him lead her to the study. Since she hadn't had any contact with her family other than Reid since her release from jail, she braced herself for an inevitable barrage of questions.

When they entered the crowded room, everyone went quiet, staring. Lifting her chin, Piper met Reid's sympathetic gaze. Alanna smiled and waved and T.C. nodded a greeting. Of course Marceline wouldn't even look at her, which suited Piper fine. Whitney, who sat next to her daughter, wore a dramatic black veil, so Piper couldn't make out her expression. On her other side sat Fowler. He appeared preoccupied with his phone, though he did glance up long enough to flash Piper a smile that looked more like a grimace.

"Here you are, my dear." Hugh released her and Piper sank into the empty seat. He continued on to the front of the room before removing an envelope from his suit jacket pocket.

"Harrumph." Clearing his throat for emphasis, Hugh held up the envelope. "As you can all see, this envelope is sealed. Eldridge entrusted me with this, the original of his last will and testament. Even though I am—was—his attorney and friend, he had this prepared elsewhere. He told me he felt I was too close to the family to be objective and made me swear not to open it until after his death."

"Which is now," Fowler put in, his mournful expression at odds with the flash of anticipation in his eyes. Everyone knew how badly he needed this made official, so he could finally take total control of Colton Incorporated.

Though Reid shook his head, he didn't contradict the oldest Colton son. Whitney sobbed once, but kept her veil in place and didn't comment. Piper began to wonder if she'd taken antianxiety medication.

With a dramatic gesture, Hugh used a gold letter opener. Hands visibly shaking, he removed a thick document and unfolded it. "I don't know that I can do this," he commented to no one in particular. "Eldridge can't be gone..." His voice broke and he looked down, clearly unable to continue.

"I'll do it." Fowler snatched the will from Hugh's fingers. "'Being of sound mind, I, Eldridge Colton, bequeath Hugh Barrington, one of my oldest and dearest friends, controlling interest in Colton Incorporated.'"

As he uttered the last words, disbelief, shock and finally rage flashed across Fowler's aristocratic face. "You," he snarled, glaring at Hugh. "You did this. Somehow, you managed to persuade Eldridge to give you my birthright."

Chapter 15

With Piper gone, even though it had only been a few hours, it felt like all the life had been sucked out of his house. Though he'd tried his damnedest to be strong for her, Cord had really wanted to beg her not to go.

But he couldn't. He'd only just begun to understand how important family was. Piper's family needed her.

So did he.

Trying not to focus on her statement that she didn't know when—or if—she'd be back, Cord roamed aimlessly, Truman right behind him, room to room, trying to put a finger on his huge sense of loss. He ended up in Piper's room, standing just inside the doorway staring at her perfectly made bed.

Her scent still lingered. Strawberries and peaches. Truman whined, appearing confused. "It's all right, boy," Cord told the dog, scratching under his collar. "I'm sure she'll come back and visit you."

Truman only stared, before jumping up on Piper's bed and settling in to wait.

Cord's heart ached, both for him and his pet, who clearly adored Piper. He wondered how long Truman would lie on her bed before he realized she wasn't coming back.

Ever? The notion seemed unbearable. Shaking his head at his own foolishness, he turned and headed toward the farmyard. Best to get outside and keep busy. Overthinking the situation wouldn't do anyone any good.

Chores waited. Maybe if he got busy, he'd feel better. Mucking out stalls would make his body sore, but might help his heart ache less.

He spent several hours cleaning out the barn, moving hay, and doing every single minor chore that he'd been putting off for months. Finally, he headed back to the house and took a long, hot shower, wishing he could wash away the haunting loneliness he felt at Piper's absence.

This. Was. Ridiculous. Or so he told himself. She hadn't gone far. It wasn't like he would never see her again.

He decided to head into the kitchen and make himself something to eat. At the last minute, he stopped and went back to her room. He couldn't believe he'd come to care so much in such a short period of time. She'd left. He couldn't blame her, with so much going on with her family. No, it was more the way she'd gone. With a casual wave and without a backward glance.

But then what had he expected? They'd made no promises to each other. He'd known she'd return home eventually. So why did her absence make him feel like he'd been punched in the gut?

His world appeared to be shrinking. He'd almost lost Ms. Berens, and he'd had to face the fact that eventually, he would. No one lived forever. She'd seemed at peace with the idea, and he'd try his best to help make things easier for her for as long as he could.

Truman still slept on Piper's bed, refusing to budge until she returned.

"Come on, boy," Cord said. "Are you hungry? It's time to eat."

Barely blinking, the dog didn't move a muscle.

"Suit yourself." Cord sighed, wondering how long his pet would remain there before realizing life had to go on. Just then Truman jumped up and gave a joyous bark, leaping from the bed and racing past him.

"Did you miss me?" Piper's voice, from the doorway behind him. Half-afraid he might be dreaming, he turned. Crouched down with her arms wrapped around the dog, she eyed Cord with a curious mixture of self-confidence and hesitation. "I'm back."

Hands clenched into fists at his sides to keep him from touching her, he nodded. "I see that. What's going on?"

Disappointment dimmed the sparkle in her beautiful eyes. Cursing himself for putting it there, he closed the distance between them, yanked her up against him and kissed her until they both were senseless.

"Wow," she murmured after, her head against his chest. "I guess you did miss me. I wasn't even gone all that long."

It took a moment for his head to clear. He didn't tell her that even such a short period of time had felt like eternity. "What are you doing here? I thought you were going home to be with your family."

"Here's the thing." She gave him a half smile, her gaze questioning. "I did. Fowler pressed for the will to be read, so it was. Hugh Carrington was left controlling interest in the company."

"Wow." Reluctantly, Cord released her. "The family attorney? I'll bet that didn't go over well."

"It didn't. I thought Fowler was going to deck poor

Hugh. And Hugh seemed as stunned as everyone else. Apparently Eldridge had another attorney draw up the will."

"What about the rest of the assets?" he asked.

"That was about what you'd expect. Whitney gets the ranch and all their homes around the world. The bulk of the fortune is divided between the kids, including me." She shook her head. "Odd how that simple gesture, including me with the others in the will, made me feel as if Eldridge really loved me."

"Of course he did. What's not to love?"

She grinned. "Thanks. Oh, and there's more. One thing for sure—it's never boring around Colton Valley Ranch. Turns out Eldridge isn't dead. Someone in the medical examiner's office got suspicious of the first rush autopsy and double-checked the results. That body wasn't Eldridge's. Dental records positively identified it as another person entirely—a drifter from Kansas who'd been living on the streets of Dallas."

"What?" Stunned, he could only stare.

"I know, right? Turns out they think someone paid off the guy that did the first autopsy. Before they could arrest him and find out who, he disappeared."

"But why? Why would someone do such a thing?"

"We don't know. Reid thinks it was all a ploy to get the will read quickly. Eldridge has been missing a long time and everything is in limbo."

"Fowler?" he asked, still trying to wrap his mind around this newest development.

"I thought that, too, until Reid reminded me we don't know who would benefit the most by having the will read."

She exhaled an exasperated puff of air and combed her fingers through her hair. "Now that we know it's

Hugh, that casts an entirely different light on things. However, with there being no proof Eldridge is dead, Hugh has no control over anything."

Cord's cell phone rang. "Fowler," he told Piper. "Just a sec."

Bracing himself for more ultimatums, he answered.

"All the charges against Piper have been dropped," Fowler said, his voice uncharacteristically defeated. "Your services are no longer needed."

Bemused, Cord knew he should stay silent and let it go, but he had to ask. "I thought you wanted me to bring her home. Remember, you gave me a two-week ultimatum."

"I know what I said," Fowler snapped, sounding much more like his old self. "But she's been here and gone. I can't say I blame her for leaving after the uproar around here." Fowler went silent, apparently realizing he'd come too close to revealing private information to Cord. "Anyway, she's in the clear. Everyone believes that Eldridge is still alive."

"They do?" Cord played along, curious to see how much Fowler would tell him. "What happened?"

"That's family business. Don't worry, you'll still get your money. I'm going to get you the balance of what I owe you. You tried, but I guess you're not as good as I thought you were if you couldn't even find Piper."

Again, Cord knew the smart thing to do was keep his mouth shut. But once again, for whatever reason, he couldn't. Maybe the fact that he felt like all along he'd been skirting too close to outright lying. "I did find Piper," he said. Across from him, Piper's eyes went wide.

Silence. Then Fowler swore, the sound low and guttural. "When?" he demanded. "How long ago? Was it before she showed up at the ranch today?"

"Yes." It felt good to finally tell the truth.

The swear words that came out of Fowler's mouth astonished Cord. He wouldn't have guessed the other man could sink to that level of vulgarity.

Cord waited for Fowler to get it all out of his system. Finally, the other man wound down.

"I'm sorry," Fowler apologized, another surprise. "It's been a very upsetting few days, but I shouldn't take it out on you. Piper's adoptive mother—Whitney—is extremely worried about her. They didn't get a chance to talk today."

Even now, Cord couldn't help but notice how Fowler had to point out that Piper had been adopted. "I'll pass that information on," he said.

"You do that." And the other man hung up without saying goodbye.

"What's going on?" Piper asked, her clear gaze wary. "I heard a lot of yelling on Fowler's end, which since he hardly ever gets his feathers ruffled, shows exactly how upsetting today was for him."

Cord grimaced. "I agree. I think he's so used to being in charge and now that everything is continually spiraling out of control, he's losing it."

"You told him that you'd found me."

"I did. And it was the right thing to do. I feel like I've been lying to him all along. It doesn't matter that I had no legal grounds to bring you in. I took his payment and then failed to do the job he hired me for. I have no choice but to return his money."

Her concerned gaze searched his face. "You can't. I know you gave some to Ms. Berens."

"True." He sighed. "And I used quite a bit to catch up on bills. It's been no secret that I've been running low on funds. I let my business go so I could have time to search for Renee. And then you found her on your very first attempt. I'm good at what I do—damn good—but I don't understand how I could have messed this up so badly."

"You were too close to the situation." She rushed to his defense, which made him smile. "Kind of like the reason they won't let surgeons operate on their own family."

The fact that she compared his job to that of a surgeon made his smile broaden into a grin. "I appreciate that," he said. "But I checked several bars. Most of them told me they wouldn't hire a bartender under the age of twenty-one, even though they could legally."

"You underestimated Renee's determination."

"I sure did."

The sound of her delighted laughter unfurled the last remnant of tightness in his chest. He caught at her, pulled her close and held her, breathing in the strawberry scent of her hair. He held on a bit too long, wishing he never had to let her go, before releasing her.

That night, though they went to separate bedrooms, he lay alone in his bed wide awake, fighting the desire to go to her. He wondered if she thought of him, or if she'd dropped into sleep quickly, without a care.

Finally, he fell into a fitful sleep, waking early. Since he saw no sign of Truman, he figured his pet had spent the night with Piper. Lucky dog. Whistling softly, Cord put on a pot of coffee before heading out to feed the livestock.

When he returned, Piper had started making breakfast. She flashed him a smile as she handed him a cup of coffee. "Take a seat," she said. "Do you want your eggs sunny side up or over easy?"

Struck by the cozy, domestic feel the morning had taken on, he shrugged. "Whatever way is easier for you."

"I like sunny side up." She turned back to her skillet. "You know, I'm really glad I was able to come back so quickly."

"Me, too," he said, his heart pounding. Now would be the time to open up, to tell her how awful he'd felt when he'd thought she'd gone for good. To ask her to never leave again.

But the words stuck in his throat and the moment passed.

"Here you go," she said, still smiling. "Breakfast!" She placed two plates on the table. Though the fried eggs had burned edges and the toast appeared barely toasted, he thought it might be the most appetizing breakfast he'd ever seen.

They fell into a companionable silence while they ate. When they'd finished, Piper carried the plates to the sink. "So what are your plans for today?" she asked. She batted her eyelashes at him, her sexy smile inviting him to answer in kind.

"I'm planning to work," he said, pushing away his regret and keeping his voice deliberately casual, even as he fought off the desire coursing through his veins. "I've got to run into the office and start getting everything in order if I'm going to have a prayer of turning that company around."

"Have fun." Her light tone matched his, in direct contrast to the smoldering heat that darkened her green eyes. "I'll see you at dinnertime? I'm making something pretty special."

Relieved, he nodded. He'd noticed the pan of dried beans she'd left soaking overnight in the sink. This, he thought. This was what happiness felt like. "Sure. I'll be back by then. And, Piper?"

A smile quirking up one corner of her mouth, she eyed him. "Yes?"

"Thanks for all you've been doing around here. I really appreciate you cooking for me."

She grinned. "You're welcome." And then she got up, grabbed him and pulled him close for a kiss. "There," she said once they broke apart, slightly breathless. "To go with the hug."

While he tried to collect his thoughts, she spun around and sashayed out of the room, wiggling her fingers at him in a goodbye wave as she left. Of course her ever-faithful sidekick Truman went with her.

Bemused and aroused, Cord got into his truck and headed into town.

Back at his office, his mood changed to serious. He knew he needed to get his business back on track if he intended to have a prayer of making a living. He had more than himself to consider now. Renee wanted to go to art school and she sure as hell deserved a chance.

Fowler still claimed he wanted to settle up with him, but Cord knew he needed to refuse. He hadn't done the job he'd been hired to do, not really. In good conscience, he couldn't accept another dime from the other man. Not only that, but he gathered the remainder of the down payment to return to Fowler. He couldn't keep it. No matter how badly he needed it.

As if thinking about him had summoned him, Fowler appeared shortly before lunchtime. He walked in, wearing his usual impeccably tailored suit, and held out a large, thick envelope. "Here you go. The rest of what I owe you."

Cord took a deep breath, then shook his head. "Keep it, man. I can't take your money. I found Piper shortly after you hired me and ended up helping her instead of doing the job you paid me to do."

Clearly not used to people refusing cash, Fowler stared. "We had a deal," he began.

"Exactly. And I didn't keep up my end of it. So there's no need for any further payment. In fact, here's most of the down payment back." Cord dropped the envelope on the desk for Fowler to take.

"I don't want the money back, despite the fact that you lied to me." Fowler said the words matter-of-factly. "Someone told me you never lied. I knew that wasn't possible."

"I usually don't. This time, I did. I'm sorry, I was wrong. Everything I did, I did for a reason," Cord began.

"You're splitting hairs." Fowler grimaced. "Save your explanations. I truly don't care."

He dropped his envelope onto the desk, right next to Cord's. "Whatever your motivation, I appreciate you looking after my sister," he said, his voice gruff. "Reid actually filled me in on everything. I know she's staying with you. And I know she doesn't want to come home, for whatever reason. I have a feeling her reluctance is due to a conversation Marceline and I had with her. I think I mentioned that to you. We were unfair and wrong."

Wow. Cord sat back in his chair and eyed the other man. "Maybe you should try saying that apology to Piper."

"I should and I will. When she's ready to hear me. Reid gave me her number and right now, she won't even take my calls." Unbelievably, Fowler appeared hurt.

"Give her time," Cord said, not sure what else to say. "She's been through a lot."

"Yes, she has." Turning to go, Fowler left the envelope on Cord's desk. "Keep the money. As far as I'm concerned, you've earned it."

As the door closed, Cord stared at the thick white envelope. For perhaps the first time since he'd met Fowler, the other man had shown a decent, almost humble side. He opened it up and took out the contents. Stunned, he counted the neat stack of hundred dollar bills three times. While he knew Fowler technically still owed him twenty-seven thousand dollars, he hadn't imagined the other man would pay it in cash.

With this, not only could he keep his business afloat until he got new clients, but he could afford to pay some of the balance after scholarships to send Renee to art school.

First, he had to get the ball rolling around here.

He pulled out a file where he kept the names and phone numbers of all the local bail bondsmen. He picked up the phone and dialed the first number. Time to start reestablishing contacts and let everyone know he was back in the game.

Just as he'd finished the call, his door opened again and Fowler stepped inside. "You got a minute? I drove down the street and turned around when I realized there was something else I needed to discuss with you."

"Sure." Cord indicated the chair across from his desk. "Take a seat. If you've come back to get your money, it's all right here." He pushed the envelope across the desk.

Sitting, Fowler eyed it but made no move to take it. "No, that's not why I'm here." He sat back, his relaxed—for Fowler—posture told Cord he meant to stay awhile. Truth be told, Cord was sort of glad. He'd never enjoyed working the phones.

"I'm guessing Piper told you the body wasn't Eldridge's?" Fowler continued. "I was all fired up to get the will read, but now I wish I hadn't. Turns out old Hugh—he's Dad's attorney—will be controlling the company."

Since no response appeared to be required, Cord simply nodded.

"I thought that reading the will would really help simplify things. With Eldridge missing, it's difficult for me to make any major decisions." Fowler grimaced. "Now, there's no damn point. Hugh has no idea how to run Colton Incorporated. Do you have any more of that bourbon?"

"Sure." Cord got out the bottle and poured Fowler a glass. "Here you go."

"You're not having any?" Fowler asked, raising his and taking a deep swallow.

"Not just yet. You were saying?"

"Too much," Fowler responded. "Forget everything I just said. It's personal, and I had no business involving you."

Cord inclined his head in a quick nod, figuring the other man would soon get to the point.

"Actually, I came to talk to you about Piper. I don't know if you're aware, but Eldridge had someone specific in mind he wanted Piper to marry. A guy who works for us named Shane Sutton. He's an upper level manager and his family is very wealthy. I like him a lot."

Cord wasn't surprised. From what he'd seen and heard of the Colton family patriarch, control was exceedingly important to him. "No. I wasn't aware. Piper never mentioned that to me. Does she know?"

"Oh, yeah. Eldridge made no secret of his attempts to push the two of them together."

"I take it Piper didn't like him?" Heart pounding, Cord waited for Fowler's answer, stunned by the depth of his emotion.

"I don't think she ever gave the guy a chance, honestly." Fowler smiled and took another drink. "You know how she is. She was upset Eldridge truly wanted to control her life. And Pipe's the type of person who will do the opposite, just because she hates being ordered around."

Relief flooded him, though he took care not to show it. "I don't blame her. That's kind of sad, don't you think?"

"Yeah." Fowler gave a short, humorless bark of laughter. "He's like that, you know. When Reid wanted to go into law enforcement rather than work on the family ranch, I thought he was going to disown him."

Cord nodded, not sure where Fowler might be going with this.

"How is Piper, by the way?" Leaning forward in his chair, Fowler focused on Cord. "I know you're helping her, but you haven't mentioned her state of mind."

"Great. She seems really happy."

"Good. Do you have any idea why she won't come home for good?"

Cord had several, though he felt sure Fowler already knew them. Whatever Fowler was getting at, his usual direct approach had vanished.

"What's going on?" Cord asked, instead of answering. "You're circling around something, which must be important. Why don't you just come right out and say whatever it is you need to say."

"Fine." Fowler gave him a half smile and a look of grudging respect. "You're absolutely right. Let me ask you something first. Do you love my sister?"

Stunned, Cord wasn't sure how to respond. Since he could only speak the truth, he did. "I don't know. I think I could, very easily."

Fowler nodded. "What about her? Does Piper believe herself in love with you?"

Funny how his heart skipped a beat at the thought.

"Again, I have no idea. If she does, she hasn't said anything to me."

"All right. This situation might not be as bad as I first thought. At least I know where we all stand. Listen, Cord." Again Fowler leaned close, his breath smelling like bourbon. "Since you think you could possibly love Piper, I want you to think about what she's giving up staying with you."

"Giving up?" Cord frowned. "I'm not sure I follow."

"Piper was raised with every luxury imaginable. Servants, cooks, even her own personal shopper. She wants to start her own business, did you know that?" Fowler rushed on without giving Cord a chance to answer. "The Colton name and my connections, as well as Marceline's and Whitney's, will be invaluable to her in getting started."

"True." Chest tight, Cord figured he knew where the other man was heading.

Fowler cleared his throat, shifting in his seat. "I know you two have a relationship going. Reid told me. Hold on." He held up his hand when Cord started to speak. "And that's all well and good, as long as you keep it casual."

"Which it is," Cord put in, biting back his growing anger.

"For right now. But if either of you are considering taking it to another level, such as, I don't know, professing your undying love, I hope you really think about the consequences."

"Which are?" Cord asked through clenched teeth.

Draining his drink, Fowler shook his head. "Look, you seem like a nice guy. And Reid tells me you've got a little farm on the outskirts of town. But you have to know, once the rosy glow of infatuation fades, Piper will never be happy there. How could she be, going from Colton Valley Ranch to a small farm?"

Cord stood, his hands clenched into fists. "I think you've said enough. I'm going to have to ask you to leave. Here." He shoved the envelope the rest of the way across the desk. It flew off and landed in Fowler's lap. "Take your money with you."

Rising, Fowler let the envelope fall to the floor. "Again, keep it. That's just a drop in the bucket to me. I know I've made you angry, but all I ask is that you think on what I've said for a couple of days. Will you do that?"

"Get. Out." Hand shaking, Cord pointed toward the door. "Now."

Making no move to pick up the envelope, Fowler shook his head and eyed his empty glass. "Thanks for the drink. Please, consider what I've said. Believe me, it's sound advice. Have a good evening."

And he left.

As soon as the door closed, Cord got up and locked it. He picked up the envelope from the floor and carried it back to his desk. Then he got his bourbon, poured his own glass and slugged it down.

Piper couldn't wait for Cord to come home. Renee had gone to work, and Piper had made one of her favorite childhood meals, a big pot of ham and pinto beans. She'd even baked some sweet cornbread to go with it. The recipe she'd used had never been written down, but instead had been passed from one Colton woman to another. Whitney had learned it from Eldridge's mother years ago before she'd passed, and had taken it upon herself to teach Marceline, Alanna and Piper how to make the Southern delicacy. This had been the only time she'd ever done anything even remotely domestic with her daughters, and for that reason, Piper cherished the memory.

Now, Piper had prepared this particular meal for a reason. Years ago, when Cord had lived on the ranch, Whitney had instructed her cook to make a huge pot of it and had it taken down to the hired hand barracks to feed all the hands. Piper had trailed along after the crew. She'd seen Cord's reaction when he'd taken his first bite. He'd told her later he'd never had anything so good. As a kid who'd tasted everything from caviar to lobster on the half shell, she'd felt sorry for him at the time.

She wondered now if he'd remember. Actually, she could hardly wait to see.

When she heard the sound of his truck tires on the gravel road, she rushed to the front door. Then, deciding she didn't want to appear overeager, she went back into the kitchen to give the pot one more stir. Truman looked up and grunted, before drifting back to sleep.

Cord came in, his expression black as he strode past her without a single word or even a glance. Her welcoming smile died on her lips as she watched him disappear into his room, closing the door firmly behind him.

Crud. What else could have gone wrong? She considered giving him a minute, but she'd never been a coward or one to back away from trouble. So she marched on down the hall to his room and tapped on his door.

"What?" The harshness of his tone made her stomach clench.

"Are you all right?" she asked.

"I'm fine," he snapped back. "I'm just not a good candidate for company right now."

She turned the doorknob and went in anyway. Cord sat on the edge of his bed, head in his hands. He looked up when she walked in but didn't move.

"You should go," he told her, his voice as hard as the look in his eyes.

"I made a special dinner." She spoke softly, soothingly. "Something you used to like a lot back when we were kids. Do you want to come eat?"

"No."

"Are you sure?" she pushed. "You're usually hungry at this time of day."

He uncoiled himself and got to his feet. "Don't make me be cruel to you." The pleading note in his otherwise cold voice made her heart ache. And his words...

"What are you trying to say?" Bracing herself, she crossed her arms and kept her head up.

"I didn't ask you to cook for me."

"No. I do it because I love to cook. And you're an appreciative audience."

The compliment bounced off him like rubber-tipped arrows on a suit of metal armor. Any other time, such a corny analogy would have made her smile. Not now, when she had a pretty good idea of what he was about to do.

What she didn't understand was why.

"I think it's time you go back to where you belong," he said. The bleakness in his eyes felt like a punch in the stomach.

"What happened today, Cord?" she asked, moving closer. "When you left earlier, everything was fine. Now just a few hours later and you act like I've sprouted a horn and grown hairy warts. What gives?"

His nonchalant shrug didn't fool her. "I came to realize you don't fit in my world," he said. "Right now, all of this simple living probably feels like a novelty. Fun, different, maybe even exciting until the newness wears off. Then, when you realize you no longer have all the little luxuries you had at Colton Valley Ranch, you'll go running home as fast as you can."

Now she got it. "You're afraid I'll hurt you."

Instead of responding, he looked down. When he raised his head again, his features might have been carved in stone. "Go, Piper. Get out. I don't want you here any longer."

Stunned, she didn't move. She knew this wasn't true—it couldn't be. But Cord didn't lie. If he told her he didn't want her, he must mean it.

"But I love you." Breathing the words because she knew deep down inside her that only the strength of this truth would give them a fighting chance.

"Really?" He shook his head. "I'm sorry, Piper. I don't feel the same way. I'll never love you, so it'd be better if you go."

"That's not true," she protested, abandoning her pride. "I know you feel the same way about me that I do you."

"Do you?" Grimacing, he sighed. "I wonder how, since I've never told you that."

"I can tell by your actions," she said stubbornly. What they had, what they might have, was worth fighting for. Even if it had begun to feel like a one-sided battle.

"Well, you're wrong," he declared.

He didn't lie. Which meant she needed to go.

Pulling her shattered heart around her like a cloak, she turned around without another word. Praying her attempt at a dignified exit would last until she made it to her room, she walked away. When she reached her room, she pulled out her bag and began loading her belongings back into it. Damned if she'd let him see her fall apart. She'd do that once she was off his property. She only wished she could take Truman with her.

Chapter 16

Cord couldn't watch her go. Seeing the hurt flash across her expressive face had been torture enough.

Since he'd met Piper, he felt like he'd done nothing but lie. However, this time he figured if he was going to tell one final falsehood, it might as well be a doozy. Even if saying the lie felt like he'd ripped his heart clean out of his chest.

Because he loved Piper Colton. He loved her so much he was willing to convince her that he didn't, couldn't and never would. Fowler had spoken the truth. Who was Cord to think a woman like Piper could ever be happy living with a man whose business teetered on the brink of collapse? He could barely provide for himself and his niece. Even once he got his business up and running, there'd be college expenses for Renee. He'd never be able to give Piper the sort of lifestyle she deserved.

Damn, the truth hurt. He'd been fooling himself all along, allowing himself to believe that even though they were from two wildly different backgrounds, they might have a future together.

Knowing he'd been wrong didn't stop the wanting.

Or the craving, or the need. Even now, he had to fight the urge to go and comfort her, because he knew he'd hurt her deeply.

For as long as he lived, for every single day he spent on this earth, he knew he'd miss her. And no matter what he did—or didn't—do from here on out, once he died he no longer had to worry about going to hell. He reckoned he had already arrived there.

When Piper left about ten minutes after their talk, he waited until he heard her car start up. Listening for the sound of tires on the gravel road, he still yearned to rush out after her, beg her forgiveness, and take her in his arms. He wanted to hold her tight and never, ever let her go.

Instead, he wandered into the kitchen. Something smelled delicious, though his stomach turned at the thought of food. Piper had left a big pot of something simmering on the stove. He walked over and turned the burner off, and then saw what she'd made. Pinto beans and ham. On the counter sat a foil-covered pan which he'd bet contained sweet cornbread.

Instantly, he flashed back to the day he'd first had this. Whitney Colton had her head chef prepare a huge pot of this along with several pans of cornbread. Her kitchen crew, along with Piper, had brought this down to the hired hands for their evening meal. That day, Cord had been helping his father with some cattle and he got his own bowl, which made him feel proud.

At the first taste, he'd thought he'd died and gone to heaven. He'd savored each bite and when he'd sopped the last bit up with cornbread, he'd noticed Piper watching him, wearing a broad smile on her freckled face.

That's what she'd meant by a special meal. She'd made this for him, from their shared childhood memories, with love. He felt, even though he wouldn't have believed it possible, worse. Instead of sharing it with her, he'd sent her packing.

He'd had to, he reminded himself. He'd only done what was best for her. Because he loved her.

Now, the thought of eating anything, especially this, turned his stomach. Instead, he went and got down a bottle of bourbon. He planned to drink until he'd demolished the pain.

Piper drove around for a while. She didn't have any idea where she was going, she only knew it wouldn't be home.

Her tears began falling before she'd even reached the end of Cord's driveway. She made it to the farm-to-market road that led to the two lane blacktop before she pulled over to the side and let herself weep. Gut-wrenching sobs shook her. The guttural sounds of her grief were something no one else could hear, so the privacy of the inside of her car seemed fitting.

And then, as she cried herself out, she started to think. The man who had spoken so callously and cruelly to her was not the Cord Maxwell she'd come to know. Something had to have happened. But what? What could have made him turn on her, push her away, when the thing between them had started to show so much promise?

Or had it all been one-sided?

No. Piper lifted her chin and wiped away her tears. She might have left, but she hadn't stopped fighting. She'd get to the bottom of this.

Once she'd composed herself enough to hopefully sound normal, she called Reid. "Have you talked to Cord lately?" she asked.

"No, why? You sound terrible. Is everything all right?"

She sighed. Of course her brother could hear the roughness in her voice that meant she'd been crying. "Cord wants me to go home."

Reid went silent. "For a visit? Or permanently?"

"I think for good." She took a deep breath. "Have you heard anything?"

"Not really. But I know Fowler was planning to go see him and bring the balance of the money he owed."

"Oh, Cord wouldn't take that. He told me he felt like he'd failed to do the job."

Silence. Then Reid cleared his throat. "Um, I think he did. Fowler got back a little while ago and mentioned he'd had to force Cord to take the payment, but that he finally did."

She should have been shocked. She should have been stunned. But Piper had come to understand her life had gotten so weird nothing surprised her anymore.

Still, that didn't sound like the Cord she knew. Of course, neither did the things he'd said to her. She had to wonder if she'd really ever known him. Or if something had happened. Something that had made him believe he had to send her away.

Fowler.

"How long ago was this?" She tried to keep the urgency from her voice.

"A couple of hours at most. Why?"

Gritting her teeth, she took a moment to consider her words. "Reid, I know this is going to sound strange, but is Fowler there? Can you put him on the phone? I really need to talk to him."

"Um. Okay. Let me see if I can find him."

Glad her brother hadn't pressed for a reason, she waited while Reid walked around the huge house, looking for Fowler, her heart pounding in her chest.

"I found him," Reid said. "Hold on and I'll pass the phone to him."

A moment later Fowler came on the line. "Hey, Piper." He sounded cheerful. A bit too much so. "I wondered if you were going to call me back. I've left you several messages, you know." There it was, a hint of reproach underlying the pleasant tone. "I was hoping you'd congratulate me and Tiffany on our engagement."

"Congratulations," she said. "Sorry I didn't call sooner, but I wasn't in the mood to talk to you."

"But now you are? How interesting. Is it something I did?"

Horror filled her. Inhaling sharply, she gathered her thoughts. Surely, hopefully, Fowler hadn't messed things up between her and Cord on purpose, just so she'd call him. No, not even Fowler would sink that low. Would he?

"Fowler, what did you say to Cord?"

"Cord?" he asked. She knew him well enough to know when he feigned ignorance. "I paid him the balance of what I owed him, even though he didn't really do his job. The man's a liar. Someone who can lie right to your face. Proves he can't be trusted."

Her first gut instinct was to rush to Cord's defense. But that's what she suspected Fowler wanted, so she refused to give him the satisfaction.

"Besides forcing him to take your money, what else did you say?" She thought he might argue, attempt to dispute the fact that he'd had to pretty much shove his money down Cord's throat. She hoped he didn't bother because no matter what he tried to make her believe, she knew the truth.

"Nothing much," Fowler answered, abandoning all pretense at bewilderment. "We talked about you, naturally."

If she could have reached through the phone and shook him, she would have. "What about me?"

"Well, let's see." Fowler cleared his throat. She could picture him, adjusting his tie and puffing out his chest. "We discussed what your life was like here at Colton Valley Ranch. I told him about your hope to start your own business, and I might have mentioned your beau."

"My…what?"

"You know. Your suitor. Shane."

"Shane Sutton?" This time, she couldn't contain her disbelief. "You told Cord what about him? Hopefully the truth, that I despise the man."

"Um, no. I don't think I mentioned that."

"What was your point?" she asked.

"My point?"

"Yes, your reason. For letting Cord in on all the supposedly wonderful aspects of my life at Colton Valley."

"That's simple. To get you to come home, of course."

Beyond exasperated, Piper knew if she told Fowler everything, how Cord had sent her packing, he'd believe his little strategy had worked and that he'd won.

"Did you threaten him?" she asked as another thought occurred to her. "Mention you'd have him and his business blackmailed if he didn't send me running back to the ranch?"

"Of course not." Fowler sounded indignant. Then, as the implications of what she'd said sunk in, he chuckled. "He threw you out, didn't he? Told you to run on back home and rejoin the lifestyle you were meant to have."

Instead of answering, she employed one of Cord's mechanisms. "Do you see me at your front door? I'm not home, I'm calling you. So whatever you hoped to accomplish, it didn't work."

"But you're on your way, right?" Apparently, he didn't

believe her. "When should we expect you? I'll let Whitney know. Honestly, we sure need your help in calming her down. She's been a mess through all this."

"I'm not coming home." The instant she spoke, she felt the rightness of her choice. "Not now, maybe not ever. I don't belong there anymore."

"If this is because of when Marceline and I—"

"Partly," she cut him off, not in the mood to hear whatever justifications he planned to cook up. "But mostly because I got a taste of how fulfilling life could be on my own, with someone I care about."

"That bounty hunter?" With disgust plain in his voice, Fowler let her know how he felt about Cord. "What kind of life could he possibly offer you?"

"A life filled with love and respect," she answered. And mind-blowing sex, though she didn't mention that out loud.

"You might think so now," Fowler insisted. "But over time, you'd come to resent him for not being able to offer you the sort of lifestyle and opportunities you have here at home. Where you belong. And apparently Cord Maxwell realized that, too, or I strongly suspect you wouldn't be making this call."

"You haven't changed at all, have you, Fowler? You sound so smug and self-satisfied, so certain your way is the only way. You're a lot like Eldridge. I'm guessing it hasn't ever occurred to you that I might want to choose my own path in life."

Finally, Fowler fell silent. She couldn't tell if her words had finally reached him, or if he was just trying to come up with another argument to sway her to his side. In reality, she realized she didn't even care.

"I'm done, Fowler. You may not realize, but the events you set in motion hurt me deeply." She took a deep breath.

"I'd hoped by you discovering love with Tiffany, you'd understand, but apparently not. Maybe you don't really understand what love is. I'm not ever coming back to Colton Valley Ranch to live. As a matter of fact, I doubt I'll be visiting there anytime soon. I'll give Whitney a call and set up a lunch date somewhere, and of course I'll keep in touch with T.C. and Alanna and Reid."

"What about my engagement party?" The sharpness in his tone wasn't lost on her. "Tiffany is throwing a huge party to celebrate. All the Coltons must be there or everyone will talk."

Once again proving he cared more about appearances that anything else. "I'll think about it," she said, more to end the conversation than anything else. She hung up before Fowler could get in another word.

Though the conversation hadn't resolved anything, she felt slightly better. Though her heart still ached, now that she had a sense of the why behind what had happened, she could plan for the future. Piper had never been a quitter. She believed in Cord, knew what they had between them had been real.

For now, time and distance would be the best thing. First, she needed to find a place to stay. No motel or hotel this time around. She wasn't in hiding anymore and she remembered some seasonal cabins on Lake Whitney. This time of year, the rent would be cheap. She'd drive up that way and see if she could claim one for the next month.

Her phone rang. "Hey!" Renee. Judging by the background noise, she was at work in the bar. "Guess what? I just heard from one of the art schools I applied to. They've accepted me starting the spring semester!"

"Already? We were just going over your portfolio."

"I know, right? The husband of one of my former art

teachers is on the admissions committee. She not only put in a word, but she hand-carried my portfolio over. He put me on the fast track, and I'm in!"

"Congratulations! I'm thrilled for you. Have you talked to Cord yet?"

"No." Renee's voice was a combination of embarrassed and defiant. "I wanted to tell you first since you helped me apply."

Which meant Renee had no idea Cord had sent Piper packing.

Piper's stomach twisted. How could she tell her now and ruin Renee's moment. She couldn't. She simply couldn't.

"I'm very proud of you," Piper said firmly. "I think you should call your uncle, too."

"I will. But it just got busy in here, so I need to go. Maybe I'll wait until I get home or if he's asleep then, I'll tell him in the morning."

"Sounds like a plan." Piper ended the call, her stomach twisted again. She felt like she'd lost more than just the man she loved. She'd come to care for Renee like a daughter. Piper hadn't been the only one to feel that way, she knew. More than anything, Renee wanted the three of them to become a family. And now their little mismatched household was in pieces.

Several drinks in and Cord didn't feel any better. If anything, with the bourbon souring in his gut, he felt worse. Especially with the old-school country music playing on the satellite radio. Even Truman had abandoned him, choosing to sit outside on the front porch, apparently waiting for Piper to return.

Which she wasn't. His poor dog was doomed to be disappointed.

Switching the station to classic rock, he continued to drink, bourbon on the rocks at first, and then straight up, hoping he could numb his pain enough to pass out long before Renee got home from work.

Her headlights hitting the front window disabused him of that notion.

Blearily, he glanced at the clock. Since he'd turned all the lights off but one, he had to squint to make out the time. Sure enough, eleven o'clock was way too early for Renee to get off work.

At least if it was someone else, Cord didn't plan to answer the door. He didn't even bother to turn the music down. Too much of an effort. In fact, he wasn't sure he could get up off the floor. Which would be fine. He could sleep there just as well as anywhere else.

Renee walked in, humming under her breath. "It was slow tonight, so they let me come home." She caught sight of Cord. "Are you all right?"

He used the bourbon bottle to salute her. "Better than I was earlier." Wincing, he realized he'd slurred his words.

"You're plastered." Without waiting for a response, she went around the room, first turning off the stereo, then turning on lights. "Did you and Piper have a fight?"

He nodded, then shook his head. When he did, the room spun, which pissed him off. "It's been a long time since I drank this much," he said, taking another swig, this time directly from the bottle.

"That's probably a good thing." Renee surveyed the trashed out room. Earlier, Cord had given in to a fit of fury and swept everything from the coffee table to the floor. She crossed to him and removed the bottle from his hand. "I think you've had enough."

"No. I haven't. I'm not passed out yet."

"Give it time," she drawled, sounding so much like

his sister that he got an ache in the back of his throat. "Where's Piper?"

"Who knows," he managed to respond. "But she ain't coming back."

"What?" Digging out her phone, Renee made a phone call. He suspected to Piper.

"No answer," she told him, sliding her phone in her back pocket. "I'll try again later."

"Don't." He tried to stand, finally managing by grip the side of the couch and using it to pull himself to his feet. "I'm sorry you had to see me this way. I'd hoped to be in bed oblivious to the world by the time you got home."

"It's okay." Her sad smile struck him as brave. "We'll figure all of this out in the morning, when you're sober. Come on, let me help you get to your room so you can go to bed."

The next morning, loud banging from the kitchen woke him. Wincing at his killer headache—what had he expected after consuming so much bourbon?—Cord sat up in his bed and waited for the room to go back to steady.

Ignoring the clattering, which sounded like Renee deliberately banging various pots and pans in an effort to get him out of bed, he made his way to his bathroom. A short while later, having showered and brushed his teeth before getting dressed, he felt human enough to go to the kitchen and rustle up some strong, black coffee.

"Mornin'," he muttered, rummaging in the cabinet for a mug. Once he'd filled it and taken a long, grateful drink, he walked over to the table and took a seat. "Renee, I'm sorry about last night."

"It's okay," she began, refusing to look at him.

"No, it's not. I was upset about Piper leaving. I had

no idea you'd be home early. I hate that you saw me like that."

"I see people like that every night at work." At least this time she glanced at him, a quick short look through her lashes. "And of course, Mom and Dad liked to party."

He winced. "You know I'm not like that. I don't want you subjected to that kind of lifestyle at home ever again."

"Thanks. Are you hungry?"

"I'm not sure." Based on past experience, eating something, anything, would do him some good. Though right now the smell of whatever Renee had cooking made him a bit queasy.

Truman, apparently having been persuaded to give up his porch-front vigil, lay listlessly in his dog bed, eyes closed.

"Did you feed him?" Cord asked.

"I tried to. Poor guy wouldn't eat." They both knew why. Cord sympathized.

"Here." She dropped a plate with scrambled eggs on it in front of Cord. "Eat."

Sheepishly, he dug in. After one bite he feared he might get sick, but under Renee's determined glare, he managed to eat it all. "Thank you," he said, pushing his plate away. "I needed that."

"Yeah, I thought you might." She pulled out the chair across from him and took a seat. "Are you ready to tell me about what happened with Piper? I checked out her room and all her stuff is gone."

"She went back home, where she belongs." He thought the words came out pretty steady, considering saying them out loud ripped him up inside.

"Bull." Renee snorted. "Piper no more belonged there than you and I do. She was happy here."

He sighed. His niece was only eighteen, a baby. Despite everything she'd been through, her innocence touched him. She still viewed life through rose-colored glasses. Like Piper. Pain stabbed his heart.

"She needed more than I could ever give her." He held up his hand when Renee started to speak. "Let's leave it at that, all right?"

"No." Renee slammed both hands down on the table, sending his plate jumping. "It's not all right. I care about Piper and I care about you. You two were pretty perfect together. I want to know what happened to make her go. Clearly, something did."

Now he looked away, trying to compose the right words to make her understand. "I told her to go," he said, pushing to his feet. The room spun slightly before righting itself.

"But why?" Renee cried.

"Because I want what's best for her." Going back to the coffeepot, he refilled his mug. "I don't want to talk about this anymore. Consider this topic closed."

"Piper's not a *topic!*"

He didn't respond, taking his cup with him as he headed outside to perform his morning chores slightly later than usual. Of course Truman, once an eager participant in the farmyard life, didn't follow.

Though Renee kept calling her phone, Piper didn't want to answer until she figured Cord would have had enough time to talk to his niece. The two of them were family—blood—and she couldn't bear to think she might somehow cause a rift in their relationship.

But Renee was nothing if not determined. She called hourly, leaving messages every other time, until finally Piper realized the teenager wouldn't stop until she picked up the phone.

"Hi, Renee," she said softly.

"Why are you avoiding me?" Renee demanded. "I'm not your enemy now, am I?"

"Of course not. I want to make sure you and Cord had time to talk."

"We did." Renee sighed. "Though all he'll say is it's all for the best. Maybe that's true, but it sure doesn't feel that way."

Though Piper wholeheartedly agreed with that statement, she couldn't let Renee know. "No matter where I live, you'll always have me as a friend."

"Really?"

"Yes, really." Piper attempted a laugh, hoping it didn't sound too forced. "You're not getting rid of me that easily."

"Thank goodness. I really miss you."

Piper's heart squeezed. "I miss you, too, hon. Tell me, what did Cord have to say about your acceptance to art school?"

Silence. "Uh, I didn't tell him."

"Why not?" Shocked, Piper wondered what exactly had gone on after she'd left. "I know he'll be thrilled for you."

"Maybe," Renee allowed. "Or maybe he'll be worried about how he's going to pay for it."

"If he is, don't you worry. We'll figure something out, I promise."

"Thanks. How's life back among the rich? Does it feel weird being back there after living like ordinary folks for a while?"

Piper looked around at the small, yet cozy cabin. "I didn't go home, actually. I rented my own place. I needed time alone to think."

"But that's…" Renee bit back whatever she'd been

about to say. "I've got to get ready for work," she said instead. "I'd like to come see you sometime soon."

"That'd be great," Piper replied, meaning it. "Just give me a call and we'll figure something out."

After Renee had hung up, Piper wandered outside her small cabin. From her front porch, she could see Lake Whitney. She found the water view soothing.

Taking a seat in the oversize, wooden rocking chair, she wondered why Renee hadn't shared her most important news with Cord. Cord had seemed supportive earlier, when Piper had helped Renee put together a portfolio.

Though she knew she no longer had a place in their family, she couldn't help but worry about Cord and Renee's relationship. The last thing she wanted was for her leaving to drive a wedge between the two of them. Of course, in reality, the last thing she really wanted was to have left.

Fowler may have initiated all of this, but in the end, Cord hadn't trusted her enough to believe her admission of love. He'd trusted Fowler's assumption of how she felt instead, and now their chance was gone forever. She'd have to come up with a way to let go of her feelings and move on.

Even though right now, all she wanted to do was curl up and die.

Chapter 17

Working nine-to-ten-hour days didn't allow Cord the luxury of wallowing in self-pity. If not for his job, he thought he might have gone crazy. He hadn't known it was possible to miss someone so much it felt like a broken bone—an actual physical manifestation of his pain. For a distraction, he'd thrown himself into reviving his business. He'd worked the phones, renewed his contacts, and as a result had several new assignments. This was a tribute to how hard he'd been working during the week Piper had been gone.

Success would have felt a hell of a lot better if he'd had Piper to celebrate with.

Alone in his office, he glanced up when the door opened. When Fowler walked into his office, Cord nearly groaned out loud. His first reaction—shock—gave way to anger.

"If you're coming to gloat, don't bother," Cord said tiredly. "You won, you were right, and I did what you wanted."

"May I?" Fowler indicated the chair across from Cord's desk. Cord jerked his head in a reluctant nod.

Fowler could sit, but damned if he would offer the other man bourbon.

"I didn't come to gloat. I came to see how you were doing."

Hope flared, unbidden and unreasonable, but there nonetheless. "Did Piper send you to check on me?"

Fowler shook his head, watching Cord closely. "No. I'm here of my own accord."

"What do you want?" Cord didn't even attempt to modulate his flat tone.

"I made a mistake," Fowler admitted. His frank tone and the direct, unabashed way he met Cord's eyes almost convinced Cord he meant it. Almost. Except men like Fowler always had an ulterior motive.

Cord decided to play along, just to see where this led. "I'm listening."

"I wanted to talk to you about Piper."

Even her name brought a sharp stab of pain. "Why? She's no longer with me. I sent her on to live her bigger and better life. At least tell me she's happy there, back at Colton Valley Ranch."

"I can't," Fowler said. "Though I truly wish I could. But after Piper left you, she didn't come back home."

"What?" Cord shoved up out of his chair. "Is she all right? What happened to her?"

"She's fine. Other than having the strangest hair cut and color I've ever seen. Sit back down." Was that amusement curling one corner of Fowler's mouth?

Clenching his hands into fists, Cord suppressed the urge to punch the other man. Glaring, he took a moment to push his anger away. Finally, he dropped back into his seat. "Say what you have to say," he ordered. "And then get the hell out."

Taking a deep breath, Fowler nodded. "I understand

your anger. It's well deserved. I wanted to let you know I was wrong. Piper didn't want any of the things I thought she needed. She doesn't care about the Colton lifestyle." He took a deep breath. "Turns out, she only wanted you."

Stunned, Cord couldn't find his voice for a moment. When he did, it came out in a croak. "Is this your idea of a cruel joke?"

Fowler bowed his head. "No. Piper called me after you made her leave. We had quite an enlightening conversation. She told me she wasn't coming home. That she loved you. And when she said she'd hoped since I'd discovered love with Tiffany, I'd understand, I realized I'd made a huge mistake. I never should have interfered in your relationship with her."

Fowler looked down at his hands, twisted together in his lap. "I'm sorry. If I can do anything to help fix it, let me know."

"Fix it? I think it's broken beyond repair, Fowler." Cord almost choked on the words. Wild pain, mingled with a desperate hope, warred inside him. "It's been a week! I made Piper hate me. I convinced her that I didn't want her or love her or even really care about what happened to her."

Anguish filling him, he stood, paced to the bookcase and returned to his desk, then dropped back into his chair. "I actually *lied* to her, Fowler. On purpose. She knows I usually don't lie, so she believed me. But this time, I didn't tell her the truth. I couldn't, because I love her enough to want what's best for her. And you convinced me she wanted more than I could ever give her."

"I know." Fowler cocked his head, his expression pensive. "Though I have to say, it's a measure of your lack of confidence in your relationship that you were so easily convinced of this. Why didn't you think to actually ask her?"

Cord cursed. Again he had to suppress the urge to throttle the other man. "Because I knew what she would say," he snarled. "I knew she loved me. I broke her heart because I wanted—want—more than anything for her to be happy. You've got a hell of a nerve saying that to me after what you caused."

"You're right," Fowler said agreeably. "I probably shouldn't have said that." His tone softened. "Honestly, you have to find Piper and tell her all of that, not me."

"Find her? Again?"

Fowler's laugh grated on Cord's nerve endings. "I'll make it easy on you. I thought you might like to know where she's living. Reid visited her and passed the information on to the family. I think even Whitney's been over there or is planning to go soon."

"Please." Heart pounding so loud he couldn't hear, Cord handed Fowler a pen and a notepad. Fowler jotted down an address and slid the paper and pen across the desk to Cord.

"There you go."

"Thank you."

"You're welcome." Standing, Fowler turned to go. As he opened the door, he glanced back across his shoulder at Cord. "And whatever you do, don't mess this up."

With that parting shot, he left.

Hands shaking, Cord pulled the address up in his phone. Out by Lake Whitney? Judging by the map, she'd rented one of the lakefront cabins that were so popular in the summer. Now, with winter knocking on the door and the Christmas holidays around the corner, she probably rented one for a song.

He wasn't usually a praying man, but he uttered a

quick prayer as he locked up his office and headed for his truck. He prayed he could undo the damage he'd mistakenly done. And he prayed Piper loved him half as much as he loved her.

The drive took him over the dam. Back when Sam was alive, the two had spent a lot of time fishing this lake. Sam had owned a little bass boat and loved taking Cord out and teaching him everything he knew about fish. While Cord enjoyed it, after Sam died he'd sold the boat and hadn't been fishing since. Seeing the lake again, he thought it might be time to change that once he got the rest of his life in order.

When he located the turnoff, the road changed from paved to gravel. As he turned down her street, he immediately spotted her car parked in the driveway of a tiny, wood frame cabin painted a deep red color. It made him smile because somehow, the place reminded him of Piper.

Parking in front, he crossed the sidewalk and headed toward the front door. Since there didn't appear to be a doorbell, he knocked. Inside, he could hear loud music playing. Something bluesy and slow. He could picture Piper dancing by herself to the seductive beat, and his mouth went dry.

Taking a deep breath, he knocked again. This time, the music cut off. A moment later, Piper opened the door, just a crack. She stared at him, her expression neutral, her bright green gaze direct. "How did you find me?" Then she rolled her eyes. "I imagine Reid gave you my address."

The impact of her beauty slammed him in the gut. Somehow, he managed to answer. "No, it wasn't Reid. Actually Fowler told me where I could find you. Can I come in?"

"Fowler?" Despite her apparent shock, she made no

move to open the door any wider. "That's weird. And as for you coming in, I don't think that'd be a good idea. What do you want, Cord?"

"You," he said. "I want you."

She froze. "For how long, this time? I don't think you realize how badly you hurt me."

"Believe me, I do. Please, let me in."

Eyeing him while he stood on the doorstep feeling more exposed than he ever had in his life, she considered. Finally, she opened the door. "You'd better start explaining. And don't try blaming all of this on Fowler."

Her words made him laugh. "I've missed you," he said.

Instead of responding in kind, she only folded her arms across her chest and waited.

"Why didn't you go home?" He knew the reason Fowler had given, but he wanted to hear what she had to say.

"I don't belong there anymore," she said, without a trace of sadness. "Home is where the heart is, you know."

Was that an opening? Did she mean her heart was with him?

Aching to touch her but not wanting to rush things, he took a step closer. She didn't retreat. Instead, she held her ground, head high, eyes flashing. Fierce and independent, two of the many things he loved about her. His heart swelled.

"I've been an idiotic fool," he said, meaning it.

"Agreed." No hesitation there.

Again he found himself smiling. "You know what? In the few minutes I've been here with you, I'm happier than I've been since you left."

"Since you threw me out, you mean." Pain flashed in her eyes before she smoothed out her expression and sighed. "And since you claim you don't lie, I have to take what you said at face value."

Desperate to make her understand, he swallowed hard. "It seems I've been lying a lot lately. I lied to Fowler, and then to you. I knew the only way I could convince you to leave was to lie. So I told the whopper of them all."

"Because?" Her voice silky with exaggerated patience, she eyed him. "Look, Cord, I know Fowler somehow convinced you that I couldn't be happy with you. He admitted as much. What I don't understand is why you believed him."

Good question. All he had was the truth. "Because it made sense."

"No. Nothing about that makes the slightest bit of sense."

Now the time had come to lay himself bare, to strip away the confidence he presented to the world, leaving only what remained of the uncertain son of an alcoholic. He swallowed hard and met her gaze. "What he said played on my insecurities. Deep down, I guess I believed someone like me could never be good enough for someone like you."

Struggling to find the right words, he continued. "You came from wealth, a world of servants and chefs and designer clothes. I own a small farm and right now I struggle to pay the bills."

She shook her head. "None of that matters to me."

"But it might, as Fowler pointed out. In the future, someday after the newness wears off and our life isn't as grand as the one you left behind. I couldn't stand it if there came a time when you looked at me with bitterness for keeping you from the life you deserved."

Now she closed the distance between him, reaching up

and cupping his face in her hands. "What about you, Cord Maxwell? What kind of life do you want and deserve?"

Holding perfectly still, even though he ached to kiss her with every fiber of his being, he answered. "The kind of life with you in it." He turned his head, kissing the palm of her hand instead. "Earlier, when I said I wanted you, you asked me for how long. The answer is forever, if you'll have me."

Though he hadn't planned this part, he dropped to one knee in front of her, still holding on to her hand. "Will you marry me, Piper? Become my wife and make me the happiest man in the world?" He didn't have a ring, but if she accepted, he figured they'd pick one out together.

She dropped down to her knees with him. "Are you sure?" she asked, the sheen in her beautiful eyes warning him she might be about to cry.

"More sure than I've ever been about anything." His heart raced while he waited to hear her answer.

"Then kiss me," she breathed. "To seal the deal. Because my answer is yes. It's always been yes."

Joy surging through him, he covered her mouth with his.

Piper packed up her belongings under Cord's loving and indulgent eye. After his proposal and kiss, one thing had led to another and they'd ended up celebrating their engagement in her bed. Now, rumpled and feeling thoroughly loved, they were going back to Cord's to find Renee and fill her in.

Tossing the last item in her bag and zipping it, Piper turned to Cord. "I'm ready."

"Great." He took the bag from her and hefted it on his shoulder. "Let's go."

In the truck, she buckled up and shook her head. "Re-

member in the old days when pickups had bench seats?
I would have snuggled right up next to you while you
drove."

His sexy grin warmed her all the way to her toes.

"Yeah, I remember. Sometimes it was damn hard to
keep the truck on the road."

This made her laugh.

"Renee's going to be so excited," he told her. "She was
pretty upset when she found out I'd run you off."

"I know. She called me." Carefully considering her
next words, she glanced sideways at him. With his large
hands draped casually over the steering wheel, he looked
relaxed and sexy. "Did you and she talk about anything
else besides me leaving?"

"No, why?"

"Just curious."

Her answer made him laugh. The richness of the sound
made her heart feel full. "You're not good at being evasive," he commented.

"I know. But it's her news to tell. I'm sure she'll mention it once she knows we worked things out."

With a quick shake of the head, he pulled the truck over
to the shoulder of the road. "Is that the best description
you could come up with?" he asked, his dark eyes glint-
ing dangerously as he undid his seat belt. "'Worked
things out' sounds so…clinical. Boring even. Nothing
like this…"

Reaching for her, he captured her mouth again, kissing
her as if he meant to inhale her. When he finally lifted
his head, she could barely breathe, never mind think.

"Well?"

Her body throbbing with desire, she stared up at him.
"Well what?"

"Give me a better phrase than 'worked things out.' Come on," he teased. "That kiss was meant as inspiration."

Dazedly, she realized they still sat on the side of the road with cars driving past. "Oh, I can think of a few phrases. But none of them are something I'd say around your niece."

He laughed again. "Let me." She loved the new tenderness in his voice and in his gaze when he looked at her. "I could admit my love and how I finally faced my insecurities."

"How about we keep it simple," she said, unable to keep from smiling. "Just tell her you proposed and I accepted."

"Perfect!" he crowed, kissing her one last time before buckling back up and pulling out onto the road. "We also need to pop in and see Ms. Berens. She's being moved into a rehabilitation facility tomorrow. She'll be thrilled."

Touched, Piper nodded. "I really like her."

"She likes you, too."

"You know, I almost feel like pinching myself to make sure all this is real," she told Cord. "And I'm not usually like that. But to be honest with you, I was confident with the way things were going before. You breaking it off came out of the blue. I can't help but feel like it could happen again."

He reached over and put his hand on top of hers. "I promise you, I won't make that mistake again. No one— not Fowler or Eldridge or anyone—can come between us."

His words released the last bit of tension she'd been carrying.

When they pulled up to Cord's place, Renee's car was there. "She's home," Piper exclaimed. "I'm so glad. I didn't want to wait to tell her."

They found her in the kitchen, hunched over her sketchbook, pencil in hand. She looked up and did a double take. "Piper?" she asked, looking from one to the other. "What's going on?"

She squealed when they told her. "Group hug!" she exclaimed, holding her arms out wide.

As they moved in, she wrapped them tight and held on. Heart full, Piper knew this was where she belonged, forever and always.

Hearing her voice, Truman came barreling around the corner, leaping at her, spinning circles and crying.

"I swear he's grinning," Cord pointed out. "He's been moping around here ever since you left."

"My sweet boy," Piper crooned, dropping to her haunches to better love on the dog. "This is the second time I've disappeared on you. I promise you, I won't do that again."

Truman let out a woof, as if he understood.

Later, over a fresh baked pan of brownies topped with Blue Bell Homemade Vanilla ice cream, Renee finally shared her news with Cord.

"That's fabulous," he said, jumping up to plant a kiss on the top of her head.

"I know it won't be easy to pay for this." She bit her lip, a nervous gesture. "But I've been looking into grants and scholarships and I think I've figured out a way to help cover part of the cost."

"We'll do it together," Cord promised fiercely. "I don't want you to worry about that. I've been getting my business back together and Piper's going to start her own. Between the two of us, we'll manage."

Piper stared. "I… How… I mean, yes, I had planned to eventually open a store and sell my repurposed furniture, but I…"

"No excuses." Moving around the table to her, he kissed her on the lips. He tasted of brownie and vanilla ice cream. "We're going for the gusto, aren't we?"

"Well, yes. But—"

"No *buts*." Then he sweetened the deal. "You can even take Truman to work with you every day. He'll love that."

Truman woofed again, staring up at Piper with adoration shining from his big brown eyes.

Piper laughed and held up her hand. "I surrender. But I was trying to tell you I thought I'd help out in your office until you could afford to hire someone."

"Were you?" He winked, grinning. "But that's going to be Renee's job, at least until she goes away to college."

"What?" Renee's mouth fell open. "But I bartend."

"And you still can, at night. I only need someone part-time, a few hours a day. Do you think you'd be up for that?"

Watching, Piper loved Cord even more. She hoped Renee understood this was his way of making an effort to include her in more of his life.

"I think that'd be fun," Renee said, still hesitant. "But I don't have any office experience."

"I'll teach you," Piper put in. "It's mostly answering the phones and handling billing, I'd think."

"And filing," Cord added. "You can't forget about the filing. There's quite a bit of filing that's piled up."

Renee nodded. "I'm sure I can file with the best of them."

Cord glanced at his watch. "We'd better get going," he said. "I nearly forgot we were going to swing by the hospital and visit Ms. Berens."

Renee gasped. "I didn't realize it was so late. I've got to get ready for work." Jumping up, she dashed to her room.

"Let's go." Reed took Piper's arm. "Tomorrow we'll head into Dallas and pick you out a ring."

"Nothing extravagant," she said. "I'm not much for big and flashy. My tastes run to more bohemian and quirky."

Grinning, he kissed her, leaving her breathless. "I'll keep that in mind."

At the hospital, they found Ms. Berens sitting up in bed, watching TV. "Well, lookie what the wind blew in," she exclaimed, muting the volume. "I'm so happy to see you both came this time."

"We did, and we have some news. She and I are engaged to be married."

"How delightful!" She beckoned Piper closer, holding out her hand. "Where's your ring, honey?"

Piper grinned. "We're going to pick one out tomorrow."

They chatted with the elderly woman for a few minutes. The effort to make conversation clearly wore her out, and when her eyes began drifting closed, they said good-night and left. Of course she made them promise to come see her in "the rehab place," as she called it.

Full darkness had fallen when they walked outside.

"What now?" Cord asked. "The night's still young. Do you want to go somewhere and have a drink?"

"Sounds great. I don't care where. Just someplace relatively quiet."

As they drove around downtown Terrell, Piper went pensive, amazed how so much could change in such a short period of time. "I can't believe we're actually engaged," she said, speaking her thoughts out loud.

"Are you going to tell your family?" Cord asked, appearing only mildly curious. "As far as I'm concerned, our life would be better without the whole lot of them."

"Cord!" Piper protested. "As crazy as they might be,

they're the only family I have. And I love them. Of course we're going to tell them."

"When?" he asked. "How about now?" She flashed him a grin. "Instead of getting a drink, let's swing by the ranch. I double dog dare you."

To her surprise, he called her bluff. "Let's go."

She thought about confessing the truth—that she'd only been teasing. She wasn't actually ready, but then, when would she ever be? "Might as well get it over with."

"My sentiments exactly."

The closer they got to Colton Valley Ranch, the more anxious she got. When they turned into the long drive, Cord glanced at her. "Where should I park?"

"There's a circular drive. Anywhere there's a space is fine."

Once he'd parked and killed the engine, he smiled at her. "Nervous?"

She nodded.

"Don't be." He hauled her up against him and kissed her thoroughly. When they finally broke apart, she had to catch her breath.

Once she'd gotten out of the truck, he took her hand.

"Are you sure you're ready for this?" Piper asked, unable to keep from smiling, drawing strength from his touch. As long as he had her hand clasped securely in his, she thought she could face anyone, even Marceline, Whitney and Fowler.

At the front door, Piper wasn't sure whether to knock or simply walk in, as she'd done when she'd lived there. Deciding, she turned the ornate handle, unsurprised to find it unlocked. "Here we go," she said.

Inside, their footsteps echoed on the marble floor. The two-sided, impressively curved staircase that led up to the second floor was also empty.

"Is anyone home?" Cord asked quietly. "At the very least, I expected to see a bunch of servants bustling around."

Piper laughed. "Oh, they are, just not out here. Let's go to the kitchen. If we can't find anyone there, I'll call and let Whitney know I'm home."

As if saying the name had summoned her, Whitney Colton appeared at the top of the landing. "Piper!" she squealed. Rushing down the stairs, her high heels clattering, she made a beeline for Piper, wrapping her in a strong perfume-scented hug. "Darling, I can't tell you how happy I am to see you."

To Piper's surprise, her own eyes misted up a bit. Once Whitney released her, she patted down her perfectly coiffed blond hair. Narrowing her eyes, she looked Piper over. "What on earth did you do to your hair?" Without waiting for an answer, she turned to Cord, batting her false eyelashes. "And you are?"

Piper answered instead. "Whitney, this is Cord Maxwell, my fiancé."

"Your what?" Dangling diamond earrings swinging, she turned from Piper to Cord, then back again. "When did this happen?"

"Fairly recently," Cord put in smoothly. "We wanted to come by and tell you the news ourselves."

"And I'm very thankful that you did, young man. First Fowler and Tiffany get engaged, and now you. Maybe we can make the engagement party a combination celebration."

Fowler would hate that. "No, that's okay. We don't really need a party," Piper said.

Pursing her red painted lips, Whitney sighed. "At least promise me you'll invite the family to the wedding."

"If we don't elope—which is a very real possibility—

we definitely will invite everyone." Piper winked at Cord behind Whitney's back. "Is anyone else home?"

For a second Whitney appeared confused, frowning as if she didn't understand the question. Then, she sighed. "No one is here but me. Fowler and Tiffany went out, Reid's off somewhere with his friends, and I'm not sure about the others. Lately, they've all been making it a habit to disappear at night. They don't understand how lost I am without my Dridgey-pooh."

Somehow, Piper refrained from wincing. "I'm sorry."

"But you're here." Whitney brightened. "Come into the study and have a drink. We need to visit so I can catch you up on everything."

"I wish we could," Piper replied quickly. "But we have to run. Tell everyone our news and we'll catch up with them later, okay?"

As Whitney opened her mouth to respond, her cell phone rang. "It's Marceline," she said. "Just wait until I tell her your news. She's going to be so jealous. Drive safely." Answering the call, she wiggled her fingers in a goodbye wave.

Once outside, Piper exhaled. "Whew. Saved by the phone. I'm glad that's over."

"She really didn't seem to mind that we were leaving," Cord commented.

"Nope. She was more interested in stirring things up with Marceline."

"You're not really going to let Whitney tell everyone you're engaged, are you? I think your siblings need to hear it from you."

"And they will. I'm going to start making calls while you drive." Raising up on her toes, she kissed him. "Take me home, my love. I need to have a chat with Truman."

He laughed. "You and that dog."

"I have to tell him I'm never leaving him again. He was very upset with me after I was gone so long."

"As was I," he said, pulling her close. "One more kiss before we get on the road."

Putting her arms around his neck, she gave him all she had. When they broke apart, both breathing hard and grinning like fools, he unlocked the truck. "Let's go. And before you start making those calls, I wouldn't mind hearing what exactly you're planning to say to my dog."

After climbing up in her seat and securing her seat belt, she faced him and smiled. "Just the same thing I told his owner. I love you and I promise to stay with you until death do us part."

She swore his eyes got a bit shiny hearing that. "Right back atcha, my love," he said. "Right back atcha."

* * * * *

Don't miss the final book in
THE COLTONS OF TEXAS *series,*
COLTON CHRISTMAS PROTECTOR
by Beth Cornelison,
available December 2016
from Harlequin Romantic Suspense.

And if you loved this novel,
don't miss the other thrilling titles in
THE COLTONS OF TEXAS *miniseries,*
available now from Harlequin Romantic Suspense!